HAUNTED

HAUNTED

by

GINNA MORAN

ISBN 978-1-942073-47-5 (soft cover)
ISBN 978-1-942073-48-2 (ebooks)

This is a work of fiction. All of the characters, organizations, and events portrayed in this novel are either products of the author's imagination or are used fictitiously.

Cover design by Silver Starlight Designs
Cover images copyright 123RF

For Inquiries Contact:
Sunny Palms Press
9663 Santa Monica Blvd Suite 1158
Beverly Hills, CA 90210, USA
www.sunnypalmspress.com
www.GinnaMoran.com

For my grandma, Lois Anderson,
You were always so very special to me, and I'll cherish all
of our memories together. Until we meet again...

PROLOGUE

WELCOME TO HELL

I NEVER THOUGHT I'd believe in fate. The idea of something being out of my control and in some otherworldly power always made me uneasy. Fate was something I could blame my problems on when things didn't go as I wanted them. Destiny played no part of my future. I got to pick what I wanted to do and who I wanted to be.

But now, as I stand in this barren landscape as fire burns all around me, darkening the sky in billowing black smoke, stealing away all the light except the brightness of the fire, I can't help but wonder if I was foolish for not believing in fate.

I spin around, taking in my surroundings, watching as

the world burns before my eyes. Heat sinks into my skin, and it's the first time I've ever felt its intensity. But the flames are nothing compared to the pain exploding in my soul. Every horrible emotion latches onto me, threatening to kill me by drowning me in the pit of lava that suddenly appears before me.

Hot tears brand my cheeks as the smoke stings my eyes. My body remains frozen in place as the fire draws closer and closer. If I don't move now, it'll consume me until I'm nothing, but I can't look away.

The mesmerizing flames dance and move, blazing fingers outstretched, curling and uncurling in a come-hither motion.

My legs shake as I take a step forward. Cacophonous noise rings out over the fire, and the closer I shuffle toward its arching doorway that leads into an endless sea of flames, the louder the screams and moans of the lost call my name.

"Cami," a voice whispers. "Welcome home."

I swallow, my throat burning. My eyes train on a fiery figure erupting in front of me. I should be terrified. I should turn and try to run, to fight off the flames, to scream out for help.

But I can't move.

I can't do anything.

My soul chose its side, and now I have to accept my fate.

Hell shouldn't be so welcoming.

ANOTHER DEMON DEAD

THE DEMON SMILES seductively at the pretty brunette woman in the gorgeous, purple sequined dress across from him. They've been here for more than an hour, chit-chatting away like any other couple does on a date. They're in the corner booth, with the demon sitting facing the mirror hung on the wall behind the woman. He hasn't noticed me yet, surprisingly, his sole attention on getting his prey to trust him enough. I know this because if he wasn't, we'd have fought it out the moment he walked in the door.

The handsome, brawny demon wears a dress shirt and tie and reminds me of a rugged movie star seen in action movies with his dusty blond hair, triangular-shaped chin, strong nose, and thick brows. There isn't a doubt in my mind that he's an upper-level demon. I bet no one has ever seen his true body, and I'm definitely opting out of that option tonight. It's one thing to see a lower-level demon and their mutated animal forms, but an upper-level demon? I still have nightmares about Malicevile, the demonic man who ruined my life, my biological father.

"Can you hear them?" Cadence asks, using her spoon to peer over her shoulder. Her deep purple hair is tied in a ponytail at the nape of her neck, showing off her delicate jawline and high cheekbones.

"No, but I can smell him." I sniff the air again, breathing in his rose scent. "He smells like he's spent some time in your grams' house."

Cadence arches her perfect brows. "That's surprising. A floral demon. What was he thinking? Doesn't he know that makes him seem weak?"

I shrug my shoulders. "I don't know. He probably wasn't. It's better than rot though."

I sip my soda, sinking lower into the booth when the demon's eyes flicker to the mirror. He stares for a measly second but just long enough to send paranoia through me. I can't risk being noticed. Surprise is the only great thing I have going for me against a demon most likely at Malicevile's caliber.

"Check, please." The demon's smoky voice reverberates through the dining room, and I shiver, the imaginary feeling of ice dripping down the back of my shirt.

Cadence bites her lip, slinging her purse over her shoulder. She slides her delicate hand into her bag, pulling out a plain metal flask.

She pops off the lid, smiling. "I'll distract. You attack."

I nod my head, scooting out of the booth. "I'll be right back. I have to go to the bathroom," I say unnecessarily loud.

Turning on my heels, I head to the front entrance where the public restrooms are conveniently located. I push the restroom door open, duck, and then head outside. The balmy night air sends sweat trickling on my forehead. I creep across the bright parking lot and station myself next to the nicest car, a Mercedes, which screams demon-owned. Not because of the luxuriousness but because it smells like him. He must travel a lot.

I peek past the rear end and at the entrance of the restaurant as the demon and his ignorant prey leave the building. His arm rests behind her back, his hand squeezing the curve of her hip. I'd admire them as a beautiful couple if it wasn't for his demonic status...oh, and the fact that he looks ready to seduce her. I'm not going to let him plant his seed of evil in her. I was never one for interfering, but this is a date that needs to end badly, at least for the demon, not for the woman or anyone else.

"Hey, mister!" Cadence calls, innocently standing behind the couple. She looks like a junior in high school in her plain jeans and tank top, long hair pulled back, and her almond-shaped honey brown eyes flickering as she blinks. "You dropped this."

Cadence waves her hand so wildly that even the speediest demon wouldn't be able to see she was holding nothing. She skips up to the man, batting her eyelashes, ignoring the annoyed stare of the woman.

Mr. Demonic Movie Star wannabe leans over, peering down at Cadence's closed fist. She slowly opens her fingers, teasingly, before revealing her empty palm.

Her smile brightens. "I'm sorry, wrong hand. I meant to show you—" Cadence splashes the flask of holy water into the demon's face before she even finishes her sentence. She ducks, sliding out of the way of his awkward attempts at grabbing her.

Flying from my hiding spot, I tackle the injured demon from behind, forcing him to the ground. Straddling his back, I smash his melting face into the rough pavement hard enough that some of his skin sticks to the ground when he struggles to get up.

The demon's date screams, an awful ear-piercing sound, making me nearly lose my focus. "Shut her up!" I yell at Cadence.

Holding her hand out, Cadence struts to the woman and says, "Cadence Dubois, demon hunter." The woman scrambles away from Cadence's proffered hand, hitting her back against a white SUV. "Whatever, don't thank me for saving your soul. Just get out of here and never trust a man who doesn't come out in the day. Be careful next time, would you?"

I push Cadence's voice away and concentrate on keeping the flailing demon under control. "What's your name, demon?" I ask.

The handsome demon thrashes, and I hold on tightly to the back of his neck, digging my nails into his flesh. Metal clanks from nearby as his car moves an inch closer. The more he flails his body, the closer the car lurches forward until it taps my shoulder.

"Knock it off," I say, absorbing his strange, exciting power. His car skids backwards, hitting the parking space bumper with a ding. "I can take whatever you have."

The demon relaxes under my tight grip. "The hunters are slacking in their ways," the demon says, huffing.

I place my hands around his throat and squeeze to cut off his air supply to wear him down. It won't kill him but will make him extremely uncomfortable. I want nothing more than for him to suffer like all the demons I've ever met made me suffer. This thrilling, new hobby is what keeps me together when my soul would rather fall apart. "I'm not a hunter. I'm a girl on a mission, and you're going to help me."

The demon leers at the ground because I won't let him meet my gaze. "I love to hear those words." He twists his arm, holding his hand out to me over his shoulder. "George

Black, at your service." Of course he'd think I'm crazy enough to seek him out to make a deal. Hunters usually don't play games. But I've learned a few things over the last few weeks. Demons think of the world as one giant game board and the rest of us are their pieces. But what they don't know is that I'm no longer playing their games. I'm rewriting the rules.

Cadence laughs, and I smile at her amusement. "George is the most ridiculous demon name I've ever heard." Insulting a demon is one way to make things more dangerously fun. Cadence always knows how to keep things interesting when we're out for a hunt.

George's car taps me again a lot harder this time. I bet he could run over the both of us if he tried hard enough. Concentrating, I imaging pushing the car back with my mind, and it works.

The demon makes a low guttural sound deep in his throat as firelight blazes in his eyes when he glowers at me from the corner of his eye since he's in no position to face me head on. "You want to make a deal or not? I could just take your soul. It's a nasty little thing. Perfect for my collection."

I roll my eyes. He's the first demon to ever call my soul nasty. I should be offended, but I am Hell-bound after all. "I'm not here to make a deal, *George*. I'm giving you an ultimatum. You can tell us what you know, or we'll kill you."

George growls, flinging his arm back at me, and I lean

away avoiding contact. Cadence stomps on his hand, pressing the pointed heel of her boot into his skin. He yells out, the mere sound of his voice shaking the ground under me. I blink as I imagine what it would be like if his power broke open the ground to swallow us all whole.

The stench of burning flowers wafts into my nostrils as Cadence drips more holy water onto George's face to get him to knock it off. He convulses, deep shudders reverberating through him and into me. His anger is so hot, I can feel the warmth emanating from him, but he'd never be able to burn me.

I yank a small dagger from my boot, holding the silver blade to the back of his neck. "You'll calm down or I'll cut your head off." I'm tired of playing games. I'm not going to waste my energy forcing a demon to talk. If he doesn't spill his guts soon, I'll spill them for him.

"Fine." He stops fighting and submits to me. "What do you want to know?" I never realized how much demons care about self-preservation until I started destroying them myself. Back at the Hunter's Academy, we were trained to intervene if they were hurting a human or trying to attack first. Cadence and I are true hunters, though. We stalk demons, sneak into their personal lives, learn all about their human facades and use it against them to take them down.

"I'm looking for a demon. He goes by Malicevile." I adjust the hilt of the dagger in my hand, easing off the demon's neck.

"Last I heard, he took his business elsewhere. I don't know where. I don't keep track of those things," George says. "Made life a helluva lot easier on me, though. He made a kingdom out of the entire west coast. Almost as powerful as Lucifer himself."

I didn't realize how far my demon dad's power and influence stretched. I knew he was powerful, but powerful enough to control such a large area? "What kind of business?" If I can find out what he does to survive in the human world, it would narrow my search down.

"Souls," he says slowly, like I'm an idiot. My hope to find my Malicevile crashes to the ground in broken pieces. The search is full of fake leads, dead-ends, and shed tears. The only reason I keep trying is for Evan, the boy who made sure I'd make it away from the Hunter's Alliance alive. I'm still angry at him for it, but I use my anger in my new obsession. Hunting the one person who has spent years hunting me first—Malicevile.

"Thank you for proving yourself useless," Cadence says, her voice as sweet as the milk chocolate we sometimes live on while we're on the road.

The demon screams in frustration, sending the ground shaking like an earthquake sent up from Hell to rattle not only my bones but my soul. Yanking his head back, I maneuver my dagger to the front of his neck. I quickly silence the obnoxious, guttural sound with a swipe of the blade, splattering oily black blood on the asphalt. His arms and legs twitch, and I pull him to his feet, levitating behind him. He continues to struggle while pouring his demon blood all over the concrete. He's one of the demons that really, really refuse to die.

Cadence saunters forward, slipping her dagger from her belt. She smiles wickedly, raising a single eyebrow at me before swiftly stabbing George through the heart enough times to cut it from his chest. She jumps back before the wave of demon guts explodes everywhere, covering me from head to toe with the slimy, burnt flower-scented remnants of a not-so-powerful demon. I thought George was an upper-lever demon, but Malicevile would've never made it this easy. George never even tried to reveal his true form—his demon body in all its hellish glory.

Even though Cadence gave the final blow, excitement washes over me. Another demon dead. It's not the same rush of adrenaline I've felt before, not the kind I've felt after surviving but better, darker. It lessens the pain I've buried deep inside me, soothing the cracks permanently damaging my soul, the dark shadows reminding me of what I've paid for my freedom.

My vision flashes red for a split second. I close my eyes, taming the demonic beast raging under my skin, claiming my soul for evil. Cadence touches my shoulder, and I snap my eyes open, quickly wiping the anger off my face.

She frowns, her concern for me obvious. "Sorry we didn't get any answers. How are you holding up?"

I bite my tongue to stop the sarcastic remark from spilling out. It's not Cadence's fault we've reached another dead-end. I think exhaustion is finally wearing me down. We've been on the hunt for weeks now with no results. For a demon who always seemed to be lurking around the corner, Malicevile has vanished off everyone's radar. I'd be happy in any other circumstance, but not this time—not with the love of my life's soul in his possession.

I purse my lips, shoving my feelings aside. "I'm fine," I say, putting on a brave face.

She squeezes my arm, a sad smile playing on her lips. "You don't have to deal with this alone, you know."

"You're here, aren't you?" I ask, playing innocent to what she's really saying. I've dragged my friends through enough. I'm not going to drag them to Hell as well.

"Cami," Cadence says, "You know what I mean. Let me be here for you. You haven't said a single word to me in weeks except when planning these hunts. I'm terrified that if you keep things bottled up for too long, you're going to fall over the edge. I don't want to lose you."

I don't know what to say. How can I possibly tell Cadence that it's too late for me, that my soul has fallen off the edge and landed on the side of darkness? She wouldn't understand, and I'm not even sure I can explain it.

"I'm fine, really." I fake my brightest smile. "And with levitation, it's impossible to fall over the edge. I'd just float."

Cadence sighs, her release of breath blowing the loose

strands of her deep purple hair out of her face. "Okay. I trust that you'll tell me if something is wrong." *She has definitely been hanging around Alana too long.*

I can tell this conversation is far from over, but I'll put it off as long as I can. I don't want everyone worrying so much about me when Evan is the one damned to eternal torment under the sadistic hand of my father. Once he serves his purpose, he'll end up as another trinket on the shelf where Malicevile keeps all his souls. *Don't think like that. You'll find him. You owe him as much.*

"I will," I say, turning toward my new car, a gift left by George. "Now, let's get out of here before someone sees us."

PROMISES

I STAND IN front of my mom's grave, staring at the beautiful, lush peonies blooming around it. The sky is a brilliant blue, and the sun shines brightly overhead. My skin glows in the luminous light as I imagine the heat of the sun burning away the evil that lurks within me. I never thought being in a cemetery could be this peaceful, and I find comfort knowing that my mother's soul has finally been put to rest. Saving her soul is the only good that has come from the hell that is my life.

"How'd you know I wanted to be here?" I ask, sensing Dylan hovering behind me. He always seems to pick the right places to meet me in my dreams. I haven't seen him in a while, but it never feels like he's far away.

"Because I know you, love," he answers, placing his warm hands on my shoulders. I stiffen under his angelic touch. I can't help it.

"Shouldn't you be running for the hills then? If you know me, then you know I'm not safe to be around." Clouds appear out of nowhere, blocking out the precious rays of sunshine. I wince when a cold drop of water hits my cheek. *Please, not another nightmare.*

Dylan might be able to pick the location of my dreams, but he can't stop them from turning into nightmares. Ever since Evan slid into Malicevile's car, I can't seem to find peaceful sleep. My heart aches with every beat at the memory. I'll bet if I woke up this instant, my pillow would be damp with my hot tears.

Dylan brushes the raindrop off my cheek with his thumb. "I tried to leave you once, and it was the biggest mistake I've ever made. I'll never do it again." He says it now, but I'm not going to hold him to it.

We're no longer on the same side when it comes to good and evil, and it's the reason he stayed behind when I had to run for my life from the Hunter's Alliance. It's when I discovered that his finding me on the bus with Alana when we first met was not an accident. His job was to monitor my soul—to make sure I headed down the right path, the one that leads me away from my demon dad and not straight into his arms.

His leaving wasn't the mistake, staying around is. The shift of my soul happened so swiftly I didn't realize it happened. I couldn't believe it. I thought my soul betrayed me—maybe it did.

But now I know that it's true. I feel different, darker, yet more alive than ever. Everything I was unsure about is perfectly clear. I know exactly where my soul is heading, and I don't care. Because that's where Evan will be after Malicevile is through with him. I'd rather be damned to Hell with Evan than spend an eternity in Heaven without him. Ridiculous, yes. Morbid, definitely. But I can't think about eternity unless it includes him.

A harsh wind swirls Dylan's crisp apple scent around me, and I turn away, bowing my head. "Dylan..."

He grabs my shoulder gently, but I plant my feet into the soft grass, my hair slicking against my wet cheeks as the sky explodes in a torrential waterfall of raindrops, soaking me. "Don't. Please, don't say it."

But I have to. Because these little drop-ins make it harder on me. They stir too many emotions with me—ones I'm terrified of.

Listen to him. Don't push him away. I look over my shoulder. "I need to be alone. I don't want you here." Dylan's face falls as the words escape my lips. I try to open my mouth to take them back, but I can't. I pray that he'll argue and convince me to let him stay. Instead, he releases me and disappears, leaving me alone to wallow in my own stormy nightmare.

"Cami? Earth to Cami."

I lift my gaze to Cadence, and she smiles at me in the mirror. Brushing her deep purple locks back, she ties her long hair into a tight bun at the nape of her neck.

"You have twenty minutes to get ready," she says, tapping the imaginary watch on her wrist.

Glancing down, I take in my rumpled shirt and stained jeans. The old me would care that I look like crap. I'd have changed the moment I had the chance. Now? I look pretty ready to me. I won't be sliding into a skimpy dress and stilettos anytime soon.

I brush my fingers through my hair, getting them stuck in a knot. "I guess I should brush my hair," I say, yanking my trapped fingers free.

Cadence sighs. She tosses me my brush before digging through her small bag and pulling out her lipstick. "Don't you want to look sexy for Dylan? You haven't seen him in weeks."

I glare at her reflection, watching her apply the plum-colored lipstick. "No, and yes I have. He's been invading my dreams every time I fall asleep." While it never really bothers me while I'm sleeping, it bugs me when I'm awake and have a chance to think about it. I know he's trying to support me, to be here for me, but I don't want to feel better. Not now.

"That's romantic and creepy," she says. "Do you guys, like you know, in your dreams?"

My cheeks heat with embarrassment, and I see them turn crimson in the mirror. "They're *dreams* not fantasies. And no. I could never do that to Evan."

Cadence's smile falters as her remark sinks in. She opens her mouth, then closes it, unsure of what to say. I shrug, smiling weakly to show Cadence that I'm okay. I don't want her to feel guilty on my account. I'm not a fragile doll that will shatter if not handled properly.

Cadence's eyes light up. "Send him my way next time. I could use some sweet dreams."

I roll my eyes. "Fine by me. He'd probably annoy you the entire time anyway." I press my lips together, getting my jealousy under control. I know Cadence would never move in on Dylan, but the thought of him walking into her dreams instead of mine bothers me. I'm torn, needing his love and company, but the moment I think about Evan, those feelings wash away. I can't be happy knowing Evan's soul is in the hands of my demonic father. It's hard to move on—even after he broke my heart by doing the unthinkable.

We pack up our bags and leave the hotel room key next to the television. I automatically start to walk to Cadence's Jaguar but then turn to the driver's side of the Mercedes, pulling the keys from my pocket.

Cadence opens her car door, leaning over the top. "I'll lead."

I nod, get behind the wheel of my new car, and wait for her to back out. The drive back to our house is long and boring. After Malicevile obliterated most of the alliance leaders, Alana thought it would be better if we left and started a new life. I didn't want to agree. I don't care if people know where I live. I prefer it. It would make it easier to find Evan again if we weren't in hiding, but Alana is still my guardian and no matter how much it hurts to follow her orders, I do so because I love her. She's my family.

The one thing she did promise is that we'd never have to run again. After all these years of running, I thought I'd be ecstatic, but I've grown so used to it that I need it. It's my way of coping with Evan trading his soul to save me. It keeps my mind off him not being around. Because when I think about it, I can't help but think of all the horrible things Malicevile could be doing to him—making him do—all to punish me.

Forcing the thoughts away, I pull into our circular drive behind Cadence in front of our two-story brick and stucco house. The five bedroom house is big enough that we all have separate rooms, which is a relief because I can hide behind my walls whenever I want without having to gaze into the eyes of the people who have given up everything so that I could live.

Alana stands in the doorway, arms crossed, and smirks as I get out of the Mercedes. I pull my bag off the front seat and sling it over my shoulder, shoving the keys into my pocket. She doesn't rush to me like she used to, and I know it has something to do with the fact that she finally sees me as an adult and not the weak little girl she rescued from the clutches of a demon.

"Please, tell me you didn't steal that thing," Alana says as I wrap her into a hug.

I pull back and smile at her. "No, it was a gift from George. He said he wouldn't need it any longer because Hell is too packed to drive around in."

Alana's eyes widen. "I guess you'll need some help putting it in your name."

"I was hoping you'd say that."

Cadence comes up behind me, and Alana steps back to allow us inside. David's in the kitchen, and the smell of roast beef is potent. I look at the floor instead of Dylan, who walks into the living room from the hallway.

I never dreamed of the day that he and Alana would be living under the same roof, but he's grown on her since proving that he wasn't out for my soul all along.

His wings flash subtly, and I resist the urge to run to him and tell him how much I've missed him, how much I need him to hold me and tell me everything will be okay despite my Hell-bound soul.

David comes into the room and saves me. He smiles sadly at me, causing my heart to ache. I don't blame him for the distance he's put between us. I can't even look in the mirror without hating myself. I sometimes feel that he only lets me stay around because he doesn't want to lose Alana again. He's lost enough already. Evan was more than just his partner. David practically raised him. I'm not sure they've ever been apart.

And who am I? A girl Evan's known for a speck of time in comparison. David sees me as I am—I'm the girl who caused his wife to turn rogue and sentence his partner to demon servitude, all in the name of love. He knows I'm undeserving of the life I now have, but he smiles and acts cordial, because if he didn't, and if I didn't have this life, Evan would be gone for nothing.

"Any success?" David asks, drawing me away from my dark thoughts.

The words lodge in my throat. I can't tell him that we've hit another dead-end.

"Cami got a new car," Cadence says instead of telling him that we've failed. Again.

David nods and turns on his heels, heading back into the kitchen. Alana follows behind him, leaving me with Cadence and Dylan, who still hasn't said a word. I push past him and head straight for my room, ignoring the apple and rain shower scent following behind me.

After opening my door, I stop just inside my room. It still doesn't fail to surprise me when I see Evan's belongings blending among my own. I just couldn't let them go.

I hear the door click closed and abruptly turn around to see Dylan behind me. He doesn't say anything as he moves closer, wrapping me in his arms. In the real world, I can't force him to disappear into nothingness. I ignore the comfort of his angelic wings promising me the hope I desperately need.

I stiffen, forcing myself to resist. Without returning his hug, even though my body craves to sink into him, I say, "I need to leave." I lean my head against his shoulder, curling and uncurling my fingers.

Being in this house and in this room with all these memories makes it too hard. The sadness makes it too hard. I need to stay active, to test my limits and push myself. I need to be reckless to remind me that in the end, I'm not some monster. I still have my humanity.

My hardened reaction doesn't faze him. "No, you need to stay, love. Throwing yourself into danger every chance you get isn't going to change anything. Evan wouldn't want you to live like this. He traded his soul so you could have a normal life, not the one you're so determined to destroy."

Anger stabs me like a sharp knife. I'm tired of people saying Evan wanted this or that. They don't know anything. "I'm not trying to kill myself." I grumble as I pad to my bed. Flopping onto it, I press my face into the pillow and inhale a deep breath of amber and patchouli. Evan's scent still clings to everything.

"You could've fooled me." The bed shifts as Dylan sits on the edge. His warm fingers trail up my back, rubbing soft circles over my spine.

I turn over, staring into his deep, chocolate-brown eyes. "I'm doing my best, okay? You wouldn't understand."

"Try me. It hasn't been easy here, either."

I give up. He's right. I don't know what it's like being here. I don't really want to know.

I suck in a small breath. "I'm sorry, Dylan. It's just—"

"I've missed you," he says, cutting me off.

Sliding onto the bed next to me, he pulls me close enough that our noses almost touch. My heart races faster than a hummingbird's as the sudden desire to kiss him overwhelms me. I can't deny how much I want him, to feel the weight of his body, the softness of his lips, the warmth of his soul. It hurts to stay still, to continue to look into his eyes. He makes me forget. I can't even smell the scent of Evan with him so close.

Just allowing him so close to me makes me feel like I'm somehow betraying Evan. Something so wrong shouldn't feel so right, but it does. I've known all along that Dylan regretted not staying around the first time. He couldn't. Still, I shouldn't allow him into my heart, but he's already there.

I swallow. "Dylan...I can't. We can't. Evan..."

Dylan brushes his fingers along my cheek. "I understand." I'm not so sure he does though. If he did, he'd roll off my bed and leave me alone to wallow in self-pity. He wouldn't torture me with his closeness or test my resolve. *Why do I want this so much?*

"I don't want to forget him, and that's what you make me do." A tear slips from my eye, leaving a warm trail as it drips down my temple and into my hair.

Dylan slumps down, burying his face into my pillow. "I'm sorry, Cami. Please, don't cry. I just—I want you to know that I'm here for you. I'm real and not going anywhere." His breath is heavy in my ear as his warm weight pushes into me. We just lay together, our scents mingling, finding comfort in each other.

After a long moment, I finally find my voice. "You know what scares me the most?"

He lifts his head and gazes into my eyes.

My heart feels like it's about to burst. "That I'll lose you, too." Because I am. As much as I feel guilty admitting it, I don't want to lose him. I've been pushing him away, hoping that it'll save me from more pain—pain that seems to have become a part of me.

He brushes his lips against my forehead, and they're cool against the heat of my skin. "I told you, love. I'm not going anywhere."

I close my eyes, my brows crinkling as I force myself to stay in control. It's so easy for Dylan to say he'd never leave me, but I don't know if I can believe him. He left me the first night we met, and then he left me again when the alliance leaders put out a warrant for my death. He lets me fight my battles alone and then shows up to pick up the pieces. What happens when the pieces are crushed beyond repair? Is that when he'll give up and let me drift away on the breeze created by his wings?

How can I give my heart to someone who can easily break it? And worse, how can I trust someone who has the power to rip my soul from me the moment he thinks I no longer deserve it? Dylan is a Demon Watcher. His job is to take souls before they're tainted beyond saving. And mine isn't close to being clean. It's swayed to the side of evil. Dylan could let me end up in Hell if he wanted to, but he can also redeem me.

"Why should I trust you?" I ask after a moment. "It's not like you've stuck around before. And how do I know you wouldn't just stay to damn me to Hell? It's what you're supposed to do." Heat burns my cheeks, but I'm neither embarrassed nor angry. I'm more hopeless than anything.

Dylan narrows his eyes, a mixture of shock and guilt lining his face. "I want to save you, not damn you. I'd fight Hell's army before I let them have you. Don't you see, Cami? I love you. If I could go back, I'd trade my soul so Evan wouldn't have had to, because I want you to be happy. I'd die for you."

Tears blur my vision. "But I never asked for any of this! It should've been my bargain to make all along. Malicevile uses people. The Hunter's Alliance uses people, too. Don't you see that I already have enough blood on my hands? The last thing I want is yours. Promise me you won't give your life for mine. Ever. You're too good for me, Dylan. Evan was, too." For the first time, I refer to Evan in past-tense.

Dylan opens his mouth to argue with me, but the look in my eyes stops him. Instead, he whispers, "I promise." But I can tell he's lying.

HAUNTED

A KNOCK ON my door draws my attention from watching Dylan sleep. I shift out of his comforting arms, guilt nudging at the back of my mind. For the first time in weeks, my dreams have been nothing. He didn't dream walk or bother me. Just held me in his arms as I thrashed about all night trying my best to find some sort of peace.

He startles awake at my sudden movement, bolting upright before leaning his back against the wall. I'm not sure what time it is, but I've been watching him for a few hours.

"Come in," I call when the person knocks on my door again.

I expect to see Alana when the door creaks open, but

Hunter Garcia steps in with raised eyebrows and a smile playing on her lips. I wasn't expecting my demi-demon instructor from the Hunter's Academy to show up so soon. She's one of the few who have stuck by my side after the destruction of the alliance leaders. They decided to sentence me to death because I didn't follow through with their punishment for accidentally using my demonic power against a human—oh, and for making a deal with my father, which I regret. If I'd never tried to save a stranger's soul by trading it for some visiting hours, Evan would still be here. The alliance leaders would be, too.

"Alana said you were back." She saunters across the room and takes a seat at one of the rolling chairs in front of the table I haven't had the chance to use as a desk. "I have a surprise for you."

"You have another lead?" I get off my bed, putting distance between me and Dylan, who remains quiet. Hunter Garcia knows a lot more about the Veiled Realm than most people. She's been sneaking information to me. "Please, tell me you have another lead, Hunter Garcia." If she does, I'll be on the road again within the next hour.

"How many times do I have to tell you to call me Jazmin?" She rubs her hands together for a moment, and I know she hasn't come to give me more leads.

I drop my gaze to my hands. "Alana asked you not to look into things, huh?"

She shrugs. "I'd tell you if I found out something important. But this isn't about Evan. It's about you."

I sigh. "What did I do now? Cadence and I have been model hunters. We're careful, we clean up after ourselves, and now you have a few less demons to worry about."

She laughs. "Thanks for all that, but you're not in trouble. The alliance has no say in what you do anymore. Plus, I said I had a surprise. You really think it'd be a scolding or something?"

I roll my eyes. "Not all surprises are good." I shift my gaze to Dylan who sits quietly on my bed with his hands over his head.

Hunter Garcia follows my gaze but doesn't say anything. She's thinking something though. I kind of wish Dylan would leave.

I lick my lips. "This isn't what it looks like." I hate that I feel like I have to defend myself for something that is nothing. The truth is that I'm afraid to be alone. Cadence is usually with me, but she went out to visit her father. I told her not to burn any bridges, because it wasn't even his fault. I know this. Even Malicevile knew. It's why Aston Dubois is still alive.

"Doesn't look like anything to me," Hunter Garcia says, shifting on the chair to reach into her tote bag on the floor by her feet. "And if it was something, it's no one's business. You shouldn't feel guilty. You're young, and Ev—"

Dylan clears his throat, cutting her off. "What's the

surprise?"

Hunter Garcia smiles, waving the envelope. "Right, sorry. Remember that test you took a couple weeks ago?"

How could I forget? The only way Alana would let me go on hunts with Cadence was if I took a test to finish high school since I refused to go back to public school. "Yeah, why?"

"You passed. Congrats!" She wraps her arms around me like I just won the lottery. Like passing some test somehow matters.

Standing with my mouth open, I stare between Hunter Garcia and Dylan for a moment before I run my finger through the seal and tug out a black certificate holder. I carefully open it and drop it onto the desk when I see my name printed in fancy, curly script.

Tears burst from my eyes at the sight of my diploma. They're not tears of happiness, though. I'm crying because another moment—one that was supposed to be celebrated with excitement—has passed me by without much consideration. Is this how my life is going to be now? Nothing will ever matter again?

Hunter Garcia quietly leaves the room. She's just another person on the long list of people who'll slowly disappear from my life because I suck to be around.

Dylan takes the diploma from my hands and peers at it. "This is a good thing, love."

"I know!" My voice sounds out higher than I expected

it to.

"Then why are you crying?"

I can't answer him. It seems so pathetic to be crying over something this trivial. It's not like I had big plans for my future. I'm not thinking that far ahead. I can't.

I chuck my diploma into the trashcan near my desk. "It doesn't matter."

"It does. This is something we should celebrate." He pulls my diploma from the trash and sets it on my desk.

I snap. My tears of disappointment shift to angry tears—tears that brand hot streaks on my face. All the anger and hurt I've buried inside surfaces as Dylan tries to tell me what's important. My skin tingles as I flick my gaze from my desk to Dylan. It was such a little thing, but I'm pissed. Not just at him but at the world.

I place my hands on my hips. "Are you kidding me? You want to celebrate? Celebrate what exactly? That I've done something normal for once? Something human?"

He tries to pull me to him, but I shrug away. I see through what he's doing. Always trying to heal me because I'm so broken.

"Why can't you let me suffer?"

He crosses his arms. "If that's what you want, then tell me to leave."

Turning away, I don't respond because I can't find my voice. I catch my chilling reflection in my vanity mirror. It's enough to slap me in the face with a reality check. I don't recognize the girl in the mirror. Not because my eyes are puffy and I look like I've slept in the same clothes for days, but because even under my pathetic, moping exterior, something lingers in my eyes, clear for the world to see.

I release a small gasp, moving closer to stare intently into my own eyes. Dark shadows swirl within my irises, and under the shadows, an emerald color, the same color as Malicevile's. It's my inner demon peering through. The light that used to shine in them vanished. I'm alive, but I'm not living anymore. Creatures would probably confuse me for a zombie, except they won't catch me eating their brains.

"Oh, God." My stomach churns, all my anger forgotten. I'm not even sad in this moment. I'm lost in the gaze of a monster who's an imposter for Cami Anders. I don't even know who I am anymore. "Have I always looked like this?"

Dylan tilts his head slightly, peering at me in confusion. I'm surprised he hasn't fled the room before I can drag him into my whirlwind of mixed emotions. It's why I've stayed away so long. When I'm away, out with Cadence with a single focus, it's easy to obsess over the hunt instead of my life. I live for the hunt.

"Like what?"

I jab my finger into the mirror hard enough that if my nails weren't so short, I'd probably break one. "Like this! You don't see it?"

"I think you need to take a deep breath." Dylan wraps his arms around my shoulders.

I shrug away and spin to face him, sounding as crazy as I feel. Closing my eyes, I gulp air to try to calm my racing heart and to try to snuff out Dylan's worry. "Don't look at my soul. Look at *me*. Do I look different to you?"

"You look scared," he says.

"No, I'm serious. Do I look physically different? Look at my eyes."

I levitate enough to meet his gaze straight on. When I look into his chocolate-brown eyes, I see his pure, shining soul smiling at me. It's something I've never noticed before, but there it is. It's beautiful—so pure and so full of good— the opposite of what I'm sure he'll find searching in mine. And then it disappears. *You need some sleep. You're imagining things.*

His fingers cup my chin as he turns my face back and forth. His dewy apple scent engulfs me, and I try to inhale even an ounce of his calmness to sooth my rattled nerves.

He leans even closer, his nose touching mine and our lips so close together that I can feel the warmth of his breath on my mouth. "They're green," he finally says. "Like two jewels shadowed with the swirls of rainbow oil."

So, I'm not imagining their change. I'm not going crazy after all.

"They're supposed to be a dull green," I say, brushing my lips against his as I speak.

His fingers tremble against my cheek like my close presence threatens his resolve. "What's your point? You're still beautiful, Cami."

"It's not about that. I think I'm turning into a full demon. I look like my father." I pull back slightly. Just enough to focus on Dylan's eyes.

His lips tip upward in a half smile. He almost looks relieved by my words. "That isn't possible. You'll always have your human half to balance your demon half."

I want to believe him. I do. But he's the one who showed me that anything is possible in the Veiled Realm. We were able to transform a hellhound back into a werewolf, which was something that was supposed to be impossible. But we did it. We did the impossible. So turning into a full demon doesn't seem impossible to me, and I think I'm turning.

"But—"

Before I can argue, Dylan wraps his arms around me and kisses me on the lips. Instead of pulling away, I kiss him back. I kiss him desperately, my heart racing out of control, a hurricane of emotions roaring in my chest. He lifts me up, and I wrap my legs around his waist, holding him tighter. A light breeze plays with my hair, our scents mingling together, his iridescent wings unfolding and covering us in their pure, golden light.

He carries me to the bed, our lips never parting as he gently lays me down. His legs straddle mine, and my fingers lock into his hair. He tastes like apples and rain, just like he smells, his lips as soft and warm as I imagined them to be.

He pulls away, breathing heavily, and I swear he's peering into my soul. I can see his love for me in his eyes, raw and devoted, and it makes me feel so terrible. It's the same love I see in Evan's eyes, well, used to see.

My vision clouds with tears, and I can't stop myself from crying. I'm lost and confused, and I don't know what to do. I love Evan. I'd give my life to have him back and safe, but with the way things are going, it feels hopeless. It feels more hopeless than finding my way back into good grace.

And Dylan, well, as much as I want to deny it, I have feelings for him. Deep-seated, unbidden feelings. Feelings strong enough to obliterate the only plan that makes sense to me—to find Evan and free him. What that means exactly, I don't even know. I haven't wanted to face the truth. That it's very well possible that the only way to save Evan from an eternity of torment by Malicevile's hands is to release him to a different, uncertain fate.

A demonic contract is binding. Possess Evan, possess his soul. I used to believe that the death of a person could save them, but I was wrong. It takes divine intervention, the kind Dylan can provide, and even that's not always guaranteed. But risking it might be worth it. I'd risk it. It's the reason Malicevile has kept him far from me.

Dylan rubs his thumb across my cheek, wiping away my tears. "I'm sorry," he whispers, shifting next to me. "I don't know what got into me. I know that you don't feel the same way I do. I just—I don't know what I was think-ing."

"Don't assume you know how I feel," I blurt, surpris-ing myself. "Why do you think this is so hard and easy at the same time? I love you, you know. And I hate that I love you." I never thought I'd say the words out loud, but there they are, and it feels like a weight has been lifted off my chest.

Guilt rolls over me in waves. How is it possible for one heart to be ripped between two people? It doesn't seem fair. It gives me twice as much to lose, and I've lost enough al-ready. I don't think my soul can handle anymore heartache.

Dylan searches my face like he'll find all the answers he's dying to know. "But you're in love with Evan."

"Yes." I glance at Dylan, a rubber band squeezing my heart. It's like the word pains him, and I hate how much it looks like it hurts, but I warned him. I told him I'd only break his heart. I didn't know I'd be breaking mine as well.

I shift on my side and slide closer to him. "But I'm in love with you, too."

"That bothers you." It's not a question. Dylan always has a way of knowing what I'm thinking.

"Love isn't supposed to be like this. It's supposed be about happiness, loyalty, butterflies fluttering in your stom-ach. Good things."

"Love has its downside," Dylan says.

"Yeah, arguments about mundane things like forgetting

to do the dishes or shrinking your favorite shirt, not about how my soul is evil or how I put my life in danger. My heart shouldn't feel like it's breaking every time I think. It's like my demon half has tainted every part of me, like I've lost the chance to find peace."

"It doesn't have to be this way. You're letting your guilt consume you. I can see it eating away at the good you have left. You have to let go of it. None of this is your fault. You didn't choose this," Dylan says, squeezing my hand.

"That's where you're wrong. I did choose this. I chose to embrace my demonic powers. I chose to make a deal with a demon. I stood by and let my father murder the alliance leaders. I even decided that I'd play on Hell's team. I should've just let you take my soul, then we wouldn't be in this mess."

"Don't say that, love." He peers into my eyes, and my grief melts away.

"Stop doing that! I don't deserve to be healed." I roll off the bed, my fists clenched at my sides. "I don't deserve any of this."

I rush from my room, plowing into Alana. Before she has a chance to figure out what's happening, I grab my car keys and fly out the door, running for my car. I've been so absorbed in my own world I hadn't even realized the sun had already set. Time is meaningless these days. It's just about getting by, and I'm barely doing that.

When I slide behind the wheel, my warm back rests

against the cool leather seat. I slam my hands on the steering wheel a few times to ease the tension tightening my every muscle.

After a minute, I turn the heater on full blast to stop the chill pouring through my veins. I need to get away. I need to run.

Pulling out of the driveway, I pop the gear in drive and hit the throttle. I speed down the road without a destination and without a plan. All I know is that I can't be in that place anymore.

Everywhere I look, all I see are ghosts. The ghost of my family, of Evan—the ghost of the girl I once was. I'm haunted.

BROKEN

MY HEADLIGHTS FLASH as I turn onto a familiar road. I'm beginning to think that leaving was a big mistake. I don't really have anywhere to go, and I didn't think to grab cash before I made my grand exit. I'm sure Alana realized this because she hasn't even called my cell phone. Dylan, on the other hand, has left ten messages.

I pass the lemon grove bordering the Hunter's Academy and imagine all the students nestled in their beds. Alana mentioned that there hasn't been much word from the Hunter's Alliance, but the whole hunters' community mourns the loss of their people by my father's hands. He's the most-wanted demon in the Veiled Realm, but luckily,

I'm not on the alliance's list anymore. Cadence's dad, one of the two remaining alliance leaders, pardoned me, yet I still refuse to have anything to do with the people who pushed my boyfriend into trading his soul for my life.

It's been weeks since I've been in this area, and a nagging feeling begs me to turn around. I have no business returning to the place that started this whole mess. To one of the many houses belonging to my demon dad.

I pull the car into a clearing in the thick forest that I think is near Malicevile's lair. I don't know the exact location of his demonic palace, but if I levitate high enough, I should be able to glimpse the stone walls.

My phone vibrates in my pocket again, and I ignore it as I bend my knees and propel myself into the air. I rotate my arms, pushing them through the air until I reach the high branch of a live oak tree. The sturdy branch doesn't move under my light weight, since I'm still levitating, and I peer around the darkness. I catch the low glow of a light about half a mile away, deep in the middle of the forest. Since nothing else is out here, it has to be coming from Malicevile's, but I know he's long gone. Maybe there's something I've missed before though. Even all the local demons I've killed swore he up and left without a trace.

I propel myself to the nearest tree, keeping to the tree tops instead of the ground in case anything lurks around. Demons are territorial, and I wouldn't put it past one to try to swoop in on Daddy Demon's precious home.

Stopping on the branch of a tree near the edge of the ominous property, I search the area for signs of demonic activity and life. The porch light glows, illuminating the front of the house. The tall pillars cast long shadows on the driveway, reminding me of prison bars. A light glows from within the house. The foyer chandelier appears to have been left on.

I sniff the air, using my sensitive sense of smell to better investigate what I can't see. I've always hated relying on my nose like a tracking hound, but it does come in handy. The lingering scent of cinnamon and clove hangs in the air, but I don't think it means anything. My father lived here. Of course the place still smells like him.

After another long moment of studying the house, I push off the branch and jump over the block wall, floating to the ground. I don't plant my boots in the grass. I'd rather sneak up on the house just in case.

The moment I glide forward, the scent of burning flesh wafts through the air. A guttural growl echoes through the night, sending a chill down my back. I'd know that smell and sound anywhere. Malicevile's hellhounds are on the loose. Of course they are. Why wouldn't he leave some of his broken werewolves to keep people away? It doesn't stop humans from coming by in the day, but they aren't the ones to worry about. It's the monsters who show up the moment the sun goes down that the entire world needs to worry about.

I search the premises, catching sight of the orange glow of firelight bouncing off white walls of the plantation-style home. A flaming figure slinks around the corner of the house, creeping through tall grass in need of a mow. The hellhound stalks me like the true predator it is, and I slide my dagger from the sheath on my hip. The poor broken werewolf needs to be put out of its misery.

I position my legs in a fighting stance to launch into the air if the hellhound lunges. The scent of the flaming beast causes me to crinkle my nose. The air is so pungent with its foul stench that I hold my breath to keep from gagging.

I aim the dagger at the hellhound. "Come closer, little beasty. I'm going to kill you and put you out of your misery."

The hellhound stops in its tracks about fifteen feet away. Its flaming hackles rise as it releases another throaty growl. Black slime drips from its jowls, sending the dry grass smoking under it.

It doesn't move and its coal eyes don't even blink. The standoff is excruciating, waiting for the hellhound to make the first move. When it comes to these beasts, I'm not an offensive fighter. I have to wait for it to give me the opportunity to send my dagger through its heart. I nearly died the last time I was bitten, and no one knows I'm here. I'll surely face my end if I'm not careful.

Another growl sounds from behind me. I shift sideways. The moment I turn my back on the hellhound in front of me, it'll attack. I can't give it the opportunity, but I also can't leave my back open for an attack from behind.

I shoot a look to the hellhound that saunters through the thick vegetation. They're surrounding me to take me out. One hellhound I can handle. Two? Not so much. I'll be ripped to shreds in moments if I try to fight. My best option is to flee to the house and hide out until the sunrise banishes the demon-broken werewolves.

I dart my gaze between the hellhounds moving in on me and then to the house. I just hope it's empty. What'll happen to me if another demon moved in? I should've put more thought into my plan. *Pull it together. You need to focus.*

Pushing my thoughts away, I take a deep breath, regretting it the moment the burning flesh smell coats my tongue. The hellhounds lurk closer, hunting me like the prey that they think I am. *It's now or never...*

Using the force behind my levitation, I launch from the ground and jump ten feet toward the house. The hellhounds bark and snap as they turn me into their favorite game of chase. I bolt forward the moment my feet hit the ground. Guttural growls echo from behind me, but I don't look over my shoulder. It'll only slow me down.

If I could feel the heat of fire, I'm sure I'd be sweating. The foul air chokes me as I run, and by the thickness of the smoldering air, the hellhounds are closing in on me. I don't think I can make it.

When I'm within ten feet of the porch steps, I bend my knees and launch forward, flying up the stairs. Crashing into the sturdy wood door, I gasp as the air whooshes from my lungs. I spin and fall, pressing my back into the door. My dagger gleams in the porch light as I point it in front of me at the first coal-eyed hellhound, a bit smaller than the one who came up behind me, as it jumps in my direction.

Its front paws sear the porch as it lands with a thud, but the larger hellhound crashes into its side and knocks it away. The two fire beasts roll, snapping and growling, sending black sludge and fire all over the pristine porch. They're competing for the kill instead of teaming up. Something's off, but I'm not going to sit here and think about why I'm still alive.

I reach up behind me and twist the doorknob. Surprisingly, it flies open on its hinges. I thought I was going to have to break a window, but Malicevile didn't lock up. Maybe he's never needed to. It's not like people stroll into a demon's lair willingly. They'd have a lot more to worry about than breaking and entering.

I scramble into the grand foyer and kick the door shut with the heel of my boot. Leaning back against the gleaming black floor, I stare up into the sparkling chandelier. My chest rises and falls as I huff in a breath of air that lingers with the cinnamon and clove scent of my father.

After a moment of deep breathing, I pull myself together. A loud thump reverberates from the front door, and I force myself to my feet to look through the peephole to watch the two hellhounds still fighting, despite the fact that their prey has escaped. *Stupid hounds.*

Peering around the house, I notice the only light left on is the foyer chandelier. The rest of the place is as dark as the night. Anything can lurk in these hallways, but I don't hear or smell anything. I'm pretty sure I'm alone.

I don't call out. If someone is here, I'd rather not draw attention to myself. My boots squeak against the black floors, and I levitate to move silently through the house I never really got to see much of. I'd instigated my father the last time I was here and pushed all the power he had given me back into him. I still regret doing it. I miss the feeling of the electricity flowing through my veins. I thought it was the power unleashing my inner demon, but as it turns out, it was my own soul teetering on the side of Hell before finally falling over.

I creep through the vast living room full of a variety of artwork—from abstract paintings to enormous pottery and even a pair of black wings hanging on the wall. There is no way they belong to a creature of this world. I never noticed them before, but it stirs dread in my stomach, imagining who they belonged to. I don't think Malicevile would hang up a pair that was fake.

I flick on the hallway light and head straight for his study. The last time I was here, I took out a shelf of glass cylinder vials that contained the souls of the people he collected. My mom's soul was among them, and I couldn't leave her behind. It makes me sick to think that Evan's soul will be on a shelf when he dies unless I can do something about it.

Tears prickle in my eyes. My heart aches remembering the last words Evan said to me, about how trading his soul for mine was the best decision he's ever made and how he wanted me to live life like I should have been able to.

Anger rushes over me, replacing the ache that never goes away, and I reach out and grab a horned statue that sits on top of a small table in the hall. The glass cools my fingers, and I chuck it at a wall mirror. Glass shatters from both the statue and mirror and cascades to the hallway runner in dazzling pieces that reflect the light from above.

I stomp over it, turning the shards to dust, but it doesn't make me feel better. Even burning down Malicevile's house wouldn't make me feel better.

Moving on, I enter Malicevile's study. The shelves full of souls have been emptied, but everything else remains the same—from the sturdy desk with the computer and phone, to the artwork and leopard skin rug. If he was planning on leaving forever, I'd think he'd pack some of this stuff up, but it's hard to tell. Malicevile is a wealthy demon with great influence in the human world. Material items are replaceable.

I release a long breath. What does it matter anyway? I

can't stay here, hoping he'll come back with Evan so I can negotiate for his soul. Malicevile would never make the trade. By owning Evan, he already has me. It's only a matter of time. Evan would never forgive me if I tried to bargain. This thought is the one thing that holds me back. It held me back the night Evan left with my demonic father.

I cross the room, trailing my fingers across every surface. A thin layer of dust coats the desk, and I grab the stapler next to the phone and throw it at a framed orange, red, and yellow abstract watercolor painting. It cracks the glass front and hits the floor with a thud. I look around the desk and pick up a paperweight and throw it at another painting. Destroying Malicevile's study helps to release the anger I'm holding.

I walk around the desk and turn on the computer, but it's password protected, and when I try to guess, it locks me out. I thrust my hands at the monitor and knock it right off the desk before swinging my arm across the surface of the sleek wood to clear everything else that remains.

"You deserve this, you know," I say out loud even though Malicevile can't hear me. "I should destroy everything."

I peer around the room. Actually, I think I will destroy everything.

It doesn't take long to tear up the leopard skin rug or tip the desk. I run my dagger along the wall, scraping the paint before I punch a few holes with my bare hand. My knuckles bleed, leaving droplets of blood behind, but I just wipe them on my jeans and head back into the hallway. It's a huge place, so it might take me a while.

I make my way through the house, destroying the room Malicevile claimed to be mine and then tear through a few guest rooms. On the second floor, I discover Malicevile's lair and hold my nose when I enter his enormous sleeping quarters that are bigger than most apartments.

A California king bed sits in the middle of the room against the far wall, flanked by sleek black side tables. It's a silly thing to own considering that he disappears when the sun rises, so he's awake all night, if he even sleeps at all. A sitting area is set up to the right of the bed, tucked in the far corner where an eighty-inch TV hangs on the wall with a couch and recliner facing it. Floor to ceiling built-in shelves fill the wall to the left, and two opened doors lead to a bathroom and a walk-in closet.

I stroll along the perimeter of the room and stop at a shiny black table with framed photos decorating the top of it. My heart sinks into my stomach when I realize that I'm among one of the faces. He has a photo of me as a child with my mom. I have no idea how he got his hands on it, but it sends a shiver through me. There's also a collage of my school photos up until I was fourteen when Alana saved me from his evil grasp. Near the edge of the table is one more photo, one much more recent, and it's of me and Alana, sitting on a bus stop bench just after sunset. It was from a few months ago, before Dylan nudged me into the Veiled Realm.

Malicevile has been watching me. I shouldn't have expected any less of him, but it makes me angry—livid. I smash all the frames on the top of the table and rip the photos free. I can't leave them here. Not if he's coming back.

As I grab one more frame, I realize I'm clutching a photo of my dead sister Melanie and Malicevile. They smile at the camera, looking somewhat normal, and I try to imagine what it was like to be raised by a demon and how on earth she turned out to be somewhat good. Good enough to want to fight everything that our father stood for. I smash the frame down and pull the picture free before ripping it in half and leaving the image of Malicevile on the floor among the destruction where he belongs.

Tilting my head to the roof, I inhale another breath as my rage melts into sadness. I'd throw some words out for my dead sister to the universe, but her soul remains in Malicevile's hands. I just want to understand her. I want to understand all of this.

I hate the confusion burrowing into my mind, making me question if my father is really as evil as I think he is. How could another being love him if he were? *He stole your boyfriend's soul. He's evil.*

I spin around without touching anything else. I can't stand to be here any longer. Every trace of his presence crushes my soul—his absence a reminder of all the things wrong with my life. I'm afraid I'll never see Evan again, yet I'm afraid of what I'll find if I do. Demons change you. I have to brace myself for anything.

I make my way back to the front door and peer through the peephole for signs of the hellhounds. My wild emotions push me to turn the knob even though it'd be safer to wait until morning. I'm just not sure I'll survive in this house until then.

I crack the door open and sniff. The faint smell of burning flesh lingers in the air. Pursing my lips, I release a low whistle. The moment the hellhounds hear me, they'll come lunging for the door.

I wait a moment, wondering if they're tricking me into thinking the coast is clear. Hellhounds are broken werewolves—they're smart. They lack humanity, but they're still as intelligent as a human with the keen senses of a wolf.

"Here, little hellhound. Come out and show your fiery self." My words echo through the quiet night.

A low whimper whispers through the air, and I crane my neck out to get a better look at the porch. One massive figure lies on its side, scratching its long talon nails against the now disgusting porch. It looks like something exploded, spewing guts and tar all over the place. I take a step out from the house, and the scent of burning flesh and decay nearly knocks me backwards.

I didn't get a good whiff of the hellhounds' scent because neither of them are burning. One lies bruised and beaten and whimpering, and the other—well, the other one is the black tar and guts everywhere. I guess Mr. Coal Eyes didn't stand a chance against his much larger brother.

I levitate over the mess and glide toward the injured broken werewolf. A low growl rips from its throat, and it snaps at me when I try to get a better look at its injuries, but then it stares me dead in the eyes. I cover my mouth with my hand when pale gray, *human* eyes gaze at me. This poor hellhound is only half-broken, and it was abandoned by the demon who failed to finish the job.

It's not the first time I've stumbled across a hellhound with humanity. Lola, the broken werewolf who I helped save before, was the reason I ended up in the position that forced me to make a deal with my father in the first place. It's what led the alliance leaders to sentence me to death.

I swallow the knot forming in my throat at the memory. It takes everything in me to kneel next to the slimy body of the injured hellhound, because all I want to do is leave this place and never look back. But, how could I leave this poor soul behind? I might be Hell-bound, but I still have a heart and soul.

I gently touch the hellhound's muzzle. "Stay with me, all right. I'm going to save you. I promise. You didn't deserve this."

Tugging my cell phone from my pocket, I notice another dozen calls from Dylan and one from Alana. I tap Dylan's name and watch as my phone lights up as it calls the one person I know who can help me.

"God, Cami. I thought I was going to have to wait for your dreams to talk to you," he says without greeting me. "I'm sorry. I'm sorry for everything. I just think we need to talk about everything—about us, whatever that means."

The words stick in my throat as tears prickle my eyes for the millionth time tonight. The hellhound whimpers again, and I force myself to speak. "That's going to have to wait," I say, shaking my head to clear my mind. "I need your help, Dylan. Can you come to me?" I don't know why I ask. I know he will. *You suck as a person. You know that, right?*

I rattle off directions and tell him to fly so he can spot my car and enter the premises without needing to break-down the impenetrable wall. He doesn't comment about me being at my demonic dad's house but just says he'll see me in a bit.

I hang up the phone and scoot closer to the poor defeated hellhound. I rest my fingers on the top of its head, the only place that isn't oozing, and hum a soft melody my mom used to sing to me as a child.

The hellhound closes its eyes, and we sit together on our tormentor's porch, waiting for our angel to arrive. I don't know who needs Dylan more, me or the hellhound. Either way, we're both broken.

STRAIGHT TO HELL

A LOW GROWL startles me awake. The hellhound's warning vibrates under my hand, and I point my dagger at a threat I'm too bleary eyed to see. A figure stands on the bottom step leading to the porch but doesn't come near.

"Cami, it's me," Dylan says, his low voice slightly cracking.

I pat the top of the hellhound's head. "It's okay. Dylan's here to help. Unless you want to stay a hellhound."

The beast whimpers and rests his head on his paws. Dylan climbs the stairs, taking two at a time, and grimaces when he notices the remnants of the shredded hellhound that tried to devour me for dinner. He tiptoes through the gore and looks down at me. I don't attempt to move. I'm too exhausted to do anything besides pet the gross greasy skin of the burnt out broken werewolf.

Dylan crouches down next to me and reaches his hand out to let the hellhound sniff the back of his hand. The hellhound whimpers again and nuzzles his nose against Dylan's fingers. People and creatures alike can tell Dylan's pure in intent. The angel blood within his veins puts most people at ease—well, except Alana. She still has a hard time with Dylan, but only because he was a Demon Watcher sent to keep track of my soul.

I release a long sigh. "He's injured pretty badly. The mess on the ground was one of the completely broken ones Malicevile left behind."

Dylan touches the side of the hellhound. "Why did you come here alone, Cami? I could've come with you. It's not the first time I've been here, you know."

I press my lips together. "It's different when it's after dark. I can't just drag you into possible danger, Dylan. I have a hard enough time protecting myself. I can't worry about you, too." I look down at the half-broken werewolf. "Now, can you help him?"

Dylan nods without another word and positions himself to the other side of the beast. He rests his hands on the hellhound, closing his eyes, and his brilliant, ethereal wings stretch out on his back. A light breeze picks up my hair, blowing the dark tendrils around my face, and I close my eyes to absorb as much of Dylan's heavenly warmth as I can manage.

A soft groan escapes from Dylan as a loud pop sounds through the night. I open my eyes to watch as white tufts of fur fight to break through the demon taint coating the half-broken werewolf. The hellhound convulses under Dylan's touch and fear creeps around my heart, squeezing it, taking my breath away.

A long howl erupts through the night as the blackened, burnt skin falls off the animal, leaving behind soft fur. The longer Dylan touches the hellhound, the more it thrashes, and then all of a sudden, the fur sucks back into human skin, and a naked, hairless man screams in agony before us.

A large gash bleeds along his side, and the top of his bald head is littered with teeth marks. The man's leg is bent in a weird angle, surely broken, and he's missing a chunk from his bare thigh.

Dylan hugs the man to him protectively, and I shrug out of my jacket and cover the man with it. When the man stops screaming, Dylan pulls away, wiping sweat from his forehead with his sleeve, and then tugs his own shirt off to staunch the man's leg wound.

"Call for help, Cami," Dylan says. "These wounds are bad."

"I can't just lead a bunch of ordinary humans to a demon's lair. Can you fly him to my car? The academy is nearby. They can help him."

Without another word, Dylan picks up the man, struggling only a bit under his weight, and carries him to the front yard to launch into the air. I get to my feet, looking around one last time, and bound after Dylan, half running and half levitating until I reach my car.

I help Dylan put the bleeding man into the backseat, and a moment later, I'm peeling out as I turn around to head to the place that nearly destroyed everything.

I just hope this time, I make it out unscathed.

⁂

The academy is exactly how I remember it, though the atmosphere is much more somber this time of night. The waning moon glows above us, and the stars pepper the black sky like pinholes in a sheet of black construction paper. The guard opens the gate when Dylan waves out the window, and I'm kind of surprised they actually let me in.

Instead of wasting time parking in the guest lot, I drive onto a cement walkway, driving half in the grass, and barrel through campus toward the infirmary. The headlights of the Mercedes shine across the window, and a man in scrubs rushes out, shielding his eyes from the light.

I thrust the gear into park and hop out before Dylan can even open his door. "Help! We have an injured werewolf. The change made his wounds worse."

The man hops into action and bolts toward the side Dylan is helping the poor reborn werewolf from. The man groans as they both take on his weight, and I follow behind them into the small medical building. It smells of antiseptic and cleaner, the scent burning the stink of demon from my nostrils.

The last time I was here was when I electrocuted Evan. Just the reminder strikes a nerve, and I have to push my unbidden emotions to the back of my mind. I need a clear head while at the academy. I'm not exactly welcome here even though Leader Dubois, Cadence's dad, pardoned me. He knew I wasn't responsible for Malicevile's actions and that I didn't intentionally go against them. If the other leaders had just listened to him, they'd still be alive.

"Tell me what happened," the man in scrubs says. His nametag glimpses in the light, and I read Dr. Hamilton. "What kind of demon did this?"

I swallow, trying to moisten my mouth. "Hellhound."

Dr. Hamilton starts cleaning the most threatening wound on the werewolf's leg. Dylan stands behind me with his arms crossed over his chest without saying a word. He shifts from foot to foot, like he's nervous to be here.

The doctor hits a button on the wall next to him, and a buzzer rings out through the air before a woman in identical scrubs rushes into the room. She stands at Dr. Hamilton's side and inspects the injuries.

"Have you seen anything like this, Dr. Hall? The girl says it was a hellhound." Dr. Hamilton shoots me a quick look. "There aren't any burn marks, but some of the tar residue is still inside the wounds."

I clear my throat. "That's because this man was a hell-hound when he got injured."

Dylan sighs from behind me. "We should go, Cami. We've done all we can."

I frown. "We need to stay. I want to make sure he's taken care of."

As the words come out of my mouth, the werewolf starts convulsing on the table. Froth spews from his mouth along with what looks like ash and burned skin. His gray eyes roll to the back of his head.

The doctors jump into action, turning the man slightly so he doesn't choke to death on the remnants of the horror he's been through, and I stand back and let them work. When the man stops, he groans, and his eyes flutter open to meet mine.

I stand over him and touch his bald head. "You're going to be okay. Hang in there."

His mouth opens and closes as he finds the will to talk. Who knows how long he's been trapped in that ungodly state. "Thank you, beautiful demon," he whispers.

Goose bumps prickle on my arms. No one has heard his words except me. My forehead crinkles as hopelessness rushes through me. Werewolves know the difference between demons and their half-human spawns, yet he flat out called me a demon.

I shake my head. "I'm no demon." I can't even hear my own words, but I can tell the werewolf has.

"I'm indebted to you for transforming me back. My soul is yours." Tears rim the man's eyes.

I touch my fingers to his warm cheeks. "I'm not a demon. Your soul is your own, and you're free."

A huge smile crosses the man's face as he stares past me toward the ceiling. A second later, his eyes roll back again, and his body thrashes as he has another seizure. I drop my hands to my sides, and Dylan wraps his arms around me from behind. He pulls me back away from the doctors and the reborn werewolf.

I can't take my eyes away from the scene unfolding in front of me. The man suddenly stops, lying lifelessly on the table, and Dr. Hamilton starts performing CPR. The other doctor, Dr. Hall, grabs a defibrillator and shocks the man's heart. Nothing happens.

Tears burn in my eyes when Dr. Hamilton states the time of death for this poor, unknown man. A sob rakes through me, and Dylan ushers me from the infirmary and nearly carries me out to the car as the weight of the werewolf's death sits heavy on my Hell-bound soul.

He plops me in the front seat of the Mercedes and navigates us back to the front gate of the academy without incident. I lean my head against the cool window, tears dripping down my face. My hands tremble in my lap as I replay the words the man said to me as he lay dying. He called me a demon. He gave me his soul, and when I didn't want it, he died. It's hard not to feel like I'm to blame. I failed him.

A gentle hand touches my knee. I reach out and link my fingers with Dylan, feeling his comforting touch as he drives us through the dark night. The last place I want to go is home. I want to run off into the night again and kill more demons. I want to make them all pay for what they do to innocent people. What they've done to me.

I sniffle, wiping my nose on my sleeve, not really caring. "I don't understand. You saved him, Dylan. You brought him back from Hell, and he died."

He squeezes my fingers. "Some things aren't meant to be understood, love. People die all the time without reason. It's just how life is."

I choke on my next words. It's hard to even spit them out. "This is my punishment. He died because of me. Because I'm not meant to save people anymore. He called me a demon, you know. Said it like it was just a fact of life." My chest quivers with my next breath. "Maybe because I'm Hell-bound, all I get from this life is the bad. Life is preparing me for what comes next."

He's quiet for a minute, and I expect him to agree with me. Instead, he says, "You can't blame yourself for Malicevile's actions. And if someone even tried to drag you to Hell, they'd have to get through me. I won't let anyone take your soul."

His words make me feel slightly better but grief still sits heavy on my chest. The more I sit here and wallow, the harder it is to handle. It's why I go on hunts with Cadence.

It's why we follow every single lead we get to hopefully find Evan and Malicevile. But now that we've run into a dead-end, I don't even know what to do.

We sit in silence the rest of the way back to the house, and when he pulls my car behind Cadence's Jaguar, neither of us opens the door to get out. I'd be okay sitting here all night if it meant I didn't have to look Alana and David in the eyes. My protectors don't need the constant reminder that I'm here when Evan isn't. It was his choice to make the deal with Malicevile, but he left me with all the damage and aftermath. I'd give anything to see him again, even if it was only to yell at him.

"I can tell you don't want to be here," Dylan says quietly.

I shrug. "Not really. It's hard, you know."

"You can't keep running forever."

I purse my lips. "I can try."

I finally give in to Dylan's pleading eyes and thrust my door open. The few pictures I took from Malicevile's fall out onto the walkway, and Dylan helps me pick them up. His face remains expressionless as he looks through them, and I snag them away and hide them out of sight.

"A souvenir," I mutter, walking next to him to the door.

"You don't have to explain," he says.

I bump his shoulder with mine. "I wasn't going to."

When I reach the front door, I freeze. The scent of cinnamon and clove wafts through the air, and I recognize the aroma belonging to my father. My heart races, my hands turn clammy, and I spin around to search the dark night. This is what I've been waiting for. I've been searching every day these last few weeks for a clue, and he's finally given me one.

"It's him," I say, turning to Dylan. "Malicevile was here. Come on. He might not be far away."

Dylan doesn't move from his place on the front porch, and I consider leaving him behind.

"Cami," he says, his voice lower than usual. "There's something here."

I spin and jog back to him where he stands at the door. He points to the potted hydrangeas, and I see the blue envelope sticking out from underneath it.

I yank it free and tuck it into my pocket. "I'll read it later. Come on. We'll lose him."

He shakes his head. "No, I can't go. You shouldn't either."

I throw up my hands. "Are you kidding me? Just stay here. Tell Alana I'll be back."

Without another word, I slide my dagger from its sheath and run off into the night to find the demon I've spent my whole life running from. Hopefully he's not leading me straight to Hell.

WORST FEAR

THE TANTALIZING SCENT that could very well be my own destruction lingers in the air as I cross Starlight Drive and head toward the main road. Malicevile is on foot, his cinnamon and clove scent clinging to everything he passes by.

But why now? Why come out of hiding now? *You destroyed one of his houses. Maybe he's come with a warning.* My hand automatically touches the envelope in my pocket, but I don't let it hold me back.

Stopping on a corner, I peer around the quiet neighborhood for signs of evil. Nothing seems out of the ordinary, so I continue half-running, half-levitating, until I reach a wide intersection. I freeze when my eyes catch sight of two figures waiting on the corner diagonally from me.

I blink, not sure if I'm seeing things or if they're real. Malicevile and Evan stand tall, watching me watch them. My chest heaves as I suck in a few breaths. I've been waiting weeks for this moment, to see Evan again. And my heart breaks all over again. He doesn't react to my presence. He just straightens his shoulders, his lips pressed in a thin line.

I refuse to even look at Malicevile.

Neither of us makes a move, and I wonder if they'd stand in that spot until the sunrises if I don't move. A million plans rush through my mind. I could attempt to make a deal, or I can beg for my father to show me some sympathy after everything...or I could take a chance and face my demon head on.

Without another thought, I charge forward, not sure what I'm going to do. All I know is I want Malicevile to hurt as much as I hurt. I want him to regret making a deal with Evan. I want to cut his heart out and stomp on it. Whatever I do, it won't involve standing here and doing nothing.

My boots thud against the asphalt as I charge straight for my father. I brace myself, expecting him to do one of two things—run or attack. I raise my dagger to throw it. I might not be able to kill him, but if I can just make him bleed and feel my pain, my world would start to right itself. It might not be the same type of pain, because Malicevile isn't capable of human emotions, but it's better than nothing.

Before I have a chance to throw the dagger, Evan steps in front of Malicevile, a darkness in his eyes that I've never seen before, and I falter. In that split second of hesitation, I leave myself open, and Evan launches a fireball at me. It hits me square in the chest, smoldering the fabric of my shirt. Stumbling back, I fall into the middle of the street, scraping my palms on the asphalt all while losing my dagger.

Headlights blind me, car tires squeal, and the sound of a horn echoes in my ears. I somersault backward, throwing myself out of the way of the speeding car that doesn't even swerve. It skids to a stop, blocking my view of Malicevile and Evan. The driver doesn't move to get out. All she does is throw me a heated glare and stomps the accelerator, leaving me alone in the putrid air filled with hot rubber, cinnamon, and my own sweat.

I push to my feet and look in the direction Malicevile and Evan were standing, but they're gone, and I've lost them once again.

Even though I know Evan is demon-tainted and controlled, his attempt to hurt me to protect my father leaves me reeling. It's like I didn't even register to him, like I'm just some girl out to hurt his master. The boy who would've once died for me now would die for the person I despise most in the world. And there's nothing I can do to change it.

My worst fear has been proven. The boy I knew and loved is just a demonic shell of himself.

I was hoping to find something human left in his eyes, something to give me the hope to carry on, but it wasn't there. The evil mirrored my father's, and I know the Evan I fell in love with is gone forever. He not only traded his soul—he threw away his heart, his mind, and everything I loved about him. He steeled himself from everything human about him. It's what the hopeless do, the ones who know that there is no changing their fates. He didn't hold onto his old life at all. That shell of a person staring me down wasn't Evan. I don't know who that boy was.

I jog from the street and plop down on the curb. Tears burn my eyes, but I don't let them fall. I can't. Not now. Not when I'm vulnerable.

I don't get up to walk home but instead pull the blue envelope from my pocket and rip the seal with my finger. I'm almost afraid to read it. Why would my father go through so much trouble to drop off something at my door instead of mailing it? He obviously knows where I live. I can't hide from him. I don't want to.

I tug a couple of fragrant, cream-colored papers free and bring them to my nose. Hints of patchouli mingle with the overpowering cinnamon, but I cling to Evan's scent like my life depends on it. His familiar scrawl scribbles across the pages, and I can't believe he's the one who wrote this.

Tears blur my eyes, making it hard to read, but I force

them away. This is what I've needed. It's not as good as hearing his voice but will do.

Cami,

I'm writing you this letter because if I don't, you'll never give up and back off like I want you to.

I meant it when I said this was the best decision I've ever made. I've never felt so powerful until now. It's like someone unlocked my soul and set me free from my human bonds, and now nothing can hold me back or stop me.

Malicevile is nothing like the evil monster the Hunter's Alliance portrayed him to be. He did them a favor by destroying their leaders. They're nothing but silly humans looking for trouble and can't see the bigger picture. Their time is over, and soon, the time of humans will be over as well. Humans no longer come first. Why should they? They're powerless and corrupt, and have no idea of the gifts they were given by just being alive. They're a mockery of the greater powers and should bow down to us. We're not the ones they should fear. They should fear themselves.

Until you realize the truth, I need you to stay away. You're only making it harder on yourself, clinging to the stupid emotions of your humanity. Your father said your soul has already picked the right side, and now your mind and heart must do the same. It's the only way for you to feel as you should— without heartache and worry. Without pain. I can honestly say I don't miss my human life. I don't miss anything. I don't miss you.

I want you to stop missing me, too, because I know deep down that I loved you at one point enough to trade my soul, but my feelings have changed. I'm sure the old me would want you to carry on, but that person no longer exists. I hope my words help you push past this. I'm tired of your father evading you. It's why he allowed me to write you. We're on the same side, you know, but for some reason beyond me, you still choose to side with the humans, with that frightened little nephilim.

I rest the papers on my knee, my heart smashing to pieces. Evan might have written these words, but that's not him talking. That's his corrupted soul. I know he doesn't mean anything, but I don't know how to fix it. If I should even try. What if he is truly happy? I know we've always had our doubts about the alliance and their "humans come first" motto, but I can't accept that he thinks so little of humans now. Alana, David, and Cadence are all human. Does he think they deserve mistreatment? That idea alone pushes me away from ever agreeing with any of Evan's new beliefs.

I blink my eyes a few times and continue reading.

They will be the people to destroy you. The nephilim was assigned to watch you. He's going to take your soul the moment you let your guard down. It's what he does. He's the reason you were given a death sentence. He informed the Hunter's Alliance of how close you were to evil. He's the reason I had to make a trade for your life. Yet, here you are, siding with him like I al-

ways knew you would.

You have such a hatred for who you are, you think being around him will redeem you, which isn't true. There's nothing he or anyone can do for you. If you don't embrace who you are, you'll be miserable forever. I don't want that for you. I want you by my side. Malicevile wants you by his. Together, the world will be ours.

If you ever really loved me, you'd stop killing our kin. You'd open your eyes and accept the power that was meant to flow through your veins. You'd put humanity behind you.

Until you can, this is goodbye. Don't try to stand against us, Cami. If you do, you'll regret it. I don't want to have to hurt you, but I will. It's not about you and me anymore. It's much bigger than that. I'll be around when you make your decision.

Regards,
Evan

At the bottom of the paper is an unfamiliar phone number. I don't know why, but I program it into my cell phone in case I lose the letter. I should burn it on the spot, but his words run deep into my soul.

When I fold the letter, I notice a short note from Malicevile on the backside of the last page. His gorgeous, swirly script makes me burn daggers at the paper.

My Dear Camilla,

I always thought I'd want to stake a claim on your soul, but as it turns out, I don't need to when I have Evan. I know you'll come around.

When you do, I'll be waiting with open arms. We'll be the family we always should've been.

Forever yours,
Father

Crumpling the papers in my hands, I consider throwing the ball into the street. Doubt is the only thing holding me back. After a minute of digging the paper ball into my palms, I slowly flatten out the pages and shove them back into the envelope.

I hate this. I hate how vulnerable I feel, and how they've made me second guess my life in a matter of seconds. The reborn werewolf was right. I'm not only a demon's daughter, I am a demon. Fighting against my heritage feels hopeless when the one I love has turned against me.

I thought Evan would be miserable at Malicevile's side. It's why I've been searching so hard the last few weeks. But he's not. He hasn't been. He's half-demon and Hell-bound. I was stupid to think I could save his soul and bring his humanity back. I don't even know what to do now. I can't even kill Malicevile without putting Evan at risk.

As the dark emotions consume me, I scream into the quiet night. I don't care if I draw attention to myself. I don't care about anything anymore. And it doesn't even scare me.

My phone rings from my pocket, and I pull it out and answer without looking at it. "I'll be home by dawn," I say.

"Cami, Leader Dubois is here," Alana says. "You need to come home. Now."

I groan. "I'm not in the mood to face him. I've had a long night."

She's quiet for a moment. "You okay?"

I shake my head no but then say, "Yeah. We'll talk about it later. Give me a few minutes, okay?"

"Sure thing. Be safe."

Never am. "Yup."

I hang up the phone and push to my feet. I know exactly why Leader Dubois has come to the house, but I don't feel like explaining to him about the hellhound or anything else. And I plan to tell it to his face. I want the alliance to leave me alone. I'm not their puppet. I'm not their problem. I'm nothing to them.

This time I'll make them get it.

<hr>

Dylan waits for me on the porch, his black hair hanging in his eyes. He doesn't smile when he sees me but just opens his arms so I can fall into them. A sob builds in my chest and forces its way out my throat, and he rubs his hand over my back for the minute it takes me to compose myself. I want nothing more than to break down and drown myself in my own tears, but I have more pressing matters at hand, so fading into my sorrows will have to wait.

I sniffle. "I saw him." My voice barely comes out, and I'm not sure Dylan heard my words. "He threw a fireball at me."

"I'm so sorry, love. I didn't want you going after them. People change when a demon owns their soul." He squeezes me against him, holding me so close I can feel his heartbeat through the burned fabric of my shirt. His apple and rain shower scent caresses me in the comfort I need now more than ever. Yet it hurts, because Evan's letter comes to mind. He knew I'd run to Dylan...*God, I feel horrible.*

I suck in a deep breath. "I knew what to expect, but it was still so hard."

His lips brush my ear. "It doesn't get easy. This is his life now, Cami. There's only two ways to change it."

I've been faced with the two options for weeks, and they're both so awful that I refuse to think about them now. One, trading Malicevile for something he wants more, like my own soul, won't even work now. He thinks he already has me through Evan. And the other option, I can't fathom. I can't even repeat it in my mind. It's not really an option to me.

I lean back and press my fingers to his lips. "I'll figure out another way. I swear I will."

"And I'll do my best to help you," he says.

The door creaks open, drawing my attention to the

house. Alana peeks her head out. Her sad eyes meet mine, and I'm not sure I'm going to tell her about the letter, because then she'll tell David, and he hates me enough as it is.

She pushes the screen open. "I know you don't want to talk to Cadence's dad, but I think it's important that you know what's going on."

I sigh and turn back to Dylan. He presses his lips together without giving anything away. I know he still helps the alliance on occasion. Something has to keep him busy while I'm out hunting with Cadence, but I try not to think about him working for the enemy. *The enemy? Do you hear yourself? There's only one real enemy.*

Pushing the thought away, I hold my hand out to Dylan. He intertwines his fingers with mine, his touch cooling the heat of my hand, helping me think more clearly. With him at my side, things don't seem so daunting. So hopeless.

When we step inside, Cadence, David, and Aston Dubois sit in the living room, drinking from steaming mugs. Alana perches on the arm of the couch next to David, and I don't bother to make myself comfortable. Instead, I just hover in the middle of the room, burnt shirt and all, with Dylan at my side. My jaw tightens as I glare into the eyes of one of the people who didn't fight hard enough to change the verdict of my death sentence.

I lick my dry lips. "I'm surprised to see you out of the safety of the academy this late."

Aston leans forward and sets his mug on the coffee table. "I'm still an active demon hunter. The night doesn't scare me, Cami."

I twist my lips to the side. I had no idea that Aston still fought in the field. I thought the alliance leaders stayed far away from danger.

"It should," I say.

Alana sighs, and I draw my attention to my guardian. She raises her eyebrows when she looks at me, and I wonder what she's thinking. I haven't exactly been open with her the last few weeks when she refused to aid Cadence and me in the hunt. She's changed since she took me to the academy, and I'm afraid she's grown soft. I used to be able to count on her for anything. Now she just always looks tired.

Everyone stares at me with pity marring their faces. I narrow my eyes, letting go of Dylan's hand to place my hands on my hips.

"What? You all need to stop that. I'm tired of the looks of pity and how you tiptoe around every subject with me. I'm okay. Really. I'm trying to live my life. I'm trying to make a difference." I turn to Aston. "You're here because of my visit to campus, right?"

He presses his lips into a line. "Sort of. Bringing in a badly injured werewolf, claiming it was previously a hellhound, was quite surprising for the medical staff."

"It was a hellhound," Dylan says, cutting in. Aston might believe him more than me. "I healed his soul. Unfortunately, his wounds were too great." A sadness lines his voice, poking at my heart like a hot iron.

Aston turns to look at David and Alana. Cadence stares at me with wide eyes.

After a long moment, Aston says, "The point is you both saved a Broken One. That's enough for the alliance to welcome you back into its good grace." He turns to Alana. "I've even asked your guardians to fill two of the empty seats among the alliance leaders. They've both accepted."

My mouth drops open. David? That doesn't surprise me. But Alana? "What? Are you kidding me? After everything we've been through, you've decided to join the leaders? One of their hunters almost killed you!" My voice rises, echoing through the room. "They sentenced me to death! It's their fault Evan lost his humanity. It's their fault he's with Malicevile. It's their fault for everything!"

Rage washes through me. Without saying another word or letting anyone else speak, I fly from the room, back to my bedroom, and slam the door. I kick over some of my still-packed boxes of Evan's belongings—the stuff I've held onto in hopes that I'd get him back. But he's not coming back. Not now. Not ever.

I pick up a box and toss it at the wall. Evan's clothes scatter to the floor in a heap that smells of laundry soap and his warm scent. I glide closer and drop to my knees. Scooping up a shirt, I bring it to my nose, feeling my heart shatter all over again.

"Why, God? Why him? Why me? Why this? Help me

understand. Do you even listen to the Hell-bound?" I sigh when I don't get a response. I don't expect one, either. Tears prickle my eyes. "I'll do whatever you want. Just help me. Please. What should I do?"

A knock sounds on my door, and Dylan walks in without waiting for me to answer. His wings flash as he drops to the ground next to me and pulls me into his arms. He pets my hair, letting me cry into his shirt.

When the sobs subside, I take a breath and say, "I don't know what to do, Dylan. Everything feels so wrong. I'm not going back to the academy. I don't even know if I can stay here anymore. It's too much." I wave my hands around me. "This—keeping his stuff—it kills me. It reminds me he's not here. And the letter—" I pull the crumpled envelope out and hand it to him. "The letter proves that he's not coming back."

Dylan skims over it and sets it on the floor. "I'm sorry, Cami. I really am. Maybe we should leave for a while. Let things settle here."

I shudder as I release another long breath. "You'll come with me?"

He nods. "Wherever you want to go."

"I want to hunt for half-broken souls. If I can't save Evan, I need to do what I can to save others. It might be my only saving grace. All I know is I can't stay here. Not if Malicevile plans on returning. Not if Alana joins the alliance leaders. I. Just. Can't."

He touches my chin. "We'll leave in the morning."

For the first time in weeks, I feel relief. I feel hope. I feel alive.

I don't know how to thank him, so I kiss him. I kiss him with every single broken piece of me until he fills me up and holds me together.

ONLY WAY TO MAKE IT

"PLEASE, CAMI. THINK this through. You're acting irrational. It'll get you killed," Alana says from my doorway.

I continue to pack my bag, taking only my necessities. I
have no idea how long I'll be gone, maybe forever, but I'm
used to traveling light. It makes for an easier getaway.

I drop my makeup bag on top of my pile of clothes.
"You don't understand, Alana. I have to go. Staying will get
you killed. I'm not the same girl you rescued. Don't worry
so much. I can take care of myself."

"What about Dylan and Cadence? Can you take care of
them, too?" she questions, hugging herself.

I don't have the answer to her question, because I honestly don't know. "They're choosing to come. They want to help me."

"Help you with what? You've been dancing around your reason since you declared you were leaving again. Is this because of the alliance? What happened last night? Please, just sit down and talk to me." Her eyes line with tears as she pleads with me.

I suck in a small breath and clench my fingers into fists. "It has to do with everything. I just—I can't talk right now. Give me time. I don't want you to talk me out of going."

She sniffles. "Cami..." Her voice trails off into silence.

It hurts me to my very soul to see how much pain I'm putting her through, but she'll thank me later. That's all I'll ever be to her—the one who causes constant trouble and heartache. I've always known she'd be better off without me, but I couldn't leave. I was too afraid I'd be worse off without her in my life. And maybe I will be, but this isn't about me anymore.

I gather all the weapons I have and set them in a leather duffle bag, keeping my favorite dagger out to carry with me.

"Cami," Alana says again. "Please." Her voice cracks. "You're what's left of my family. Haven't we lost enough?"

I flinch at her words. "Just stop. I've made up my mind. I have enough guilt to last me for eternity. You don't need to add to it."

With those final words, I sling my bags over my shoulder and cross the room. I wrap my arms around Alana and hug her like it's the last one we'll ever share. Tears line both our eyes, and I don't pull away until she lets me go.

I smile weakly and leave her hovering in the doorway to my bedroom. As I make my way down the hallway, I don't look back. It'll just make leaving that much harder. In my soul, I know this is the right thing to do. Alana will understand. At least, I hope she will.

Cadence and Dylan wait for me in the living room. David is nowhere to be found, and I doubt he'll come to say goodbye. Dylan takes my bags from me while Cadence holds a box in her hands.

She gives it to me. "I didn't think you wanted to leave these here."

I clutch the box in my hands without opening it. "Thanks," I whisper.

It's a memento box that she helped me put together containing items like a picture of my parents Alana had stolen from the Hunter's Academy Research Center, Malicevile's file and the letters he's written me, notes Evan and I wrote each other, some photos of everyone I care about. I even added the letter from Evan to it last night.

Dylan heads to the door first, and we follow him out. The backseat of the Mercedes is still covered in werewolf blood, so we all climb into Cadence's Jaguar. I sit next to Cadence in the front, and Dylan sits behind me, resting his hands on my shoulders. His apple, rain shower scent fills the car, calming the anxiety tightening my muscles.

We sit for a moment, and then Cadence reverses. I shift in my seat and watch my house disappear. My heart hangs heavy in my chest, but I know this is the right thing to do. This is the only way I'm going to make it in this world.

❧

The blazing sunset hangs low over the ocean as we drive down the Pacific Coast Highway to a non-alliance affiliated safe house. It's tucked in the small town of Moonlight Shores, only a couple hours from the academy.

I used to fear the setting sun, but now it doesn't bother me. I can tell it still puts Dylan and Cadence on edge though.

"We'll make it just in time," Cadence says from behind the wheel. She taps her fingers along to the soft music, the AC blowing her purple hair behind her. She has the vent circulating fresh air to make sure I can catch the scent of any possible threat.

Cadence turns onto a street that ends at the ocean and makes a right into an eclectic beach community full of bungalows, duplexes, a few mansions, and a church at the end of the block. I know that's where we're heading before she can point it out.

She pulls into the driveway of a three-story mansion, surprising me. After she cuts the engine off, none of us moves to get out. The mansion was built on the beach, so the back door would lead to the ocean. The wall-like windows reflect the surrounding palm trees, preventing us from seeing inside. The arched entrance shows off a red door, and the house looks like a series of curves and lines, all the windows arching and the roof flat with what looks like a glass wall. I bet the ocean looks amazing from the roof setup.

An earthy scent, like wet dirt and grass, wafts into the car, causing the hairs on my arms to rise. Before I even have a chance to touch the hilt of my dagger, two giant fists bang on my window, startling me. I meet the eyes of a bulky man with shoulder length, blond hair and dark brown eyes. He bares his teeth, a weird noise that sounds like a growl, creeping in through the crack in my window.

My heart races, and I shift my gaze to Cadence who starts the car. As she tries to reverse, a man and a woman step behind the car and block our way. She'd have to run over them to get out. Another two men come up on her side, and she glances at me.

"Open the door," the man at my window says, banging his fists again.

I raise my eyebrow. "We've changed our minds about staying here. If you'd ask your pack to move, we'll be on our way."

He glowers. "Can't do that. You reek of demon. You'll send your master to collect us at nightfall."

Pulling what looks like a small bronze screwdriver from his pocket, he punches it into the glass, breaking it. I unbuckle my seatbelt, refusing to be trapped in place and slide my dagger from its sheath on my hip.

The man reaches in and grabs me by my hair despite Dylan's protests. He throws me to the ground, and I somersault to my feet and point my dagger in his direction.

"This is a big misunderstanding," I say. "Look at my friends."

"I don't have to. The whole car reeks of demon."

Someone grabs me from behind, and I thrash as I watch the other werewolves pull Dylan and Cadence out. Dylan elbows a man with a bald head before opening his wings and launching into the air.

Cadence steps on another man's foot when he becomes distracted and flees to the street and out of reach.

I don't move. The last thing I want to do is provoke a pack of werewolves. That ended badly for me last time.

"Let Cami go," Dylan says, his wings stirring a breeze that smells of apple and ocean air. "We're seeking shelter. This is a safe house, right? Katie Bauer sent us." Katie is a nephilim who runs a safe house near the academy for those the alliance won't protect.

The woman holding me loosens her grip but doesn't let go. The werewolves stare at me in silence, not paying attention to Dylan and Cadence, like I'm still trying to fool them. It's not my fault I smell like a demon. I am half one.

"I'm not here to hurt you. I'm a demi-demon. It's why I smell like a tainted one," I say.

The woman sniffs my hair. "She smells more than half," she says to her pack leader, the blond who broke Cadence's window.

Cadence scoffs, folding her arms. "Are you serious? The sun's still up."

The pack alpha rubs his chin as he looks at me. "Your friends can stay, but you can't."

A door slams, and a woman with a super-short pixie cut, caramel skin, and light brown eyes jogs toward us. She runs her hand over her black hair and offers me a huge smile. She flings her arms around me, hugging me all while pushing the other woman away. I open and close my mouth in confusion.

"I can't believe it's you. You're my real-life angel." She pulls away and points at Dylan, who now stands on the grass a few feet away. "And so is he." She rushes to give Dylan a hug, too.

"I told you to stay inside, Lola," the alpha says.

She pulls away from Dylan and comes back to my side. "You don't understand, Joshua. This is Cami, the girl who saved me. Without her, I'd still be a hellhound."

I didn't recognize Lola. The last time I saw her, she was naked, covered in black slime, and hairless. So much has happened since that night, I never asked Dylan about her. I knew she was safe and that's all that mattered.

The alpha, Joshua, tilts his head to the side to study me. His face softens, his serious eyes crinkling in the corners as a wide smile crosses his face. He opens his arms, surprising me, and lifts me off my feet in a tight hug.

My muscles loosen, and I slide my dagger back in its sheath. The other werewolves crowd around me, each giving me a welcoming hug before turning to welcome Dylan and Cadence. They unload the Jaguar without asking and guide us inside with the promise to fix the window first thing in the morning.

The attention is overwhelming. I'm kind of embarrassed by how they're treating me. It's the first time I've been treated with such kindness and adoration outside of my family.

Once our stuff is in our rooms and we eat dinner, Joshua invites us to the roof. Spiral stairs take us to a gigantic roof deck with a glass wall surrounding the perimeter. A pool table sits off to one side and a picnic bench to the other. Lounge chairs face the dark ocean, and a portable spa sits in the center of the open space. This is definitely the perfect place to relax.

A hot werewolf around our age introduces himself to Cadence, and she winks at me as she walks with him toward the picnic table set up with snacks and drinks. Dylan rests his hand on my back and guides me to the empty lounge chairs. The moonlight sparkles a silver path on the ocean, and I lean my back against Dylan as we share a lounge chair.

We're silent for a few minutes, just sitting in the cool ocean air and smelling the scent of the saltwater. I feel safe and relaxed—the first time I've felt this way since before I lost Evan. I hate myself a little for feeling okay, but I immediately shove the dark emotions to the back of my mind. I can't think like that. I need to stay in the here and now.

I tilt my head back to gaze at the stars. "Do you believe me now? About changing into a full-blooded demon? I'm afraid that one of these mornings, I'll just disappear with the sun."

Dylan breathes softly into my hair. "Demons aren't capable of possessing humanity. You're safe, Cami. I promise."

"Until I'm stripped of that, too. Like Evan," I say. "How much do you really know about us?" I don't have to tell him I mean demi-demons for him to understand. "Most demons accidentally kill their half human spawn. What about the ones who don't?"

He sighs. "No half demon has ever transformed into a full demon, Cami. Even if it were possible, the Demon Watchers would never allow it. But it's not. You're worrying about something that can't happen to you."

"Then why would the alliance leaders want you to take my soul? Why were they so worried? And don't lie to me," I say.

I can't see his face, but his muscles tense. "They assumed you'd turn against them and would return to Malicevile. Disappearing didn't help. But they were wrong in their decision and acted out of line. They don't know you like I do."

"Then why did you tell them my soul shifted to the side of Hell?" I ask, thinking about the letter Evan gave me.

He sighs and shifts me so I have to look at him. "That's not exactly what happened. The state of your soul isn't even the alliance's business. When they asked for my help, I didn't even know they had caught you when I entered that basement. I assumed it was a tainted human. Please, you have to know I'm always on your side. I'd never do anything to hurt you."

His dark eyes plead with me, and I believe him. "I hate that you were put in that position," I say.

He kisses my temple. "That's behind us. Let's keep moving forward, okay?"

I rest my head against him. "Okay." I still have a million questions for Dylan, but I can tell he doesn't want to talk about everything. He's always had his secrets. I just wish he would share them with me. Maybe he can't. I'm Malicevile's daughter after all.

A shadow crawls across the lounge chair next to us, and Joshua slides into the seat, crossing his arms over his chest as he reclines to look at the stars. His blond hair is tucked behind his ears, and he's a lot less threatening now that he's not waving his giant fists in my face.

"I wanted to apologize again about earlier. It never hurts to be safe," he says without meeting my gaze. His earthy scent wafts over me, and I shift to lay my cheek against Dylan's chest to push away the werewolf smell. It still brings back bitter memories of the time the pack of Desertville tried to kill me for the same reason these werewolves confronted me in the driveway.

"It's fine," I say, sucking up my hurt feelings. "I'm just glad Lola was here to intervene. How is she anyway? She's been through the unimaginable."

He finally glances my way but just for a second, like he can't handle to look at me. "She's come a long way since I picked her up the night of her transformation back. I knew her pack and remember when that monster of a demon imprisoned and broke them all. It hit our community pretty hard. Lola said she was sold to the demon the alliance had killed like a pet."

The newfound knowledge sends a chill up my spine. I knew that Lola's pack had been broken, but I never had the chance to ask her more. She was alone in the house, and I thought she was dead, but she had only been stunned. I don't even have to ask Lola to know that my father was behind her hellhound transformation. He's basically the devil on earth and well known. And he has a thing for breaking werewolves. My stomach flips just thinking about it.

"You might want to give the academy a call tomorrow. Lola's not the only werewolf we've saved," Dylan says, speaking up, saying what I didn't want to even think about. "Unfortunately, the man didn't survive because he was injured when we found him, and the change back was too much."

Joshua sucks in a deep breath and whistles. "So, you work for the alliance? I didn't think they did this type of thing. Bringing a werewolf back is unheard of. How did you even do it?" He sits up and swings his legs off the side of the lounge chair. "Are you willing to help us? I lost a few pack mates a few months back. Still know where they are. I can pay you, if that helps."

I wait a minute, hoping Dylan will answer, but he just looks at me. I stare at the dark ocean. The waves roar in my ears, louder than the small voice in the back of my mind that tells me not to give this man hope. Having hope in a terrible situation will only destroy you when it's snuffed out. But I can't help admiring his hope—the hope I've given him. Maybe I'm just jealous.

I shake my head. "I won't take your money, Joshua, and you have to know that it's not as simple as it seems. To bring back a werewolf, the hellhound can't be fully broken. It must still have some of its humanity. It's also dangerous. I'm immune to their fire, but their bites are deadly."

"Just think about it, will you?" he asks.

I brush my windblown hair from my face. "I don't have to. I'll do some investigating tomorrow, okay? If I think there's a chance that we can help, I'll do it."

A smile spreads across his face. "We'll be indebted to you."

I raise my hands. "No. Don't say that. Giving us a place to stay is more than I can ask for."

He leans over and squeezes my shoulder before jumping to his feet to probably tell his pack what I've offered to do. Giving myself a task will help keep my mind off things, and I really do like to help.

"It never hurts to have a werewolf pack owe you a favor," Dylan says.

I twist in his arms to meet his gaze. "Yeah, sure. Knowing my luck, I'll wake up as a demon and find myself in possession of a bunch of werewolf souls."

He smirks, flashing his dimples. "But you're already in possession of souls, you know."

I raise my eyebrows. "What?"

"I've given you mine."

A SOUL LASTS FOREVER

SUNSHINE POURS IN through the sheer curtains on the bedroom window. I still can't get Dylan's words out of my mind, and they've made it impossible to sleep. I have no idea how owning and possessing souls works, but it's never bad to be too careful. It's different than giving someone your heart. A heart can last a lifetime, but a soul lasts forever. Dylan basically promised me forever, and I don't know how I feel about it.

I shift to my side, bouncing the bed, and Dylan's arm slides around my waist. As my tank top strap hangs down my arm, his warm breath tickles my shoulder before his lips brush against my bare skin.

"You didn't sleep," he whispers into my hair. Only he would know something like that. I sometimes think he knows more about me than I know myself. It shouldn't bother me, but it does.

I turn over to face him, pressing my forehead against his. "Couldn't. I didn't feel like facing the nightmares. Not now."

He sighs against my lips. "You should try now. I'll stay with you. Promise."

Just as I'm about to consider his offer, a knock on the door sounds through the room. I pull away from Dylan and adjust my shirt before sliding out of bed and padding across the thick rug covering the gleaming wood floor.

"Yeah?" I ask without opening the door.

"It's me," Cadence says.

Without hesitating, I swing open the door and glance at my best friend who holds a tray of iced coffees from what looks like a local café. She moves past me and sets the tray on a side table next to a crystal vase full of fresh flowers. Her gaze flashes to mine before turning to Dylan and back to me. We were each given our own room, but I didn't want to be alone. Nothing happened, but I can see a million questions on Cadence's face.

She bites her lip to stop a smile from crossing her face. "Hey, Angel Boy. Mind if I borrow Cami for a few hours? I want to scout the area. Josh mentioned he'd like to talk to you more, and Lola made a gigantic breakfast. I figured you could stay."

Dylan stretches his arms over his head. "Sure. Call me if you need anything." His dark eyes hold mine while he says it, and I know he's talking directly to me.

"We won't," Cadence responds. She hooks her fingers around my elbow, and I shrug at Dylan who watches with an amused smile. "Hurry up and get ready. We're leaving in ten."

<hr>

Cadence strolls the beach next to me, kicking up warm sand. I clutch my iced coffee in one hand while using my other to shade my eyes from the afternoon sun. People in the Veiled Realm have the weirdest sleeping schedules, staying up all night and sleeping halfway through the day. I don't know how anyone functions with a day job, but I guess if you live in a safe house, falling into a human schedule can be easy.

"I know you and Dylan have a complicated relationship, but I was surprised to see you two together this morning. I'm happy for you, Cami. You deserve some good in this life," Cadence says.

Staring off into the endless blue ocean is a lot easier than meeting her curious gaze. She's been waiting for me to say something for a while about Dylan, but I'm afraid to admit the feelings that have been overflowing in my heart. When Evan left, my heart was empty. Dylan fills it. My love for both of them is so completely different; it's hard to express it in words.

"It's not what you think," I say. "Dylan's—he's—" I pause.

"Not Evan," Cadence says.

I frown. "Yes and no. It's complicated."

She rolls her eyes. "You always say that. It's time to uncomplicate things. Do you like Dylan?"

I purse my lips. "Of course I like him. You know that. I've liked him since the first day we met."

She slows down and scoops up a seashell. "Does he make you happy?"

"Yeah."

"Okay then. There you go. You like Angel Boy, and he makes you happy. Is that really so complicated?" She pulls me to a stop, and we face the ocean. "I can't even imagine what it's like losing someone you love—and you've lost so many people—so my advice is to live in the now and love as much as you can and be as happy as you can."

I bump her shoulder. "Did you age fifty years over night, oh-wise-one."

She tilts her head toward the sky and laughs. "Totally."

As we walk further down the long stretch of beach away from the parking lot where Cadence parked the Jag, fewer people stroll the shoreline until it's just us. The ocean roars in my ears, and salty air licks my face. We should be coming up to where Joshua had mentioned demon activity. If the demon breaks werewolves, he's of Malicevile's caliber.

That's why we're here in the day to get a feel of the territory.

The scent of sugar and nutmeg mingles with the sea breeze, and I lock my arm through Cadence's and pull her to a stop. That smell, like baking cookies, could actually be someone in the kitchen, but it could also be traces of a demon.

"Hey, this is a private beach," a masculine voice hollers from the yard of a mansion made of glass and concrete, almost like a seaside fortress. It's the only one around before the bottom of a cliff cuts off the beach.

A stocky man hops a small brick wall instead of using the gate and jogs in our direction. I release Cadence and touch the hilt of my dagger.

"We didn't know," Cadence says. "Sorry to have bothered you."

The man, wearing a suit, looks ridiculous on the sunny beach. He crosses his arms and blocks our way. "My boss will kill me if he senses that I allowed trespassers on his beach. Turn around and head back in the direction you came from."

People use the word "kill" as an expression all the time, but the way he says it with fear in his voice makes me think things are more literal for him.

The ocean breeze picks up again, and the sugar and nutmeg scent washes over me. It's coming directly from the man. He reeks of the sweet scent, and he doesn't look like the baking type, especially dressed in formal wear.

I step closer. "You live here?" I point at the beach fortress.

He nods. "With my boss."

I levitate a few inches to match the man's height. "Is he home? I'd like to have a word with him."

The man's eyes widen, and he huffs in exasperation. "He won't be home until tonight. You're insane to want to talk to him. Trust me. He's bad news."

"Then why do you work for him?" Cadence asks.

The man balls his fingers into fists at his side. "I don't have a choice."

She steps up beside me. "Everyone has a choice."

"Not me!"

The man thrusts his hands out, pushing Cadence back before pouncing on her. She knees him in the stomach with enough force to knock the wind from him. I slide my dagger from its sheath at my hip and stand over him as he holds his knees to his chest in the fetal position.

When the man sees the sparkle of my knife in the sunlight, he freezes. Cadence vaults to her feet and stands next to me.

I glare at the demon-tainted man. "Here's how things are going to go. You're going to tell us everything we need to know about the demon in that house, and we'll free your soul. Or you can resist and fight us, and we'll let you live long enough for that demon to kill you for disobeying him, and then he'll get to keep your soul."

I brace myself for a fight. The tainted ones always fight for their masters. They don't have a choice otherwise.

No one moves or says anything until the man's bottom lip quivers, and he starts bawling his eyes out, sniffling and snotting into the sand. He wipes his face on the back of his sleeve, and after a long moment, he finally calms down enough to talk.

"I can't help you. If you don't leave, I'll have to kill you," he says, wiping his hands across his wet face. Sand sticks to his cheeks, and he really looks a mess.

Cadence laughs in his face. "I'd like to see you try." She turns to me. "Come on. Let's go inside."

Before I can even take a step to follow her, the man roars as he launches to his feet. He yanks a gun from his waist, the favored weapon of demon-tainted humans. His hands tremble as he tries to aim it at Cadence. Her nose crinkles, and she slowly lifts her hands.

The man releases a breath, dropping the gun to his side. He focuses on Cadence, who takes a step back in the direction we came from to show that she's backing off. I don't move, though. Instead, I raise my dagger, aim, and throw it at his hand. The hilt hits the gun, and he pulls the trigger, shooting the sand before the gun falls from his grip.

Bending my knees, I launch at the man and crash into his side. We tumble to the sand, but I levitate to stop myself from hitting the ground. I swing out my arm and pop the man in the nose. He wails as he thrashes, and I sucker punch him in the throat, stealing his air from him.

His face burns a bright red before his eyes roll to the back of his head. He might not be out for long, but it'll give us a chance to bind his wrists to get him to cooperate.

Cadence unbuckles her belt and tightens it around the man's wrists. I grab the gun from the sand and aim it at the man when his eyes flutter open. He struggles against his restraints before trying to push to his feet to make a run for it.

Cadence grabs the back of the man's suit jacket and tugs it so he falls back to the sand. "I'm not in the mood to chase you, so you need to either stop fighting and come with us, or I'll knock you out and make you cooperate. What's it gonna be?"

"I can't!" he screams.

With those words, I pick up a paver from the stone walkway that leads to the mansion and swing it, hitting the man in the head. He face plants into the sand, and I flip him over before Cadence helps me drag him to a private street at the front of the fortress.

I pull my cell phone from my pocket and dial Dylan's number. He answers on the first ring.

"Hey, we need your help. Cadence left a spare key for the Jag in her room in the nightstand. Pick up the car from the lot a block over and come pick us up." I glance at the house number and the street name. "We're at 1666 Lava Rock Road. Oh, and bring something to use as a blindfold and let the pack know we're bringing home a guest who might have info on their Broken Ones."

"Do you think it's a good idea to bring one of the tainted here? Sunset's approaching. The demon can probably track all his minions." Dylan's voice creates static in the phone.

I grimace at Cadence. "What about that church at the end of the block? If things go wrong, the werewolves will be a safe distance away. I'm not leaving this man here."

Dylan sighs. "I'll see what I can do. See you soon."

He hangs up, and I turn my gaze back to Cadence. She faces the fortress of a house like she's trying to summon some X-ray vision to see through the walls. Her mouth falls open, and she points at one of the windows. A blond-haired girl with sky blue eyes, probably twelve or thirteen, watches us from a window. I raise my hand and wave, and the girl disappears, closing her curtains.

"What a monster," Cadence says. "That poor girl."

I suck in my bottom lip. "I have to come back for her. She's a halfie like me. I know it. She doesn't deserve this fate."

I ignore the dread seeping into my soul as I stare at the curtained window. I was lucky when Alana rescued me from Malicevile's clutches. This girl, she needs someone like Alana to fight for her. She needs me. She deserves a better life.

But who could give it to her? The Hunter's Alliance? I'm not so sure. I guess any life would be better than the one she's living, trapped within a fortress owned by a demon with human minions who threaten to kill anyone who crosses their paths.

"I can call my father if you'd like," Cadence says. "I bet he'd send in reinforcements."

I think about her suggestion for a moment. "No, I can handle this. I'll give Alana a call to let her know, but I'm not putting my faith in the alliance anymore. They might try to kill her to save themselves any future trouble."

Dylan pulls to the curb in the Jag, cutting off her response. We get the man into the trunk, and I watch the window where we saw the girl. *I'll be back for you. I'll save you. I promise,* I think, imagining she can hear me. I just hope I'm successful.

MY OWN WORST ENEMY

"TELL ME ABOUT the girl." My low voice comes out more as a growl, bouncing off the walls of the altar, as I pinch the tainted man's chin.

He squeezes his eyes shut like I'll disappear if he wills it to happen. "I—I don't know what you're talking about."

"Come on, James. We saw her. The clock is ticking as the sun goes down," Cadence says, twirling her dagger between her hands. "You don't want Raphael to come looking for you to discover that you've been indulging us with his secrets now, do you?" All it took was a little fear to get the man, James, to give up information on his demon master.

Demons tend to go after the weak-willed, which makes this a lot easier. People forget their soul's on the line when they have to worry about self-preservation. Cadence is a natural in getting people to forget.

"Please, leave Faith out of it. She's just a child," James says. This is the first time I've heard a tainted one worry about someone other than themselves. This proves the man still has a tiny bit of humanity left. He's not as far gone as I assumed. "She's safe. Raphael is a good father."

So, I was right. She *is* a demi-demon. Just like me.

A million thoughts cross my mind as I think about Faith and how she was probably taken the way Malicevile tried to take me. I was terrified when I met Alana, and it took me months to trust the crazy woman who spoke of the monsters of my nightmares as if they were real. It only took seeing a lower-level demon to believe her. I want nothing more than to protect Faith from all this...

But that's where Alana went wrong.

Faith doesn't need to be protected. Alana spent so long keeping me away from demons, not teaching me to fight because she was afraid I'd discover the truth about my heritage. But Faith already knows that. She needs to know the truth about her demon father and be trained. I can't do either, but I know Alana can. I know she'll do things right this time.

I take a deep breath and pull my cell phone from my pocket. The man watches me as I dial Alana's number and listen as the phone goes to voicemail. I say, "Hey, it's me. I'm sorry how we left things. Can we talk? Love you," before hanging up.

I shift my attention to James. "The girl won't be harmed. I'm going to save her."

He shakes as he laughs. "You really do have a death wish. I should've just let you come inside. And to think I was the one trying to save you."

I eye Cadence. "That's exactly what I want. I have a deal you won't be able to refuse."

His face grows serious. "I'm listening."

"I'm going to release you so you can go back. When Raphael leaves, which I'm sure he will, you're going to let me in. If you try anything stupid or tip Raphael off, I'll kill you."

"What's in it for me?"

I link my fingers together. "I know someone who can save your soul." *If it's not already too far gone.*

"Deal."

My blood cools as I process the deal I've made. After everything, it looks like I'm capable of bargaining like a demon after all.

And it feels good.

<hr>

I glare at my phone.

"Still no answer?" Dylan asks while brushing his fingers along my knee.

I shake my head. "I'm worried. She always calls back. What if she's so angry with me that she doesn't want to hear from me again?"

He takes my hands in his. "I doubt that's it. She's probably busy with all the new responsibilities that come with taking the alliance leader role."

Ugh. I didn't need the reminder. It's harder than I thought to accept that I'm not Alana's number one priority anymore. She was the one person I could always count on, and I took her for granted. But I can't pack up and head back now. I've only been in this small seaside town for a day, but it feels like I've invested a lifetime. It's more than trying to redeem myself and tip my soul back to Heaven's good grace. It's about these people who are affected by this demon, Raphael. It's about the lives he's ruining. It's so much more than me.

I meet Dylan's gaze without responding to his thought about Alana. His brooding eyes hold mine as he tries to figure out what's going through my mind. I reach out and slide my hand around his neck and pull him closer so that I have to shift my legs over his to sit comfortably with him. His apple and rain scent clears the swirling thoughts from my mind until everything fades away, and it's me and him, alone in the quiet world where nothing can get to us. It's the same feeling as being in a dream, except I'm awake, and the nightmares can't touch me.

"You have that look," he whispers, resting his head on

my shoulder.

My brows crinkle together. "What look?"

"The one that says you're about to try to take on the world and no one can stop you." The feathery softness of his wings caresses my very soul as he wraps them around us.

I half smile. "You understand why I have to do this. Why I have to try, right?"

His nostrils flare as he breathes in a long breath through his nose. "She reminds you of yourself. I get it. I do. But you don't have a plan. You're not prepared. You're not—"

"Alana?" I ask.

He closes his eyes for a second. "No, I was going to say backed by the alliance. She knew the enemy. You do not."

I gently push him back to meet his eyes again. "But I do. Raphael is an upper-level demon no different than my father. He's probably just as ruthless, but he has his weaknesses. I only have to find them."

"But—"

I cut him off with a kiss. His lips brush against mine as his argument fades away. I pull him closer and shift onto his lap, wrapping my legs around his waist. His fingers gently dig into the skin on my lower back under my shirt, and he kisses me deeper.

He moans against my lips, and I smile against his. He tastes exactly how he smells, and I run my tongue over his bottom lip before sliding it into his mouth. A cool breeze plays with my hair, and he lifts me up and spins me around so I'm lying on the bed.

My hands trail down his shoulders, exploring the tight muscles in his arms as they hold his weight above me. I can't help but wonder if it's possible to convert his soul to the side of evil with mine. I smirk through kisses as I think about trying.

I tug at the bottom of his T-shirt and pull it over his head, and then I strip out of my own. His brows lower, his dark eyes drinking me in, and he looks more devilish than anything. I suck in my bottom lip as he trails his fingers along my collarbone to my bra straps.

Something flickers in his eyes. It's like a small thought awakens something in him, pushing through his desire for me.

I don't like the sudden change in his expression.

Reaching up, I lock my fingers onto his taut shoulders and try to pull him against me, but he resists.

He rolls off me and stares at the ceiling. "Cami, we can't do this."

I sigh, leaning up on my elbows. "Why?"

He doesn't look at me. "You're not in a good place. I'm—"

"What's that supposed to mean? Is this because my soul is Hell-bound, Angel Boy? You afraid I'll corrupt you?" Anger rushes through my mind, and I grab my shirt and shrug into it before I push from the bed. When I thought that before, I was joking, but it's like he might've heard my inner conversation. "I don't understand you."

"Cami, please. Let me explain. I love you, and I want things to be perfect, but look around you. Look at what you're going through. Do you really want this?" He waves his finger between us.

"I—I—" I stumble over my thoughts as his words catch me off guard. Dylan has been the only consistent thing in my life lately. He takes away my pain, and he stands beside me no matter what crazy idea I have. So why can't I answer his question?

My heart's being pulled in two different directions. It's hard to let go of the past—to let go of Evan, because he's not the same person I loved. He's changed. *You've changed, too.*

Dylan swings his legs off the bed and closes the distance between us. He kisses the top of my head. "This is what I meant, love. And it's okay. I'll always be here. I just don't want you to regret anything."

My anger doesn't dissipate. I brush him off and turn away. I can't look at him when I say, "You can't tell me what I will and won't regret. I wanted this. I wanted you. When I'm with you, I forget. I need to forget. It's the only thing that helps me. I don't like being me, Dylan. I don't like knowing that I'm Hell-bound or that my demonic father is waiting for me to breakdown and just give in."

"Cami, love. Forgetting isn't the answer. You need to

remember. You need to feel every little thing in your soul. It's what makes you human," Dylan says, his voice barely above a whisper.

I run my hand over my face. "We'll talk about this later, okay?"

He grabs my hand. "No, we need to talk about this now."

"I *said* later." I yank my hand away and bolt from the room.

What was the perfect moment is now ruined by all the darkness looming in my soul, waiting to slip out and destroy all that's good in my world. If I stay with Dylan a moment longer, I'm afraid I'll say or do something I'll regret. Because he's wrong about what makes me human. Remembering all the bad brings out the worst in me. It turns me into the monster I'm most afraid to lose myself to.

It turns me into my own worst enemy.

<hr>

"You don't seriously think I'm going to let you go into that demon's lair alone?" Cadence calls from behind me. "I thought we were meeting at midnight?"

I trudge through the sand. "I needed to clear my head and figured I'd scope out what we're dealing with. James said Raphael leaves around eleven. I wanted to watch him go."

"I was down the hall. You still could've told me," she says.

I blow strands of hair from my face. "Sorry. I was in a hurry after Dylan turned me down."

Her eyes widen. "He what?"

"I guess he's too angelic compared to my demonic tendencies."

She laughs, her melodic voice echoing above the sound of the surf. My lips pull up in the corners as a smile overtakes my face—as much as I wish it wouldn't. When I say it out loud, it sounds hilarious. It doesn't stop my lingering anger at his rejection.

She catches up to me and bumps my shoulder with hers. "Angel Boy has been pining after you since before the day he showed up at the hospital after Malicevile forced his power into you. I doubt it had anything to do with the fact that he's half angel. I've met plenty of them, and they have no problem with—"

"Ugh." I groan as I tug at my stray curls. "I don't want to think about this anymore."

She nods. "Well, I'm here if you need to talk."

"I just want to save some souls and send Raphael back to Hell."

"Sounds like a plan."

She tucks her hair behind her ear, and it appears black in the night instead of purple. Silence falls between us the closer we draw near the beach house fortress. The silver flask she pulls from her pocket reflects the white moonlight as she hands me her extra bottle of holy water. I tuck it into the pocket of my leather jacket for safe keeping. Holy water has saved me on more than one occasion.

We kick the sand as we stroll down the beach with only the sound of the crashing waves to break the silence. My heart beats in my ears the closer we get to Raphael's. So many things can go wrong. The only demon's lair I've ever been to was Malicevile's, and it was a lot less terrifying than I imagined. It's why fear doesn't rattle me to my soul even though it should.

Lights shine from within the beach fortress as we reach the stretch of private beach. I tug Cadence to a stop long before we cross the invisible barrier in front of the house. If Raphael is responsible for kidnapping and breaking were-wolves, I'm sure hellhounds lurk in the night, guarding the place from intruders.

"Let's go around front. He'll be leaving by car," Cadence says.

I nod in agreement. "We can climb the small hill a few yards back."

She follows behind me as I hike up the hard packed dirt that'll take us directly to the street of the demon's mansion. Reaching back, I grab Cadence's hand and use levitation to get us to the top when the ground becomes too steep to climb without help.

When we reach the top, a black iron fence greets us, blocking our way to the street. I bend my knees and propel to the top, careful not to catch myself on the dull spikes. I offer my hand to Cadence and pull her up before lowering her to the ground.

And then I see it.

A flash of fiery light radiates a soft glow through the lush, perfect landscape. Like Malicevile's lair near the academy, this demon's fortress is away from human life. All he has are cliffs and the ocean, both protecting him from unwanted visitors—or maybe they protect the outside world from him.

Cadence glances at me, not noticing the hellhound stalking us.

"Grab my hand," I whisper.

"What? Why?" She raises her arms above her head while she asks.

But it's too late.

The hellhound charges from its hiding place and bolts straight for Cadence. She spins on her heels, raises her hands up to protect her face, and I think of the only thing I can do.

I jump and collide with the flaming beast and close my eyes as it opens its mouth to tear the flesh from my neck.

PERSONAL HELL

THE HELLHOUND SCREECHES, and black slime pours over my face, coating my skin in the smell of burning flesh. It slumps on top of me, the flames of its burning body snuffing out with its life. The hilt of Cadence's dagger protrudes from the neck of the beast, and I tug it out while pushing the poor broken werewolf off me.

I can't help feeling sorry for the hellhound. It didn't choose to be evil. The demon turned it into its guard dog just because he could. This could've been any member of Joshua's pack, and now I'll never know who it was. The pack won't even have a chance to give their former mate a proper goodbye since the body will disappear with the sun.

Cadence grimaces as she helps me to my feet. I use the back of my sleeve to clear the hellhound goo from my face, trying not to gag as it sticks to my hair. This isn't exactly how I wanted to start the night, and I'm sure I'll frighten Faith the moment she sees me.

"That's so gross," Cadence says, covering her nose with her hand.

"Better than having my throat shredded." I hand her the slime-covered dagger. "Thanks for that, by the way."

She offers a brilliant smile. "I should be the one thanking you."

The hum of a garage door draws our attention away from the dead hellhound, and I push Cadence toward some tall beach grass that lines the sand along the fence line. Headlights flash over the street, and a Ferrari rumbles as it pulls from the garage. Of course Raphael drives an exotic red car. I wouldn't expect anything less.

The tail lights disappear as he turns the corner to leave the cul-de-sac, and I rush ahead with Cadence running right behind me. It's best to get in and out as fast as we can. There's no way to tell how long Raphael will be gone, and I'd rather not face him before Faith is safely out of his reach. I'll come back to finish him off once I can save as many poor souls as I can. If only hellhounds could come out in the day. If I kill him now, they might disappear with him. It's hard to say. I think the only reason Lola didn't disappear with her master was because Malicevile was the one to break her. I'm pretty sure Raphael is a do-it-yourself type of demon.

"Keep your eyes open for hellhounds," I whisper as we head toward the concrete and glass fortress.

Cadence only nods. It's best to stay quiet and listen for signs of threats. I inhale a deep breath through my nose, catching the scent of sugar and nutmeg, which clings to everything we pass. I crinkle my nose at the potent, sweet smell, but at least it's better than the burning flesh of the broken werewolves.

I lead the way to the front door. There's no point in sneaking around. Raphael isn't home, and James is expecting our arrival. A motion detecting light flashes on as we stride up the walkway to the front porch lined with potted azaleas.

The wall of glass surrounding the door gives me a clear view of the grand foyer with sparkling marble floors, a metal and glass light fixture that looks more like an art piece hanging from the ceiling, and a long, burgundy painted wall with all sorts of weapons hanging from it. I doubt he's ever used any of them. Demons have enough power as it is. They'd never lower themselves to human standards and use something human-made.

"Look," Cadence says, pointing at a familiar dagger on the wall. It matches the one the alliance gave her when she first started going on hunts. "He collects the weapons of the hunters who have tried to send him back to Hell and failed."

Fear knots in my stomach for the second time tonight. And both times I've felt it was because Cadence has been by my side. I'm afraid for her. I know she's a skilled fighter and a damn good hunter, but allowing her into a demon's lair with me suddenly feels reckless. I'm endangering my best friend.

She raises her hand to knock.

I grab her hand. "Wait. I have a bad feeling about this. Maybe you should go back to the safe house."

She raises her perfectly ached brows. "Okay, who replaced my best friend? The one who wanted a desk job so she would be safe from demons."

I force myself to smile. "That girl didn't know she was a demon."

"Half," Cadence corrects.

I sigh, my expression falling serious as worry causes my hands to tremble. "If things turn badly, I want you to run and leave me to fight. Most demonic power can't hurt me."

She narrows her eyes. "We've always fought together."

"Not tonight. The plan isn't to fight. I want you to take care of the girl. I trust you more than myself. I know you could protect her like Alana protected me," I say.

She offers a stiff nod. "Okay. You're right. I'll handle Faith and you handle the hellhounds."

"Perfect," I say as I lift my hand and knock on the door.

James shuffles from the shadows in a creepy fashion fit for a demonic minion. He probably has nothing better to do while his master is out. He smiles—more like bares his teeth—as he unlocks and pulls the door open. He bows to us, and Cadence gives me a familiar look, pretty much confirming that something isn't right.

I straighten my shoulders and enter the beach mansion. "Two things. Where does Raphael keep the hellhounds, and where is Faith?"

James swoops his arm toward a dark hallway. "Faith is in her room. Why do you want to know about the guard dogs?"

Cadence steps inside without closing the door. "We encountered one out front. You can't expect us to walk in unprepared. Now hurry, I don't trust that your demon won't come zooming back at any moment."

Without arguing, James says, "This way," and leads us down the darkened hallway. He flips on the light as we head deeper into the mansion, past closed doors I wish I could peek in, but we don't have the time to map out the entire place. There are dozens of rooms, and I'm sure James isn't aware of everything. Demons are too smart to divulge their tainted humans with information that could be used against them. Some are never truly broken until they lose their life.

We stop at the last room at the end of the hall, one that faces the street instead of the ocean, and James brings a finger to his lips. He creaks open the door, and I spot a small figure sleeping in the middle of a California King bed. The shiny, pink duvet covers Faith's head, and I quietly enter the room with Cadence on my heels.

"Faith?" I whisper. "Are you awake?"

Light shines from the porch outside the window, easily guiding my way to the bed. A variety of porcelain dolls line the shelves anchored to the walls, and an open wardrobe displays more clothes than I've ever owned at once. A flat screen TV hangs on the wall above a dresser, and a desk with a computer and a giant monitor is stationed in a sitting area with a towering bookshelf filled with books.

The door slams closed behind us, and I swivel just as I hear a key turn in the lock. Cadence rushes to the bed and pulls back the covers to reveal a few pillows. She pulls her dagger from its sheath and stabs the bed, tearing a hole through the sheets and mattress.

"I knew we shouldn't have let him guide us. That bastard doesn't want to be saved," she says. She waltzes to the window and punches the glass, but it doesn't break. She shakes her hand in front of her. "We're trapped."

I clench my fingers into fists. "We're going to be okay. We have time to think of an escape plan."

Headlights flash through the sheer curtain.

"Or not," Cadence says, fear lining her eyes. "If we can't get out of here, I want you to kill me. I'd rather be dead than tainted, and I don't know how long I could keep my soul safe. Promise me."

My mouth falls open. "I—Cadence, don't talk like that."

"It's our reality, Cami." She pulls the flask of holy water from her belt and takes a sip. "We need to prepare for the worst."

I pull my phone from my pocket. "Okay." I dial Dylan's number and wait for him to answer. Before he says a word, I say, "Don't freak out, but things have gone to Hell, and now we're locked in a room with no escape. I just thought you should know."

"I'm coming," he says.

"To do what? You'll get hurt or worse. We can handle this, okay?" My sinking heart isn't so sure. "And Dylan?"

"Yeah?"

"I love you."

I hang up before he can answer. He doesn't need to tell me for me to know he loves me. I wanted him to know because of how I left things. I ran out the door, hell-bent on clearing my head and putting myself to work, and I didn't even tell him goodbye. I'll have to live with that for eternity. I'm sure all the things I've screwed up or left unsaid will be front and center in my personal Hell.

My chest rises and falls as my breath quickens. Voices erupt from the hallway, and I motion Cadence to hide by the door. There's only one door to this room, so if Raphael comes through it, she can attack from the side while I face him head on.

"If one of us gets out of this alive, it's going to be you," I tell her.

She frowns but doesn't argue. She knows me well enough to know that I mean what I say, and there's no way in Hell I'm going to take the opportunity to escape before her.

A tap sounds on the door, and I hold my dagger at my side though I won't need it. My best weapon is that people don't know what I'm capable of. I can feign being human long enough to have a fighting chance.

"Little hunters, it was so nice of you to drop by my humble abode," a smooth, deep voice says, caressing my ears.

Demons have such a charisma and way with words that even if you're terrified, you can't help but be enchanted by them. Their presence is truly captivating.

"I'd like to make things easy for you both. Stand down and let me in without attacking, and I'll spare your souls in trade for your services." Our services? Is he joking?

"And if we don't?" I ask.

"I'll kill you."

I raise my eyebrows at Cadence. "Death it is, I suppose."

Cadence braces herself.

The door swings open, and I freeze when I see the most angelic looking girl standing in front of a handsome man with thick blond hair, a square jawline, and the bluest of eyes. Even bluer than Evan's. The girl, who I assume is Faith, holds a glowing red orb in her fingers. Tears line her eyes before she closes them, and then she throws the orb in my direction.

I feign fear as I raise my hands, like I'm protecting myself, but then I catch it and fling it back. The demon ducks instead of catching the orb. It flies past him, and the murderous scream of James echoes through the hallway. Cadence jumps from her place next to the door and swings her arm out, sending a waterfall of holy water onto Raphael's face.

All Hell breaks loose when he pushes Faith out of his way and runs in the room, his face smoldering and burning from the blessed water. As he tries to wrap his hands around Cadence, I bend my knees and launch from the floor, crashing into him. We collide with the wall, my head hitting the flat screen TV and breaking it.

Stars burst in my vision, but I don't need to see clearly when the demon is blindly lashing out.

"Grab the girl and run!" I scream at Cadence.

"No!" Raphael hollers, grabbing hold of my messy hair. He lifts me off my feet, and I levitate, not letting him get the upper hand on me.

I elbow him in the face, and he drops me, but not before digging his nails into my leg. Bones crack as he transforms into his true demonic self, and I flick my gaze to make sure Cadence does what I say.

Cadence pulls the girl's arm, but she doesn't move from her place in the doorway. She's either too scared or already too far gone. Either way, I'll not let my best friend lose her life tonight.

"Go without her!" I yell.

Raphael pulls me to him, ripping my jeans as I thrash away from him. Cadence steps back into the room, aiming her dagger at the demon, and then she throws it, hitting him in the shoulder. He roars and throws the same red orb Faith had tried to throw at me. Cadence drops to her knees, and it explodes on the wall behind her, melting it like acid.

I reach up and pop the demon in the chin, jerking his head up. It takes his attention away long enough for her to get to her feet.

"Get out of here!" I scream. I press my hands into the demon's shoulder, keeping him away from me. His eyes glow orange and a crown of horns peek through the blackening skin on his forehead.

I don't have the chance to watch Cadence leave, but I know she's gone. I'm alone, facing a demon that is as scary as my own father.

He breathes hot breath into my face, leering with sharp teeth, and then he roars at me, blowing my hair out of my face.

I close my eyes. I'm a defensive fighter when it comes to power. I have to wait for the demon to attack. I just hope he doesn't use blunt force.

His weight shifts, and he restrains my hands with one of his own. I peek through my eyelashes as he holds his free hand above me. A red orb materializes above my chest, and he drops it without much force.

But still, the demonic power knocks the air from my lungs before I absorb the hot energy into my skin. Heat flows through my veins as the demon within me awakens. Darkness reddens the edges of my vision, and I thrash when he drops another orb onto my chest.

"Where is it?" Raphael asks, a low growl lacing his words. His features morph once more and he looks human again apart from the blistering skin marring his forehead and cheeks.

I swallow, my throat burning from the rush of his demonic energy. "Where's what?"

"The amulet. I know you have one. It's why my power isn't working on you," he says.

My mind wanders, thinking about this magical amulet. I wonder how I can get my hands on one. I know a few people it'll be useful for.

The demon narrows his eyes when I don't respond. "Tell me, and I'll make your death swift."

I blink a few times. "On the cord around my neck." It's a flat out lie, but I'd say anything at this point.

He tugs my necklace free from my shirt, revealing the sun stone that Annabelle, the forest nymph from the academy, had given me to keep my demon side at bay. It feels like forever ago, but I never take it off.

When his fingers wrap around the yellow stone, it sparks in his hand. He screams, and the scent of burning mingles with the sweet smell of sugar and nutmeg which emanates from his pores.

Before I have a chance to brace myself, his fist flies at my face, and pain bursts in my head. The world spins as I struggle to hold onto my consciousness, but it's no use.

The demon outmatched me, and I've lost.

I say a small prayer as the world fades away, and I wait to be dragged to Hell.

FAITH

THE FEATHERY SOFTNESS of wings wraps around me, and the warmth of Dylan's touch pulls me from the darkness I was almost positive was the gateway to Hell. I twist in his arms and gaze into his dark eyes. Worry lines his forehead, sending fear into my own heart.

"I'm dead, aren't I? But how did you manage to get to my soul?" I suck in a deep breath of his fresh apple scent. It's enough to calm the dread swirling around my heart.

He blinks glittering tears away. "I didn't. You're alive, love. But you're hurt."

My lips form an O-shape. "I'm still in Raphael's lair?"

His bottom lip puckers. "I'm afraid so."

"Cadence?" I ask.

"She's here. She's grabbing more weapons. She convinced a few of the pack members to help her," he says.

"Don't let her go. It's suicide. If I'm not already dead, then Raphael doesn't plan on killing me yet. I'll figure this out. You have to trust me." My voice cracks. I can't even trust myself.

He brushes his lips against my forehead. "I do, love. It's the demon I don't trust."

I bury my face against his shirt. "Tell Cadence to give me until sunrise. I'm not worth risking everyone's lives for."

He nudges my chin with his fingers so I have to gaze at him again. "You're worth risking it all for, Cami. I'm not the only one who agrees with that."

The ground shakes, and Dylan squeezes me tighter. I tilt my head up and kiss him sweetly. I pray this isn't the last kiss we'll ever share, but I'm afraid it might be.

"I have to go," I whisper. "Reality's pulling me back."

"Be strong, love. Don't go down without a fight," he says.

Fear grips my soul and I ask, "What happens if I die? I'm scared."

His wings expand on his back, their golden light setting me aglow. "Think of me. I'll be there. I promise."

I cling onto his words for as long as I can before the darkness rips me away and spits me out. I open my eyes and find myself lying on the floor right where Raphael knocked me out. I'm alone though, and the door's closed once more.

I scramble to my feet and search for anything I can use to break what I'm guessing is bulletproof glass. Of course Raphael wouldn't leave his home open to attacks. But just because the window is bulletproof doesn't mean it's unbreakable.

My eyes fall onto the spot on the floor where I had passed out, and I notice my cell phone and the flask of holy water lies on the carpet. Raphael didn't bother to search me either.

My phone displays the time, and I frown. Dawn is still hours away. I couldn't have been out for more than a few minutes, which means the demon will be back for me. He might've tried to go after Cadence. At least I know she's safe.

I sigh as I stare at my screen. I can't just wait around and hope for the best. It wouldn't work out for me.

Don't do it, I think to myself. *Just try to think things through. You're smart. You're the daughter of the most power-ful demon...*

I scroll through my contact list and close my eyes when I hit the call button. I can't believe I'm resorting to this, but I don't want to die tonight. Not in some demon's lair, all for nothing. I haven't saved Faith or the broken werewolves. It can't end like this.

"I honestly never thought you'd call."

Tears spring from my eyes as I hear the sound of Evan's

voice for the first time in what feels like eternity. I never knew how much I missed it until this moment, even if he sounds slightly different, colder, but I didn't expect anything less.

I sniffle. "I didn't want to, but I'm in trouble, and I'm pretty sure I'm about to die."

"So, you need something," he says.

My heart splinters, threatening to puncture my lungs. It's hard to breathe. "I—" I snap my mouth shut. This is pointless. The demon taint controls him now, not his heart. "Never mind. I'll accept my fate and face eternity."

Before I can disconnect, Evan says, "Wait, Cami. Don't hang up."

With those few words, a beacon of hope lights up the heavy darkness suffocating my soul. He sounds almost normal, like the boy I fell in love with. Somewhere, deep down, Evan still carries a spark of his humanity. I just need to set his whole soul ablaze.

"It was stupid for me to call, but I don't know where to turn," I say, my voice quivering. "Don't assume this is about your letter. I'm still me. I'm not going to change. I was just hoping that you might not actually want me to die, especially by those you've asked me to stop hunting."

"Where are you?" he asks.

"A demon's lair in Moonlight Shores. 1666 something. He goes by Raphael." I stiffen when voices hum from the hallway. "And please, don't ask what I'm doing here. I won't tell you."

"I know of him," he says. "He has some serious power."

Of course he does. He's probably aware of all the upper-level demons by now. From the letter, it sounds like Malicevile treats him at his level instead of under him like he does his collection of tainted humans.

"Oh, I know."

"You okay?"

"Do you even care?"

He's quiet for a moment. "No. Human habits are hard to break."

He's right about that. I squeeze my eyes shut as tears threaten to weaken me. I can't cry, not now, not when Evan can hear me. I pull the phone from my ear and sniffle, wiping my face with the hem of my dirty shirt.

"Figured as much." I move from the floor and head toward the wall so I'm out of sight from the door. "So, will you come? I don't know what to do."

"Does he know who you are?" he asks.

"Only that I'm a hunter. He thinks I'm wearing some sort of amulet that prevents him from using his power on me," I say.

"Good. Keep it that way. Be there soon."

He hangs up without a goodbye, and I slide my phone into my pocket so if Raphael does come back, he'd have to fight me to get it. I'll die before I give up my lifeline to the world outside this house.

Hours go by as I wait to discover my fate. Just when I think that I might go crazy from the unknown, I hear voices in the hallway again.

As they draw closer, I pop off the top of the flask of the holy water, pouring some into my hands before I rub it over my neck and face, washing away my tears with one of the few things demons can't handle. While the effects don't last long after it dries, it'll make it uncomfortable for Raphael to put his hands on me.

The door swings open, sending a tidal wave of fear over me. I push the emotion away. It's been too long since I've feared a demon. I don't like it. I got cocky, and it made me reckless.

Raphael storms into the room with Faith on his heels. She tugs at the sleeve of his blue dress shirt. The blisters on his face burn a deep red, and if he could murder me on the spot with his icy blue eyes, I'd be staring at the fiery gates of Hell already.

"Dad, please. You don't have to kill everyone who sees me." Faith's eyes line with tears when she meets my gaze. "Please. I know you have it in you not to kill her."

I like this girl.

"She's a hunter for the alliance!" His voice booms through the air, and I wince. "Her partner already knows. They'll take you away from here. Is that what you want? After everything I've given you?"

I clear my throat. "I'm not a hunter for the alliance."

He spins toward me, fire lighting his eyes, and points. "Do not speak! You tried to kidnap my daughter!"

"Dad!" Faith yells. "You kidnapped me first."

My mouth falls open.

"I saved you." His voice lowers to just above a whisper.

She pats his back while holding my gaze. My stomach twists, witnesses the two of them show affection toward each other. I wonder if that's how Malicevile was toward my dead sister when he raised her. He's been all over the place with me, so I can't imagine.

I can't imagine ever caring for a demon. It makes me sick. *Yet people care for you.*

"That's why you shouldn't kill her. She thought she was helping. It was all a misunderstanding, right?" she asks me.

Nope. Still isn't. Still want to take you away. "Yeah. I'm super sorry. Can I go? I won't bother you again." *Tonight.*

He growls at me and steps forward. Reaching down, he grabs the front of my shirt and pulls me to my feet. I levitate enough so I'm not in pain but not enough for him to notice. Evan told me not to reveal who I was for a reason. I can't imagine what he'd do with that kind of information. Demons are about being on top. If he had something over Malicevile, it could end badly for me.

"Of course you can't leave! I still haven't figured out what to do with you now that I'm granting my daughter her wish." He drops me, and I land in a crouch.

Annoyance seeps into me. It'd be a lot easier if he'd let me go so I didn't have to rely on dear old Daddy Demon to save me. I don't like being indebted to him. He might not be able to hold me to anything, but the reminder is enough to ruin a good day.

I cross my arms. "Well, you better figure it out. I don't make deals with demons, and I don't break easily."

"Is that what you think?"

I hold his steely gaze. "Yeah, I do."

Faith slides between us and pushes her demonic dad back. I'm impressed how well she handles him. If I were her at that age, I'd have probably let him kill me. She's tough and confident—the perfect candidate for demon hunting.

The doorbell rings, drawing Raphael's attention away from me. He relaxes his shoulders and steps back. I tuck my hands in my pocket, feeling the cold metal of the flask of holy water. Like a baby blanket, it keeps me calm.

He turns to his daughter. "Faith, stay with the hunter. If she tries anything—"

"She won't," Faith says.

He sighs before leaving the room without another word. When the door closes, I tilt my head back and say a quiet prayer. No one has to tell me who's here. I can smell the scent of cinnamon and clove as it wafts through the walls. I could smell Malicevile through water from a mile away if I tried.

Faith motions for me to move to the sitting area, and I

plop down next to her. Crossing my legs at my ankles, I bend my arms and rest my elbows on my knees. A million questions run through my mind. This is what I've wanted all along. A few minutes to talk to the demi-demon who reminds me of myself.

I lick my dry lips before I say, "So, you like living with a demon?"

"It was better than my foster home. Now those people were the real demons," Faith says, leaning back on the small lounge chair. "My dad has a temper, but he has good intentions. Demons are misunderstood."

"And how's that?"

"They don't prey on the innocent. They target people already heading to Hell. They want justice for the harm caused to others," she says.

I raise an eyebrow. "Is that what your dad said?"

"Yeah, and I believe him. He doesn't lie."

"And what about the innocent werewolves he's broken? They weren't all damned to Hell. I know this for a fact." I twist my lips to the side as I think about all the people I couldn't save tonight.

"Sacrifices must be made for our protection," she says, folding her hands in her lap.

"They're people!" My voice booms out louder than I intended it to.

"They're animals."

I cover my face with my hands. "If you met the werewolves I have, you'd agree with me."

"I haven't met one at all."

"I thought your father doesn't lie to you?"

"He doesn't."

"He did about the werewolves."

Her gaze drops to the floor, and she doesn't respond. Her blond hair hangs over her shoulders, and now that I can study her, I can see the resemblance to Raphael.

After a long, quiet moment, she releases a breath. "I don't know why, but I believe you. Something about you is so familiar."

I shrug. "I don't know, but I can teach you things your father won't." It takes everything in me not to tell her that she feels that strange pull to me because we're alike. We both have power and demon blood flowing through our veins. Faith couldn't have met many other half-demons, and her father is sheltering her from the world to keep her away from the alliance. She's in the dark almost as much as I was until recently.

"I told you. I'm not going with you," she says.

I reach out and touch her hand. "I never said you had to. You know as well as I do that Raphael can't control you during the day. What if we hang out sometime? I could come back if you want. We could have lunch on the beach."

She presses her lips together in thought. "Is this a trick? My father won't allow you to leave."

I shake my head. "No, absolutely not a trick, and your

father, he's going to let me out any minute. I can feel it." I lean closer and whisper, "That connection you feel between us, it's real. I can't explain it now, but I will if you'll meet me. How about this afternoon? Do you have a pen?"

"Yeah." She hurries across the room to her desk. Scooping up a pen and piece of paper from the printer, she brings them back to me. I scribble my cell phone number without my name.

"I want you to call me any time. I'm staying in Moonlight Shores for a while, so you can count on me for anything you need." I hand her the paper.

"I still don't think my father is going to let you le—"

A knock on her bedroom door cuts her off. She tucks the folded piece of paper into the pocket of her jeans and stands up, motioning me back to the spot I was originally standing when Raphael burst in.

She opens the door. "What's wrong, Dad? I was hoping the hunter could stay with me until sundown tomorrow."

He steps into the room. "Sorry, Faith. She must come with me."

Faith frowns. "What? Why?"

Raphael locks his fingers around my arm and tugs me with him. "Stay in your room, Faith."

She stays hot on his heels as he yanks me down the hallway. A red stain on the floor almost looks like a rose. I shiver, remembering the power I had thrown at Raphael, which flew past him. That's all that remains of traitor

James.

"Dad, please. Let me keep her." Faith rushes and blocks our way before we enter the cavernous living room.

"Move, Faith. This doesn't concern you. I'll get you another human," her father says.

Cinnamon and clove hang heavy in the air, and my heart sinks into my stomach at the potent, familiar scent. My reaction to my father's scent won't stop anytime soon, if it ever does at all.

"My dearest Camilla." Malicevile's melodious voice wraps around me, pulling me closer to the demon I want to kill most in the world. "I'm so happy you're safe. Raphael told me about the trouble you've caused him. You owe him an apology."

I narrow my eyes at my father but stop when Evan steps out from behind him. The world freezes as I meet the aqua gaze of the boy I've lost forever. It feels more like a dream, having him so close I can smell the warm spiciness of his skin.

I shake my head. "Never."

Malicevile reaches out and snatches me by the hair, dragging me toward the door.

I scream, surprised by the sudden pain bursting in my scalp. Thrashing around, I try to escape his strong grip, but it's useless. I let my guard down, and now I have to pay for it.

"You're in a lot of trouble, girl!" he roars in my ear.

Fear nearly stops my heart as I catch the horror on Faith's face. She screams, trying to bolt past her father, but he scoops her up, petting her hair with something that resembles concern on his face.

"Dad! Please! You can't do this. Please! He'll murder her." She never takes her eyes away from me.

I reach up and wrap my hands around Malicevile's, digging my nails in until he loosens. "Faith, I'll be okay," I manage to say.

The cool night air wraps around me, and Evan shuts the door, cutting off Faith's screams.

The world whooshes around me as Malicevile drops me to the grass and stands over me. "I'm so happy you called, Camilla. I knew you would."

"I didn't have a choice," I say, rubbing my aching scalp.

"Oh, but you did. You could've chosen to die." He reaches down and offers his hand. I let him help me to my feet.

I crinkle my nose as his scent overpowers me. "Maybe I should've."

He laughs. "Still a feisty one, I see." He points to a gray Maserati. "Get in."

I shake my head. "No, thanks. I'll walk."

"It wasn't a suggestion."

"Cami," Evan says, moving closer to me. "Will you please just get in the car?"

My mind tries to resist his pleas, but my heart won't allow it.

I get in the car.

SAVED AND DESTROYED

MALICEVILE PULLS THE Maserati into a small beach hotel nestled in downtown Moonlight Shores. The sky lightens from midnight blue to deep purple, and I can sense the sun on its way to light my day. With the sun, Malicevile will vanish, and I'll be home free. I can't wait to crawl into bed and sleep for a few hours. I must return the Raphael's to let Faith know I'm alive. I need to tell her the truth.

Malicevile swivels in his seat to meet my eyes. "You owe me fifty grand for what I spent to buy you from Raphael, and I don't take payments."

My jaw drops. "You know I don't have that kind of money. I don't even have a job. I rely on handouts to live."

"I don't get why you choose such a difficult life. Things could be so easy," he says.

I don't respond. Instead, I drop my gaze to the floor and think about calling Alana to see if she could get the Hunter's Alliance to lend it to me. I'd rather owe them instead of a demon.

"I like my life, Malicevile," I say.

He lowers his brows. "Even now? Even after everything you've been through? I know you blame me, but I'm not the one who put you in this position. Humans did. Even your own mother. Had she held up her end of the bargain, I wouldn't have had to take her soul. *She's* the one who wronged *me*. Not the other way around. I only punish those who need to be punished. It's what I do. It's why I'm on this marvelous plane."

Curiosity snuffs out the anger trying to set my blood ablaze. No one ever talks about what comes next with much detail. I honestly don't think the alliance knows. They know of angels and demons and all of us half children and other creatures, but angels don't get involved and demons would never tell them. It's life's biggest mystery. And here I sit, hoping to find out.

I force a laugh. "Yeah, you're forgetting corrupting souls to send them where you want."

He waves his hand. "My poor, clueless daughter. This is why I hate humanity. They've ruined you!"

I throw my hands up. "Who are you? What happened

to the demon who gave me nightmares? Who tried to kill me for not complying? Who destroyed my life?"

I push the door open and step into the night air. Hugging my arms against me, I try to push away the sudden chill that seeps into the heat of my bones. Uncertainty has always been prominent in my life, but my evil, demonic father has always been the constant that I've known. Now, as he sits in the car, staring off into space, thinking about the questions I've thrown at him, I don't even know if that's true. There has to be an explanation. Maybe it's because I'm Hell-bound. I just can't see his ways as clearly as I used to.

The sky lightens as the sun peeks from the horizon. The time for answers is running out. Malicevile stiffens as light pushes the darkness away. He climbs from the car, tosses the keys to Evan, and turns to me.

"Time has run out for me tonight, dear Camilla, but if you remain with Evan throughout the day and join me for dinner at sundown, I'll consider your debt paid."

"That's one expensive dinner," I comment.

"Would you like it to be fifty thousand of them?"

Ugh. That'd be the rest of my mortal life and then some. "No," I say quietly.

"I didn't think so," he says. He leans over and kisses my forehead, shocking the heck out of me. I jerk my head back like his lips burn my skin. "So, until tonight." He smiles as he strides away and enters the building to the hotel.

Thirty seconds later, the sun hangs low in the sky, and

I bathe in its light, letting it wash away the demon scent that surely clings to my skin.

Evan clears his throat, drawing me away from my thoughts. I never thought I'd get to spend time with him ever again, but now that I have to spend an entire day, I dread it. All it does is remind me of the boy I lost. The boy who saved and destroyed me all in a matter of seconds.

"You look like Mal asked you to stand on broken glass for the day. I thought you'd be happier than this," he says.

Something in his voice strikes me in the heart. It's warm and inviting like it was before he traded his soul.

I can't look at him. "I did, too." I stare at the double doors that lead into the hotel. "Do you have a room here? Can we go to it?"

Fire lights his aqua eyes like the sunset painting the ocean. "Yeah, I'd like that."

Heat crawls up my neck and settles in my face. "I meant so I can sleep. It's been a long night, and I'm exhausted."

The side of his mouth pulls up in a lopsided smile. "You want to spend our day together sleeping?"

I shrug. "You say it like you care."

He closes the distance between us and slides his arms over my shoulders, forcing me to hold his stare. His amber and patchouli scent wafts over me, awakening something dark within my soul and sends my heart racing. My body responds to him though my mind wants to build a wall between us.

Tilting his head down, he hovers an inch from my face. His warm breath caresses my lips as he says, "Is that what you want me to say?"

Yes. "No." I force myself to step away from him. He's more charming than ever. It takes all my willpower to remind myself that he's playing games with my head. He's purposely cutting my skin open to bury himself under it. He's just like a—like a demon.

He laughs as he pulls away. Without motioning to me, he turns and strolls toward the hotel, only looking once to see if I'm following. I am.

What am I getting myself into?

⁂

"Love?" Dylan's voice cuts through the darkness of my foggy mind.

A pinprick of light blossoms in front of me as I fall deeper into sleep, finding reprieve in my own dream since my reality turned into a twisted nightmare.

Translucent wings sparkle in golden sunlight before Dylan's figure appears in front of me. He opens his arms wide, and I fall into them, letting him pet my hair and kiss my forehead.

We stand still in each other's arms for what feels like eternity before I force myself to break away and meet his chocolate eyes. Worry creases his forehead, but he doesn't throw the million questions probably running through his mind at me. He waits for me to say something first.

My gaze drifts to the pale blue sky as I gather the courage to tell him the truth. That I'm with Evan, the boy I chose over him before my choice was taken away. I'm technically not with Dylan. We haven't defined our relationship, but I'm sure we're long past that. We love each other, and that's what's important...but I love Evan, too.

"I'm safe," I finally say. "Faith stood up to her father on my behalf."

He frowns. "So, where are you?"

I crinkle my nose. "You have to understand. I was desperate. I didn't know what else to do."

"Cami, spit it out. You're worrying me," he says.

I lean forward and rest my head on his shoulder. "With Evan. I'm with Evan." I grip him as he tries to pull away. "It's not what you think. I swear."

"You don't know what I'm thinking." His low voice opens a deep cut on my heart.

Tears blur my eyes. "Then tell me."

He puffs a breath of air through his lips. "It doesn't matter. What matters is that you're safe. Can you tell me where you are so I can come get you?"

I imagine a shovel falling at my feet as I'm about to dig myself deeper into this mess. Maybe if I dig a hole deep enough, I can fall in and disappear.

"You can't come get me. Not yet at least. My father paid off Raphael. Well, he technically bought me. I'm obligated to spend the day with Evan and then have dinner with Malicevile. It's the only way I won't owe him," I say.

"They're trying to get to you, Cami. I know it," he says. "How much did he pay for your freedom? I have some money in savings."

I smile. I can't help it. I doubt Dylan has fifty grand in his bank account. It's the thought that counts, though. "Fifty thousand dollars."

He grimaces. "Let me make some phone calls."

I shake my head. "No, Dylan. By the time you get all that together, it'll be past dark. It's one dinner, and the day will fly by. I'll be okay."

"Cami," he says.

I kiss him. "Have some faith in me. I'll call you the moment dinner is over, okay?"

"I don't like this."

The ground quakes under my feet. *No! Not yet. Please, give me more time.* Clutching onto Dylan's shoulders, I will the world to stop shaking. But it's useless. The world fissures as reality drags me away from my angel without allowing me to say goodbye.

The bed bounces as I snap my eyes open. Evan lies on his side next to me on the queen-sized bed, shaking the mattress with his elbow. My eyes trail from his smiling face to his bare chest, and I scramble back and fall off the bed. Before I hit the floor, I stop myself by levitating and remain on the floor as still as possible.

Evan's laughter sounds through the air. He peeks his head over the mattress and grins at me. His blond hair hangs over his forehead, damp with water from the shower, and he takes pleasure in surprising me.

I groan, dropping to the carpet. "What the hell?"

He waves my cell phone. "Someone is calling you every few minutes but when I answer they hang up."

I sit up and snatch the phone away. Waving my hand at his bare shoulders, I say, "Can you put a shirt on or something?"

"Am I tempting you?"

Ugh. Yes. "More like annoying me."

"Uh-huh."

I roll me eyes before turning my attention to my cell phone, ignoring Evan the best I can as he watches my every move. I wish I knew what he was really thinking. Too bad my demonic abilities don't include mind reading. Of course, I might not like what I hear.

A text message flashes on the screen. I realize there are a dozen of them all from the same unfamiliar number. It matches the sixteen calls Evan answered and the seven he missed. I'm almost afraid to find out who it is. What if something happened to Alana?

If this is the hunter, please, call me back, the text message reads. It's from Faith. I know when Malicevile dragged me from Raphael's like a prisoner, a dozen terrifying thoughts flew through her mind.

I don't respond to the text but instead call. Faith answers with a quiet greeting after a few rings.

"I'm okay, Faith," I say. "Sorry it took me so long to call."

"Oh, my goodness. I was so scared. My dad said that man owned you, and there was nothing he could do to save you. I thought you were dead, especially after that guy kept answering. I didn't want to believe it, though," she says. Her words gush out like she can't say them fast enough.

I'm quiet for a second, not wanting to say too much in front of Evan. Then I glance at his grinning face. *Screw it.* "About your dad. He sold me to Malicevile. Fifty grand."

"What?" Her voice rises in pitch. "He lied to me."

I don't confirm or deny her thought even though I want to tell her that I told her so. Demons love to lie. "Still up to meeting me? As long as I leave by sundown, all should be fine. I have some stuff I really want to talk to you about."

She breathes static in the line. "Sure. I can meet you on the beach out back. My dad hasn't had time to re-place...James."

Stupid traitor James. I don't say it though. "Good. See you soon."

Evan studies me with a raised eyebrow when I hang up the phone. Amusement sparkles in his blue eyes, and I wonder how much of a fight he'll put up. His combat skills are a million times better than mine, but I'm used to sparring with him, so I can easily predict his next move. We practiced every day together while I was at the academy. His lessons are something I could never forget. He's the only trainer to reward me with kisses...

Using the edge of the bed for support, I pull myself to my feet and stand over Evan, looking down at him when he rolls over onto his back. He raises his arms over his head, stretching his torso, and tightens his abs. He's even more toned than I remember. I bet he spends all his sunlight hours at the gym training.

I shift my gaze from his stomach to his eyes. "Get dressed. I have somewhere I have to be."

"What do I get out of this?" he asks, half smiling.

"My irresistible company," I say. Two can play this game. Evan's trying to get to me—not in a lustful way, but he's trying to use my humanity against me. If he wants to be a jerk or play with the love I have for him, I'm going to have to mess with his Hell-bound side.

"I already have that." His grin grows into a full blown smile perfect enough to melt my already fiery heart.

Maybe I'm not so good at this game. "I'll let you in on a little secret."

"I'm listening," he says.

I bite my lip, thinking about my next words. I'm not going to just give him any secret. I'm going to give him a secret that would hurt him if he still had his humanity. "I was turned down by Angel Boy."

His smile disappears. "You mean—"

I shrug. "Maybe next time."

A spark flickers in his eyes, and I think I might have struck a nerve. I'm sure of it. Demons, which Evan is half, love competition. He doesn't have to admit it for me to know that the idea of me being with a half angel makes this game he's trying to play even more important to him. He's going to want to win. And that's where he loses. I'm not a game or a conquest. My heart is split in two, but the more Evan reveals his newfound hellish behavior, the more my heart comes together to lock him out completely. It's like he's not even trying to fight against Malicevile's control. If he was, he'd be a lot more conflicted.

A long silence hangs between us. I caught him off guard. He still has all his memories of us together, and he knows I meant the world to him, but he just can't feel the same feelings he did. Doesn't mean he won't think about what I'm sure he considers my betrayal. I won't speak the words out loud, but I feel like I betrayed him, too. Our relationship will never be the same.

He opens and closes his mouth a few times before narrowing his eyes, looking sexier than usual with his brooding expression. It stirs the raw emotions within me I force to stay locked away.

I close my eyes and imagine Dylan's wings comforting me in their ethereal light.

"You know, I had hoped we could be together again once you came to your senses," he finally says. "How could you—" He huffs a breath and clenches his fists. "With him. He'll destroy your soul. It's what he does."

I hug myself. "He loves me. He's been here for me and stands up for me. He protects my soul."

Fire erupts in his hands, and he tosses the flames back and forth between his fingers as he scowls at the floor. "He doesn't deserve you, Cami. He's not even on your level. How can he protect your soul if he can't even fight for it?"

I run my hands through my hair. I never imagined ever having this conversation. "Wow! You actually sound like you care, Evan. But you're not going to fool me, and I'm done discussing this." I grab my dirty jacket off the back of a chair. "Now, I gave you a secret. It's time to go."

With that, I stride from the room. I swipe hot tears from my cheeks as I reach Malicevile's Maserati. When Evan appears at the driver's side door, I turn away.

I won't let him see that his words got to me.

I won't let him see me cry.

LOSING BATTLE

FAITH SPRAWLS OUT on a purple blanket under a giant, colorful beach umbrella right on the beach outside her father's beach fortress. I search the area for signs of tainted humans like the man James, who tried to scare me and Cadence away, even though Faith said there was no one new yet. Evan strolls next to me, keeping a foot of space between us. He hasn't said a word since we left the hotel, and I'm not sure if he'll say anything else to me ever again. And I hate that I'm not okay with that.

"Faith," I call, not wanting to startle her.

She tilts her head back to peer in my direction. When she spots Evan, she scrambles to her feet and ignites a glowing, red orb between her fingers. Reaching out my hand, I block Evan and force him to stop with me. The heat of his chest through his shirt warms my fingers. He's hotter than ever, both physically and temperature wise.

I drop my hand back to my side when I'm sure he won't move. "It's okay, Faith. Evan won't hurt you."

She extinguishes her demonic power and rushes to me, throwing her arms around me. I stand frozen, unable to move, and Evan meets my eyes with raised brows.

She releases me and burns Evan a look dark enough to mirror the same one her father had given me. "Why's he here?"

"It's a long story," I say, motioning her toward the blanket.

"Do you have time to tell me?" she asks.

We sit together while Evan stands in the sand behind us, checking the area every few seconds. If I didn't know any better, I'd think he was being protective of me, but he's probably just making sure no one comes to try to take me to where I really want to be.

"Some of it. A lot of my story is hard to talk about, and you have to realize that you're living with a demon. I can't risk certain details," I say. I dig the heels of my boots in the sand in front of us, staring at the faint stains from the hellhound blood. Even without a shower, the sun took care of most of the gross, dried goo.

Faith pouts her bottom lip. "I get it. It's just—you're

not what I expected. When my dad spoke about hunters, you and your friend weren't what I imagined. I pictured a hunter to be scarier, and the type to kill without asking questions."

"Well, yeah. Hunters kill demons without asking questions, and that's because demons do the same to hunters. But I'm not that kind of hunt—"

"But aren't you?" Evan asks, interrupting me. "You may no longer be with the Hunter's Alliance, but you still kill all the same."

Faith turns her gaze back and forth between us but doesn't say a word.

I glower as anger and annoyance seep into my mind. Without raising my voice, I say, "Because I was looking for you, and you know it. Now why don't you take a walk or something? This doesn't concern you, Evan."

A fireball erupts in his fingers, and he surprises me by throwing it at the ocean. Faith stiffens next to me, and I pat her knee as Evan strolls closer to the waves and away from us. My eyes never leave his back, and he doesn't glance at me over his shoulder like I expect him to.

After a long, quiet moment, I say, "I'm sorry about Evan, Faith. Unlike us, his soul belongs to that demon who bought me from your father. His humanity shut off, and he has a mean streak."

"I don't get any of this," Faith says.

"I don't either half the time," I say, laughing, hoping it

lightens the mood. "I've only known about the Veiled Realm for three years since my parents were killed by a demon." I should mention that Malicevile was responsible, but that's something I'd like to keep from Faith. For now at least. I wish I knew why I felt this way, though.

"My mom died after I was born," Faith says. "My grandma adopted me, but when she passed away, no one else in the family would take me so I ended up in foster care. It wasn't until I met my dad that I understood why my mom's family didn't take me in. They knew the truth and were scared."

"Can you blame them, really?"

She shrugs. "No. I don't blame them at all."

The white-capped waves crash into the shore in front of us, and I imagine how cool the water would feel against my hot skin. Saltwater sprays my face when the tide rolls in only a few feet away.

Staring at the ocean helps me gather my thoughts for the reason I asked Faith to meet me. She's loyal to her father, but she's also so young and easily influenced. How can a girl not like the person who wanted her and brought her into a lavish home most only dream of? If Malicevile hadn't murdered my parents and set my house on fire, I might've gone with him. Demons are so damn charming.

After a quiet moment, I finally ask, "Are you happy?"

Faith glares at her hands without answering right away. "This is going to sound ungrateful because of everything

Raphael has done for me, but he's so overprotective...I'm lonely. I can't leave this beach except after nightfall, and even then, the only people I ever get to meet are the disgraced and corrupt. You're the first good person I've hung out with in months."

Her perception of me stings a little. "I know what it's like. I was isolated from the world for years because of—"

"Cami," Evan says, interrupting. He turns away from the ocean to look at us. It doesn't surprise me that he's been eavesdropping all along. "Think about what you're going to say next and how it'll affect your life. She's a demon's daughter."

I stiffen my shoulders. "And so am I, and you're a demon's son."

Faith's eyes widen. "What? You're both like me? My dad said my kind was rare."

I shrug. "You are rare, Faith. You're being raised by a demon. Neither of us has lived with our demonic parents. In fact, Evan's mother is dead. He killed her."

"You what?" Fear lines Faith's eyes, and I regret ever mentioning that part.

"We've all made mistakes," he says, flaring his nostrils at me.

"Yeah, we have," I say. "But Faith, I want you to know that I'm here for you. You don't have to be lonely all the time. I can teach you about the parts of the world Raphael wouldn't dare show you. But you have to promise you won't tell him about me. He can't know I'm a demi-demon. He can't know you talked to me at all, okay?"

"You want me to lie to him?" she asks.

I nod. "It's not like he's being truthful."

Evan scoffs. "He's protecting her, Cami. You're just going to put her in danger."

I ignore him. "Don't listen to him. He's trying to manipulate us."

"Do you hear yourself?" he asks me. "I'm trying to protect you. It's bad to get involved in demonic affairs. Trust me."

I jump to my feet and levitate to meet his eyes all while jabbing my finger into his chest. "Trust you? You want me to trust the boy who wants me to give up my humanity? You're crazy."

"No, you should trust me *because* I gave up my soul for you, Cami. I'm like this because I wanted you to live. I loved you so much that my eternity didn't matter to me. And it still doesn't. You're what matters." He leans over and kisses me, pulling me closer to him until I'm wrapped in his arms.

His warm lips are better than I remember them, and my body awakens to the memories I've tried so hard to shut out. I've waited for this moment forever, to be with Evan again, but it's not how I imagined it to be. His words tug at my heart, pulling it apart piece by piece. He said he *loved* me. Past tense. How on earth can I really matter to him?

Not in the way I want. I matter for the sole reason that I'm a demon's daughter, and he's under his control.

I press my hands into his chest and push him back. "You can't just do that to me anymore."

I turn away, blinking the stupid tears from my eyes for the millionth time today, and I face Faith, who looks as surprised as I am. Her hands shake as she cups a blazing, ruby orb in her grip. She was ready to attack Evan. For me. That gesture alone makes me feel even worse that she had to witness that.

"I'm okay, Faith. Give me the power," I say, holding out my hands. She tosses me the orb, and it sinks into my skin where I save it for another time. It's one of the only good things I learned from having Malicevile force his power into me—I learned to store it, along with any other power a demon, or in this case, demi-demon throws at me.

"Where'd it go?" she asks.

"I'm saving it for later in case I need it. Unlike you, I can't make my own," I say. I stroll over to her, ignoring Evan hovering behind me, and I offer her my hands. "Here, let me walk you back inside. I don't have much time left, and I want you to think about everything I told you. If you call me tomorrow, it won't be so complicated. My date with the demon will be over tonight."

She bobs her head up and down. "I promise not to tell my dad."

"I know."

With a quiet goodbye and a quick hug, I leave Faith at her beach fortress. As long as Malicevile lets me see tomorrow, I know I can save her from her prison in disguise. I just hope she lets me.

⁂

"You know I could kill you, right?" Cadence says as she huffs into the phone. "What have you been doing all day that was so important that you couldn't let me know you were okay after Malicevile *bought* you from Raphael?"

I wince at the fury in her voice. "I'm sorry, Cadence. I slept most of the morning and met with Faith this afternoon."

"After she basically spit in our faces for trying to help her?" she asks.

"It's not like that. She didn't know."

I drum my fingers on the bathroom counter. Steam fills the air from the shower I got out of a few minutes ago. I never thought things could be awkward between Evan and me, but the silence between us now is even more uncomfortable. I'd rather hide in here until sundown than be alone with him in a hotel room.

"Then what's it like?" Cadence asks after a moment.

"She loves the guy, and she doesn't want him hurt. He rescued her from a bad situation. She's willing to meet with me during the day, though. I want to show her what it's like in the real world around people. I want to show her the damage her father causes. Maybe she'll change her mind about him." I gaze at my foggy reflection. "We can talk about this later."

"You sure there's going to be a later?" She listens to every word I say but doesn't respond with anything except for questions. I wish she'd give me something so I know what she's thinking.

I sigh. "Yes."

"I thought you might have abandoned us to be with..." Her words fade away before she finishes her sentence.

"I'd never choose Mal over you."

She clears her throat. "I meant Evan."

Hot emotions run through my veins hearing her say his name out loud. I'm pissed and confused and hurt and maybe even a little bit excited about the kiss he surprised me with. But that's all it was and will ever be. A spur of the moment thing that left me momentarily thinking of impossible possibilities.

"Of course not. He can try all he wants to get to me, but I'm not turning my back on the people who are here for me now. The old Evan wouldn't want me to," I say.

She breathes a deep breath into the phone. "I'm so happy to hear you say that, Cami. I know things are complicated between Dylan and you, and I never thought I'd say this, but I'm on his team. Wings don't prick like horns."

I smirk. "Come with Dylan to get me after my date with the devil?"

She laughs. "Of course. Someone's gotta protect him

when you're not around."

"Love you, Cadence. See you tonight."

I hang up after she says goodbye and force myself to turn the shower off. My wet hair clings to my shoulders, and I wrap a fluffy, white towel around me. Cracking the door open, I peek into the spacious hotel room and find Evan sitting on the edge of the bed, wearing a suit, with his elbows on his knees. He gazes up and catches me staring.

"What kind of dinner is this? I only have my dirty T-shirt and jeans. Does Malicevile want to humiliate me or something?" I ask.

Evan sighs, pushes from the bed, and crosses the room to the closet. The door creaks as he slides it open, and hanging on the single bar is a dress bag with what I'm sure is a gown Malicevile probably picked out for me. He's always prepared.

Evan doesn't move to bring me the dress, so I roll my eyes as I fling open the door and pad across the soft carpet in only my towel. His eyes trail from my neck to my legs, before making their way back to my eyes. He holds out the dress, dangling the hanger from his index finger.

"You can't deny that there isn't still something between us, Cami," he says as I snatch the dress away.

I grip my towel tighter. "Why do you enjoy torturing me so much? If you ever cared about me, you'd just stop. This isn't how to win me over. You know I love you. You know I would've never agreed to the exchange you made.

It's like you're blaming me for your decision. You say it's the best one you ever made, but then you say it's my fault. Which is it?"

He reaches out and grabs my shoulder. "I don't know, Cami. I don't know anything. But I still like being around you. You stir something within me that I forgot about. It's like I'm still living."

"We can't be together, though. As long as your soul belongs to Malicevile, I can't be with you," I say.

His jaw twitches. "You keep saying that. It's not that you can't be with me. It's that you don't want to. It's because of *him* isn't it?" He can't even spit out Dylan's name. I don't blame him. We were all friends once.

I pull away and put distance between us. "Stop. Just stop. You'll never understand."

He fists his hands at his sides. "That's because you won't tell me the truth. Do I need to get rid of the nephilim? It feels like he's the one standing in my way."

Rage builds in my chest, and I summon the power Faith gave me. The molten liquid seeps into my hands, moving and swirling until it forms a perfect orb. I hold it up. "If you dare threaten Dylan again, you will regret it."

He raises his hands up in surrender. "Then tell me the truth."

I squeeze my eyes shut as I let the words fall from my lips. "Because I'm afraid, okay? I'm afraid that I'll like being around you and Malicevile. I'm afraid of turning against all the people I love. I can't handle thinking that maybe I'm not meant to be in Heaven's grace. I'm afraid because I don't even care if I am."

Evan embraces me as my emotions get the best of me, and I start to sob uncontrollably. When his rugged patchouli scent wafts around me, I realize how much of a losing battle this all is. How can I trust him after everything he's told me? I'd be a fool to believe for one second that we could go back to how we were before. But something in his hug, the way he holds me tight, letting me cry into his suit jacket, makes me believe that maybe it's not his humanity that allowed him to love me—maybe it wasn't even his soul. It could be everything else in his essence. His heart, his mind, his power—all the pieces that fit perfectly together to make Evan who he is could love me just as much as his soul. There's no other explanation.

After my sobs turn to hiccups, and my knees strengthen enough for me to stand on my own, Evan lets me go. He peers into my eyes, a flicker of light breaking through the shadows that dull his once crystal clear irises, but it disappears just as quickly as it came.

"The sun is setting, and we can't keep your father waiting," he says instead of trying to convince me that my fears aren't legitimate.

All I can do is nod and shuffle away to get ready for an unwanted date with my demonic dad.

DATE WITH A DEMON

I BLOW A loose curl from my forehead as I step into the empty hotel room. Evan left fifteen minutes ago when he announced the sun had set. I told him I needed a bit more time to get ready. I lied. I just didn't want to be alone with him when I stepped out in the gown Malicevile had picked out for me.

The gown couldn't be any more perfect. Apart from not being able to run because of the mermaid cut, the embroidered fabric in an emerald green that matches my eyes is gorgeous. It's a perfect fit, like it was tailored just for me, and I can't stop glancing at myself in every reflection I find. The sleeveless, V-neck cut allows me to show off my sunstone necklace, which complements the green color of the gown.

My strappy black heels sink into the soft carpet as I walk, and I realize I have no where to put any of my weapons. *You'll be fine. You don't need a weapon, remember?*

I leave all my belongings in a small pile near the door. I set a new makeup bag, which was stored in the bottom of the dress bag, on top of my jacket, and then I saunter toward the door. I'd give anything to have a dinner date with Dylan instead of my father, because I don't think he's ever even seen me dressed up, and knowing me, by the end of the night, this gown will be tattered and covered in demon goo like all my other clothes at the end of a night.

The door whines when I open it, and the hallway outside the room is empty. I don't even pick up the faint scent of my father. Feeling self-conscious, I hug my arms over my chest and stroll through the hotel with my eyes trained on the patterned carpet until I reach the lobby. A few guests and the hotel concierge stare my way, their eyes following me as I cross the room to the automatic door. I refuse to stand here and be the center of attention, so I exit the building and let the cool sea breeze wrap around me.

A low whistle sounds through the air, and I draw my attention to a black limo idling in the parking lot. My father and Evan stand near the rear end next to our chauffeur. My hands tremble as I drop them to my sides and stroll closer.

Malicevile meets me halfway, his arms opened wide, and a dazzling smile playing on his face. His intense green eyes sparkle in the light from the hotel when they meet mine. I stop in my tracks before he can embrace me, and instead, he swings his arm around my back and guides me toward the limo.

"Camilla, you don't know how happy I am that you're here. You look spectacular," he says, lightly pressing his warm fingers into my back.

The driver opens the door, and Evan quietly gets in before offering his hand out for me to take. I slide across the seat and regret not moving, because Malicevile follows in behind me, and I'm stuck in the middle of a demonic sandwich, wearing impractical clothing to fight in and without any spare weapons for when Faith's power runs out.

I inhale a deep breath, forcing my panic away so I can keep a clear head. The scent of cinnamon mixing with the earthiness of patchouli makes it hard to think.

When the driver gets on the road, he closes the partition, giving us privacy. I almost wish he'd keep it open so Malicevile's forced to play human.

After a long, quiet moment, Malicevile says, "I hope you two had a pleasant day. Do anything fun?"

The question throws me off. He *is* playing human, pretending to care about my day. This whole situation feels ridiculous, like I'm having a lucid dream that includes people from my nightmares in a more pleasant setting.

"It was fine," I say before Evan can open his mouth. "I slept mostly and then went to the beach."

"I never thought you to be much of a swimmer," he says.

I frown. "I'm not, but I enjoy the sun." I say it the way I do to show Malicevile how different we really are. Or maybe it's to remind myself. I don't like the uncertainty coursing through me. Knowing my enemy has helped me survive for years, but now I'm not so sure if that was the case.

Malicevile hums in response, unfazed by my attempt to bother him. "You're going to love this restaurant," he says, changing the subject. "The food is splendid."

I raise an eyebrow. "You eat?"

He smirks. "Why wouldn't I?"

"You're a demon. I'm pretty sure you survive by devouring souls," I say.

Laughter erupts from Malicevile's mouth, startling me, and I grip Evan's knee to stop from levitating to the roof. Malicevile slaps his knee while shaking his head, looking more human than ever, and when the limo comes to a halt, he sucks in a breath to compose himself.

"You really do know nothing, dear Camilla," he says. "While I know you were joking about the souls, you must know that I, like every other demon on earth, follow the laws of the living."

"Except for the sun," I say.

He presses his lips together. "Except for that."

The limo door swings open, cutting off anything else Malicevile was about to say, and we all climb out and stand in front of a swanky, beach-front restaurant. A glittering sign reads, *Bella Oceano,* and soft music hums through the air from the restaurant. When we enter the dim place, I peer around at candle-lit tables with cerulean tablecloths and covered chairs, and minimalist sea-themed paintings on the walls. I direct my attention to a wall of glass that leads to a terrace above the beach with a view of the night-darkened ocean.

The moon hangs high in the sky, and the stars shimmer like tiny pearls sewn into a black, satiny blanket. The low lighting from a string of lights around the perimeter and fake candles in glass centerpieces filled with sand and shells allows for a clear view of the night around us. It reminds me of the night sky in Desertville and how clear everything was without the light pollution from the city.

The maître d shows us to a table in the corner, away from all the other diners, and offers Malicevile a bottle of his finest wine. When he leaves, I draw my gaze toward the roaring ocean. If I don't look at Malicevile or Evan, I can pretend I'm somewhere else.

"You know, Camilla, I'd almost given up hope on you. I never imagined you'd be sitting down to a lovely, quiet dinner," Malicevile says. "You haven't even tried to hit me."

Yet. I tighten my jaw, forcing my sarcasm to stay under

wraps. He can pretend all he wants that I'm here by my own freewill. If it makes this dinner less excruciating, then I'll play along with his twisted thoughts.

"I didn't either. If we're being honest, I never expected you to act civilized toward me at all. What changed? You're growing soft, Mal." I tuck my hands in my lap so I don't lean my elbows on the table, though I really want to.

He narrows his eyes and flashes a small glimpse of his demonic self in his irises. My skin crawls, remembering when he interrupted my execution and went full-on demon, murdering almost all the alliance leaders. "I wouldn't say I'm growing soft, but I am changing. And you're the reason for this. Demons don't procreate for the sole purpose of spreading their evil seed. We can't have more than one child at a time. If we could, the world would be quite different. The human race would've probably died off altogether."

This information is new to me. I wonder if the alliance knows about it. Any other time, I wouldn't let Malicevile open up any sort of dialogue, and I'd keep my questions to myself, but I'm going to be here for at least another hour. Might as well learn something interesting.

I turn to Evan. "Did you know this? You grew up with the alliance. Do they know?"

Evan shakes his head. "They know nothing, Cami."

"And how exactly am I changing you?" I ask Malicevile. "I haven't done anything."

"You are a part of me, Camilla. My blood runs through

your veins. The longer we're around each other, the more your essence comes back to me. Through you, I'm given a gift that all demons crave—angels, too—I'm given part of your humanity."

"And why the heck would you want that?" Demons hate humans. They think they're inferior to them.

"Power. Humanity makes it easier to rally other demons to me. It makes it easier to know and understand humans, too. I can't rule the world if I constantly act on my demonic nature."

Those are some hefty goals. I don't say it though. I can't help thinking what a parasite he is. "You're the reason I feel like I'm turning into a full-blooded demon," I say without having time to really process my thoughts. "You're why I'm changing, too."

He reaches out and rests his hand on mine. "You're not changing, Camilla. You're just starting to live up to your potential. You have so much power and influence waiting to come out. All the alliance has ever done, what your guardian, Alana, has done, was hinder your ability to grow as a half breed."

Sure, Alana spent almost all the time I've known her keeping me away from the Veiled Realm and all the creatures within it to the point that I couldn't even defend myself, but I wouldn't say she hindered me in the way Malicevile implies. She gave me a life—one among humans, like I thought I was—and kept me safe. I sometimes miss the simplicity of going to public school, only worrying about the occasional demon every few weeks. Malicevile didn't show up regularly most of that time either. I miss not being involved. It was easier.

Closing my eyes, I rub small circles on my temples. I hate admitting it, but what he says about him and me makes sense. I've always been drawn to Malicevile, but my good senses kept me away. The rational part of me would never let me forget that demons are evil beings. But now that my soul is Hell-bound, I'm finding it easier to make excuses. To give reason to the evil deeds he commits. *What's wrong with me?*

"He's right," Evan says speaking up. I never thought I'd see the day where he would ever agree with my father. "Do you really want to spend the rest of your life struggling to fit in among the humans who fear you? Or hiding your darkest sides from the n—"

I snap my eyes open. "Shut up. Don't even go there."

My father chuckles. "I already know about the nephilim, Camilla. You don't have to fear for him. I know you'd never allow him to take your soul." I bet he didn't take my heart into consideration. Malicevile sees Dylan as an inconvenience and not a threat. If he only knew how invested I've become, how much I've come to rely on my self-proclaimed guardian angel, he'd probably reconsider his thinking. He's capable of ripping Dylan away from me without a second thought. He murdered a nephilim in the name of Melanie—it's the reason the alliance killed her. They blamed her for the half-angel's death.

"Did you make Melanie the same promise?" I ask, surprising myself. Melanie is probably the one subject I shouldn't bring up. She was the perfect daughter who loved her demon father, like Faith does in a way. I probably could never compare to her in Malicevile's eyes. I've been more of a nuisance and an annoyance over the last few months.

Malicevile leans his elbows on the table, linking his fingers together. "No, I did not. And Camilla, you're nothing like your sister if that's what you're thinking."

"You don't know what I'm thinking," I snap.

A smile pulls at the corners of his mouth. "Care to share why you're making that unpleasant expression then?"

Seriously? "This is my face."

Evan chuckles, wiping his hand over his face as he looks between me and Malicevile. I'm glad someone is amused.

I straighten my shoulders. "If you must know, I was just thinking about how on earth Melanie could ever love you. You sure you still want me to share the rest of my thoughts? I'd gladly tell you."

"There's the feisty girl I've grown to tolerate," Malicevile says with an annoying smile. "If it makes you feel better, tell me whatever the hell you want. Lay it all on the table. You might actually learn something for once."

The conversation starts to head into uncomfortable territory. The last thing I want is to divulge my thoughts to Malicevile. That's what people do who're trying to build some sort of relationship. Of course a father would want to know more about his daughter. I'd rather remain a mystery. Surprise is one of the only things I ever have going for me.

Stretching up, I search around the terrace to see where our server is. This dinner is taking longer than I expected, and now, all I want to do is hide in my room and think. It's a lot to take in.

"For being such a fancy place, service sucks," I mutter, hoping to change the subject.

"I apologize. I put a hold on our dinner to give me time to talk to you. I know this might be the only chance I have. I'm not wasting the opportunity," he says.

Great. He could keep this up all night, and I'd never get to leave.

I crinkle my nose. "If I promise to meet with you again will you stop stalling? I have people waiting for me, you know."

"How about tomorrow night?"

I drop my shoulders. "Fine, but I get to wear jeans."

"You have a deal, my dear."

<hr>

"I'm okay, but it's taking longer than I thought. Malicevile says dinner isn't complete without dessert, and he's taking me somewhere else," I say into the payphone. After rushing through eating my salmon, I excused myself to the bathroom but instead left the restaurant to use the payphone out front. I knew Dylan would accept my collect call since I'm penniless and phoneless at the moment. *Stupid, impractical, yet stunning dress.*

Dylan breathes into the line. "He's so manipulative. I can't wait for this all to be behind us. Next time, I'll pay the fifty grand."

I laugh, my voice catching with nerves. "About that."

"What now?" I can almost feel his stress through the line.

"I kind of made another deal with him. I was getting annoyed because he was putting off being served dinner so I told him I'd meet him tomorrow night if he'd just get on with dinner," I say.

"Seriously, Cami? Are you crazy?"

And impatient, annoyed, frustrated, curious, impulsive. I cringe. "It's not so bad."

"This is what I was afraid of." Anger laces his words. It's not directed at me though.

I glance over my shoulder. I'm taking too long. "Don't worry about me. I'll call you when I'm ready. I have to go."

"Cami, wa—"

I disconnect before he can beg me to stay on the line. Hanging the phone back in its holder, I hurry inside, ignoring the dozens of eyes on me as I stride through the middle of the restaurant and to the terrace where I watch Malicevile take care of the bill.

He and Evan stand when a server opens the door for me, and I remain in place by the door. There's no way he's getting me to sit down again, because I'm sure dessert will take just as long.

I place my hands on my hips. "So, this dessert deal. Can I pick the place?"

Malicevile grins. "Of course, Camilla. I want you to enjoy yourself."

"Ice cream," I say. "Somewhere with lots of flavors and toppings."

He rubs his chin. "You're in a gown."

Evan cracks a smile behind him. He's not laughing at me, though. He's as amused as I am. I can't think of anything funnier than dragging an upper-level demon, in his finest suit, into a sweet ice cream shop where he has to order ice cream with names like Apple Burst or Chocoholic Love.

"Then I'll make mine fancy with sprinkles," I say.

Malicevile heaves a sigh while closing the distance between us. He opens the door for me, and Evan lingers behind us until I motion him to catch up with a quick nod of my head. A boy my age, dressed in a tuxedo, smiles at me as I pass by, and Evan slides his arm around my shoulders, pulling me to him. Jealousy is kind of funny on him. I guess I do stir something in him. Maybe that's his weakness.

Within a few minutes, we arrive at a brightly lit ice cream shop with narwhals and starfish painted on the glass windows. Arctic Ice Cream seems to be the place of choice for people after dinner, and the whole room goes quiet when I stroll in.

Awkward.

I regret choosing a normal place immediately. Sitting in the corner of the shop, eating a spoonful of ice cream, is one of the younger boys from the Moonlight Shores pack. A pretty redhead sits across from him, but I don't recognize her. She must be human.

His mouth drops open when he sees me, and I gape at him with startled eyes. I turn and do the only thing I can think of. I grab my father's hand and yank him toward the counter. I stand closest to the wall so when he looks at me, he can't see anyone behind me.

"Can you order me something chocolate with lots of toppings?" I ask. "I'm going to save us the last booth. I don't feel like sitting in those rickety chairs."

His eyes light up. "Evan, escort her. Wipe those lustful looks off those humans' faces while you're at it. Camilla is off limits to them."

What? Is he kidding me? I'm pretty sure most of the place is drooling over him.

Shaking my head, I stroll away with Evan trailing behind me. I plop down in the booth behind the boy and turn in my seat. "You need to run. Now. Go home and stay inside. I can't believe you're even out here."

The werewolf nods as he jumps to his feet, abandoning his date without a word. He rushes through the ice cream shop, and the bell dings as he leaves. I glance toward Malicevile at the counter, and my heart slides into my stomach.

He's already gone.

DEMONIC AFFAIRS

THE SCENT OF cinnamon and clove lingers in the air outside the ice cream shop. I hover in the doorway, searching my surroundings for signs of Malicevile. He must've spotted the werewolf the moment we entered the shop, and he took the opportunity of me leaving his side to go after the poor creature. I thought I was helping the werewolf by telling him to leave, but now I'm sure I just handed him to Malicevile on a leash.

I kick off my pesky heels and leave them on the sidewalk as I jog the best I can in my restricting dress to the end of the block where a set of stairs leads to the beach. I bet that's the direction the boy went. It'd have been faster for him to change and run home as a wolf.

Bolting down the stairs two at a time, I reach the beach in seconds. The dark waves crash against the shore. White foam coats the sand, giving me a glowing trail along the beach. I suck in a deep breath of salty air, picking up the scent of cinnamon and something earthy, like damp dirt, which I know must be the werewolf. They have to be nearby.

A spark of light catches my eye in the distance, and an energy orb flies across the sand, sputtering out inches from a figure on the ground. I hike up my dress and start running as fast as I can. Bending my knees, I propel through the air, but it's not easy having to land in the soft sand. It's hard to get a quick start without pushing against a firm foundation.

Another ball of electricity flies through the air, the flash blinding me just as I'm about to hit the ground, and I lose my concentration. My feet slide in the sand, sending me tumbling. I spit out a mouthful of sand and push onto my hands and knees. I can't let Malicevile take the poor werewolf. I just can't.

"Stop!" I scream as I stagger, trying to get to my feet in the stupid dress. The scent of patchouli and amber sneaks up on me.

Strong arms wrap around me from behind, pulling me away. I thrash, elbowing Evan in the stomach. I spin to watch him fall to his knees, and I do the only thing I can think of to keep him away from me. He'll try to stop me if I go after Malicevile. I'm surprised he didn't attempt to grab me sooner. Scooping up a handful of sand, I throw it in Evan's eyes.

"Malicevile! Leave him alone. I swear, if you hurt him, I'll never give you the time of day again. You can bet on it," I say, anger lining my words.

It's enough to make my father stop in his tracks. He turns from the werewolf, who scrambles to his feet and starts running in the opposite direction.

"I'm willing to take my chance, Camilla," my father says as he turns back to the fleeing werewolf. He launches another energy ball in his direction and misses the boy by a foot. "You should blame yourself for my need of new guard dogs."

I grimace. "Why don't you just get a pet dog? They're just as effective at keeping people out."

He smacks his hand to his chest while saying, "You think *I'm* worried about humans? Come on, Camilla. I know you're smarter than that. Hellhounds protect my property from other demons—angels even. I don't know how you managed it, but I'm still wondering how the hell you killed two of my best guards at my home. You killed one of Raphael's, too."

I open my mouth to answer, to tell him *I* technically haven't killed any Hellhounds, but I decide it's better to make him think I'm capable of killing three monstrous beasts on my own.

"Well, it was that or be ripped to shreds," I say. I turn my attention to the beach, the werewolf gone from view.

Malicevile follows my line of sight before turning to Evan. "Take her back to the limo and wait for me. The werewolf is still nearby. I'm going to finish the hunt."

I smack Evan away when he tries to take my hand. "Dinner is over. You can't control me anymore, and I'm not letting you hurt the boy."

Malicevile laughs, the sound deep and throaty, and it crawls under my skin. "I don't want to fight you, Camilla."

"Then give up on your twisted hunt. I'm willing to face you in your darkest form to protect that werewolf. I know him," I say.

"Then I'll break him quickly for your sake. Hell, you could use some extra protection. He can be yours," he says. He nods to Evan. "Now take her."

Malicevile turns away and starts strolling down the beach like he's sure he'll catch up to the werewolf before he can take shelter in a safe house. He doesn't even bother to look back. He thinks I'm outmatched, and no matter what I try, he'll win.

Evan touches my shoulder. "Come on, Cami. Don't make this hard. I don't want to drag you away. You can't fight your father and win. You know this."

"Thanks for the encouragement," I say, sarcasm lining my words.

I close my eyes for a second and conjure some of the

power Faith gave me. I have enough for at least two shots, so I need to get as close to Malicevile as possible. The ruby red orb warms my fingers, the same sensation I used to get holding one of Evan's fireballs. It's not as exhilarating as one of Malicevile's energy balls, but I'm sure it'll sting him a little. Hopefully, it'll slow him down.

When Evan reaches for me again, I hold up the glowing orb. "Don't think I won't use this on you. Just stay out of it."

He spreads his arms, relying on the fact that I don't really want to hurt him, and comes at me. Swiveling out of the way, I bend my knees and launch into the air higher than he can grab me. I descend toward the rushing waves, concentrating on levitating over the ocean. Saltwater splashes the bottoms of my bare feet, and I narrow my eyes at Malicevile's back.

The rolling tide steals the sound of Evan's voice from the air, and I wind my arm back and pitch the lava-like ball of power at Malicevile. A flash of red light bursts into the air as the power burns through the back of his designer tuxedo. He thrashes as he rips the sizzling fabric away, spinning in a circle to face his attacker.

I don't hesitate. I throw the remaining power at him, hitting him in the chest. The power eats through his shirt, and he yells out, hitting the sand to try to rid himself of the liquid-like energy that he can't rub off without burning his hands.

I float back to the sand and head in his direction instead of fleeing like I want to. He's pissed and about to take out his wrath on me. But I can't back down. Not this time. I meant it when I told him I didn't want him breaking more werewolves.

"I warned you," I say as I draw near. "You didn't think I had it in me, and you underestimated me. Your power isn't the only one I can absorb and store, you know."

I raise my hand, pretending like I'm going to throw another ball of power at him, and a heavy body smashes into me, forcing me to the beach. Evan's patchouli scent wafts around me as he presses my shoulders into the sand so I can't get up. I don't fight back.

Malicevile jumps to his feet, his shirt and tuxedo jacket now smoldering in the sand. His bare chest, ripped with hard muscles, glows a faint pink where the power had touched his skin. His intense green eyes glower at me as he composes himself, and then he rushes toward me. I wince when sand flies into my face.

He crouches down. "Let her up, Evan."

I roll my shoulders as Evan's weight lifts off me.

Malicevile offers his hand to help me up, and I reluctantly take it, letting him pull me to my feet. Crossing my arms over my chest, I narrow my eyes in probably the most pathetic glower possible when it comes to facing a demon.

"Where did you get the power?" he asks.

I suck in my bottom lip. "A demon."

He narrows his eyes. "Raphael?"

I don't answer. Instead, I train my gaze on the hem of my dirty gown.

He reaches out and touches my chin, forcing my head up. "Camilla, you need to be careful. If another demon discovers what you can do, they'll try to harm you."

I suck in a breath through me nose. My father's cinnamon scent burns my throat. "I *am* careful, and no it wasn't from Raphael."

"Then who?"

"His daughter," Evan says, giving away my secret.

Tears burn my eyes as his betrayal sinks deep into my bones. I knew that Evan was loyal to Malicevile. He has to be. But I also had hoped that a small part of his loyalty lay with me. There's no way for me to hide the fact that I visited Faith now. I doubt he'd believe that she gave me some of her power the night he picked me up.

"Camilla!" His hot, cinnamon breath hits my face. I stumble back out of his reach and fall on my butt in the sand. "What were you thinking? You can't just meddle in demonic affairs. That girl is off limits. You'll ruin her just like the alliance has ruined you."

I blink a few times without answering. He actually sounds how I imagine an angry father to sound like. I'd give anything to hear who I consider my real dad sound this angry with me. Malicevile stole that chance though.

I push to my feet and turn away from Evan and

Malicevile. I can't look either of them in the eyes. All I want to do is find my way to a phone so I can call for a ride and get out of this dirty gown. So much for looking hot when Dylan comes to get me.

"Where do you think you're going?" Malicevile asks.

It takes all my willpower not to flip him off. "My temporary home. I completed my obligation to you for the night. I need to be around people who don't think I'm a ruined mess, thank you very much."

"I expect you at the hotel tomorrow at sundown, Camilla," my father calls, ignoring my remarks.

I wave my hand behind me. "Yeah, okay. Whatever."

I don't look back as I head to Ocean Mist Road, the main street in downtown Moonlight Shores, to find a phone. Thank God dinner with my demonic dad is officially over tonight. Now, all I have to do is survive my return to the house of werewolves. If I'm even allowed back in.

⁓ ⁂ ⁓

"I think we can salvage it," Cadence says, running her fingers over the embroidered fabric of my dress. "I hate to see such pretty things ruined by dinner dates with demons. That would've never happened if you were with me and Angel Boy."

I smirk, leaning my elbows on my knees. "If you can fix it, you can have it. I won't be wearing this gown again."

Wrapping her arms around me, she squeezes me against her. "I love you, you know. I'm glad you're back. I thought

I had lost you forever."

I rest my head on her shoulder and peer at Dylan's reflection in the rearview mirror as he drives us back to the safe house.

He offers me a small smile. "We'd have never let that happen."

"Damn right," Cadence says. "Dylan had to stop me from returning to Raphael's last night."

"He'd have regretted ever messing with you," I say, laughing.

She wags her eyebrows. "I know."

Dylan pulls the Jag into the long driveway of the beach house. No werewolves greet us outside this time. They're probably all tucked away, safely inside, where they should be with my father in town.

Dylan climbs out and strolls around the hood of the car to open my door. He slides his arms around me, holding me against him, and I suck in a breath of his fresh apple and rain scent. It calms the bunched muscles in my back, and for the first time in twenty-four hours, I can relax.

Cadence opens the front door before us and stops in her tracks. The entire pack of werewolves hangs out in the living room just off to the side of the foyer, and they get to their feet when they see me.

Among them is the boy who I gave a fighting chance to on the beach. Mixed emotions cross all the werewolves' faces, and I freeze on the welcome mat, unsure if I'm still welcome here or not.

Joshua strides forward, his hands balled into fists at his sides. I brace myself for a punch to the face, but it doesn't come. Instead, his muscular arms pull me away from Dylan, and he lifts me off my feet, hugging me against him while spinning me in a circle.

I rest my head on his taut shoulder, relishing in his appreciation of me. I needed this firm werewolf hug after everything. It proves that my father was wrong. I'm not ruined.

"The pack owes you for what you did for Gregory," he says as he sets me on my feet.

I shake my head. "Let's call it even. You're giving me a place to stay."

He grins. "Well, you have us if you ever need us."

"Thanks," I say, turning away.

As I head back to the bedroom, the boy from the ice cream shop stops us in the hall outside of the bedroom I share with Dylan. I motion for Dylan and Cadence to head inside, and I let the boy hug me.

"I didn't tell my pack anything more than you saved me from a demon," he says.

"Oh, well, thanks. I don't usually have dinner with my father, but it was either that or owe him fifty grand for my failed mission to Raphael's."

His brows knit together. "I'm not sure how to feel about this. I thought you were a goner, but I'm glad you knew the demon well enough that he didn't kill you."

I shift from foot to foot. "It's all really complicated. I'm just glad I was able to fight him long enough for you to get away. You should know better about being out in the open after dark."

He blushes. "I know. I just really like Jamie."

"Enough to lose your soul and be damned to eternal demon servitude?"

"When you put it that way..." His voice trails off.

I touch his shoulder. "I hate to cut our conversation short, but I'm exhausted, Gregory."

"Call me Greg," he says. "And if you need anything at all, let me know."

A thought pops into my mind as I think about what's to come tomorrow. I promised I'd see Faith again, and despite my father's demand to stay out of Raphael's business, I'm not going to just abandon her.

"Actually, there is something," I say.

"Yeah?"

"Can I introduce you to my friend? She's a halfie like me." Calling myself a halfie out loud reminds me of the first time I heard the term, back in the church the day after I had met Evan. I push the invading thoughts away.

"During the day, right?"

I smile. "How about first thing in the morning?"

"Sounds like a plan."

Greg turns and strides back to where I hear his pack laughing and having a good time in the living room. Entering my bedroom, I don't even wait for Cadence or Dylan to turn around while I unzip the side of my dress and step out of it, leaving it crumpled on the floor.

Cadence watches Dylan watch me, and I ignore them long enough to shrug into a hoodie and a pair of track pants I left lying in a pile on the floor near the bathroom.

"You look like you have a lot on your mind," Cadence says, pushing from the bed. "Wanna talk?"

I yawn. "Maybe tomorrow."

She nods. "Tomorrow then. We still need a plan to break out those hellhounds from Raphael's."

A smile creeps on my face. "I have one. I'll explain it tomorrow."

She gives me a quick hug before leaving, and I turn my gaze to Dylan when she shuts the door with a soft click.

Before I have a chance to take another step, he rushes forward and embraces me. He kisses me deeply, running his fingers through my sandy hair, and I press against him until he falls back on the bed.

"I'm so sorry, love," he whispers through kisses. "I should've never let you go without making sure you were okay first. I feel like it's my fault you weren't thinking clearly and got yourself trapped at Raphael's."

I shake my head and kiss the apology from his lips. "It would've happened regardless. James set us up."

"Is he?"

I suck in a breath. "Yeah. By my hands."

He tilts his head back to look me in the eyes. "You okay?"

I roll off him and stare at the ceiling. "I don't know. A lot happened. I'm having an information overload hangover at the moment. And—" I snap my mouth shut, trying my best to think of how to put what I'm going to say next. "I'm a bad person. Evan was trying so hard to get to me, and I let him." My words barely come out as a whisper. "I let him kiss me."

Dylan stiffens next to me, but he doesn't charge from the room like I expect him to. He links his fingers with mine and stares at the light on the ceiling just like I am.

"I'm sorry you're in this situation, Cami," he finally says after a minute. "As much as I want to be angry and hurt, I don't really have that right. You're not my girlfriend, and I've known that there would always be a possibility that you'd find Evan again. You need to be careful, though. He's not the same person."

I squeeze his fingers. "I know. He's turned into someone I hate that I still love. His loyalty lies with Malicevile. I saw that tonight."

He sits up and looks down at me. Caressing my cheek with his fingers, he says, "If I could take away your pain, I would. You know that, right?"

I nod, sucking my trembling bottom lip between my teeth. "You're too good for me. How can you even love me like this? How can you risk putting your own feelings on the line? I can't promise I won't break your heart."

"I'm not asking you to promise me anything, and a broken heart doesn't scare me. You should know that by now. Even if this—" He waves his hand between us. "Even if this doesn't last or you decide you don't want anything more than my friendship, it would've still been worth it to me. You—your soul—you're the most beautiful person I've ever known."

Tears prickle in my eyes. I wish he didn't say things like that. It hurts just as badly as everything else. "I don't want to break your heart, Dylan. The last thing I want to do is hurt you."

He leans down and kisses my forehead. "I know, love. But I'm prepared for if it happens."

I frown. "Dylan."

He hovers over me. "Don't think I'll give up without a fight."

I hold his gaze, losing myself in his chocolate-brown eyes. "I wouldn't expect anything less."

A DEAL IS A DEAL

SNEAKING AROUND RAPHAEL'S beach fortress during the day beats coming here after dark. Now, all I have to worry about is whether or not he has another tainted minion to watch over the house and Faith while he's trapped by the sun.

I tap my finger on Faith's window and step back. The curtains flutter for a moment, and then she pulls them open completely.

I point and motion for her to meet me on the beach since her window is sealed, and there's no getting in or out of it.

When I reach the soft sand, I say, "She's coming. I

want you all to stay back. If she's scared, she might throw a lava bomb at you, and then things will get messy."

Greg's eyes widen as my words sink in, and he shifts to stand partially behind Dylan and Cadence. What better way to introduce Faith to the real Veiled Realm than introduce her to people who don't associate with demons. Dylan might even change her perspective with a flash of his wings.

The back door swings open, but Faith doesn't come running out like I expect her to. Instead, she stays just inside her house. I jog forward through the sand and to her back patio. Meeting new people is scary. I get it.

I smile as I offer my hand out to her. "I'm sorry I didn't call. I left my phone at Evan's hotel." *Along with your clothes and weapons...* "But I wanted to introduce you to some of my friends. They're nothing like Evan, so don't worry. You can trust them."

She purses her lips, staring curiously past me, and then takes a step forward. "Are they like us?" she asks as she looks Cadence up and down, training her gaze on Cadence's bright purple hair and black tank top with fishnet sleeves.

"Cadence is human," I say. "You sort of met her the other night."

Faith places her hands on her hips. "You threw acid in my dad's face."

Cadence tugs a flask from her belt. "This? No, it's holy water. Your demon would've killed me otherwise."

Faith doesn't respond because she knows Cadence is

right.

I take Dylan's hand and guide him closer to take Faith's attention away from Cadence. "This is Dylan. He's my guardian angel."

He blushes. "I'm only half."

Faith's eyes widen. "Dad said people like you steal souls from people like me."

I huff a breath of air through my lips. "Not true. If he did, I wouldn't be here." *If he didn't love you, you wouldn't be here.* I push the thought away. This isn't going exactly as I planned. Raphael's filled her head with so much information already. It might be harder to sway her.

Faith narrows her eyes at Greg. "And who's this?"

"Greg is a werewolf. He's the reason I came to your house in the first place," I say.

"The guard dogs," Faith says, remembering our previous conversation. "My dad did lie to me." She steps closer and tilts her head as she studies Greg. "This is what the hellhounds were before?"

Greg straightens his shoulders. "Yes, and your father kidnapped some of my pack mates."

Faith's hand flies to her mouth, sadness lining her sky blue eyes, and she flings her arms around Greg. He jumps back, startled but doesn't push her away.

"I'm so sorry my dad did this. I swear, I'm going to yell at him the moment he appears for lying to m—"

"No, you're not," I say, cutting her off. "You need to

pretend you don't know."

She runs her hands over her head. "Why?"

"Because we need your help. I need you to get me into the kennel so I can find out if we can save any of them. The completely broken werewolves—sadly, they're lost. But sometimes, a werewolf's will is too strong to break and they get trapped in their new fiery state with their humanity. If you let me in, I can tell for sure. Then Dylan can save them." I pull Dylan closer to me and smile into his dark brown eyes.

He shakes his black curls from his forehead. "At least I can try."

Faith turns toward her house. "I think I know what you're talking about, Cami. There's a hellhound—I call him Flamey—he's unlike the others. His eyes are brown and not fiery. He's the nicest of them all."

I beam a smile. "That's exactly what I'm talking about. So will you help us?"

She bobs her head. "I don't think it's a good idea for you to come back here after sunset, but I can bring him to you somewhere. My dad has some meeting at midnight. I was supposed to go with him, but I can fake being sick."

"That'll work," I say.

Cadence claps her hands. "You sure you like living here, Faith? If you ever change your mind, I know somewhere you can go."

She smiles weakly. "I'm okay here for now."

I hope it'll always be okay for her.

———⁂———

"You've been avoiding me," I say as I comb my fingers through my loose curls. Cadence's cell phone rests on the edge of the seat as I get ready for another—I'm sure to be ridiculous—evening with Malicevile before I meet with Faith in the middle of the night.

Alana sighs into the phone. "Yes and no. I'm trying to adjust to the changes in our lives."

I drop my hands to my sides and stare at the phone as if she can see the disappointment crossing my face. Maybe I shouldn't have called her. If adjusting to a change means cutting me off, then I'm setting myself up for heartache. After all these years, I never thought Alana would distance herself from me. It's not what I wanted. I just didn't want to stay.

I clear my throat. "Well, if you would've answered your phone, I could've told you that I found Evan. I also found another demi-demon."

She sucks in a breath. "David will be so relieved."

Picking up the phone, I turn off the speaker and press it to my ear. "Don't get his hopes up, Alana. Evan's changed. He wants nothing to do with any of us." The lie comes easier than I expect. Telling Alana that Evan actually does want everything to do with me would only upset her.

"Oh," she says. "I shouldn't have expected anything different. Of course his humanity would be gone with the ownership of his soul." She's quiet for a long moment before she adds, "Now what about another demi-demon?"

"She's a tween girl. Lives with her demonic father," I say. "He pulled her from the foster system where she ended up after her grandma died."

"This isn't good. That poor girl," Alana says.

I frown. "She's fine. She's not a prisoner or anything, and her humanity is still intact. She's actually helping me tonight by bringing one of her father's hellhounds to me so Dylan can heal him. He's only half broken."

"Cami," Alana says. My name hangs in the air as she gathers her thoughts for whatever she wants to say next.

When she doesn't say anything more, I ask, "What? I thought we were past secrets."

She huffs a breath of air into the phone. "Be careful, okay? You're playing a dangerous game."

I grip the phone. "It's not a game to me at all. Who else will stand up for the werewolves? The alliance won't."

"That's unfair," she says. "We're trying our best."

I scoff at her words. "I still can't get over how after everything you chose to be one of their leaders. Don't you remember the last three years? Or how about the hunter almost killing you? Did you just happen to forget they sentenced me to death?"

She sighs. "There's no point to defending my decision when you're clearly still too upset to listen."

I growl, digging my nails into my palm. "Then I guess

this is it. You've chosen the people you want to be with. I hate even thinking this, but Malicevile was right about everything."

"Don't say that, Cami," Alana says. "You don't want people thinking you're siding with a dem—"

I hang up before she can finish her sentence. How dare she imply that I'm siding with demons? She didn't have to say it, but reminding me about what others might think shows that she's the one to have those thoughts first.

I chuck the phone at the door and slide to the floor, resting my back against the cool tub. The door opens, and Dylan peers in, picking Cadence's phone off the floor. Without saying a word, he crosses the room, folding his legs to sit down next to me, and then he wraps his arm around my shoulders and pulls me to him.

I'm so livid I can't even cry. "Alana's out of her mind. Do you think the alliance is forcing her to cut ties with me?"

He rests his head on mine. "If anything, they'd want her to be closer to you to keep a better eye on you. She's doing this by her own freewill. Maybe it's not as bad as you think, though."

Shifting my legs, I swing them over his lap so I can face him. "It's awful. I don't think I can ever go back. I'm not sure what to do with my life now. I have no money, no permanent place to live, and no idea what to do next. We can't stay here forever."

"I have enough money to hold us over for quite a while, Cami, and we can go anywhere and do anything. If you want to continue to demon hunt, we can head to Los Angeles or Seattle or even New York City. If you don't, I know of a small town in a nice area that is demon free. We could get jobs and live a normal life."

I smirk as he helps me imagine our future...together. "Why do you make having a normal life sound so boring?"

He chuckles. "'Cause it is, love. I've known since the moment I laid eyes on you that nothing about your life should ever be normal."

Closing my eyes, I imagine the day I met Dylan, the boy on the bus with black hair and dark eyes who smiled at me before flashing his wings. "I hate that you're probably right."

A knock on the door draws my gaze away from Dylan as Cadence steps in. She puckers her bottom lip as she sees us on the floor. "About thirty minutes to sundown. You ready to go?" she asks.

I groan into Dylan's shoulder. "No, but a deal is a deal to a demon."

Ugh! The last thing I want to do is hang out with Dear Old Demon Dad. There's no way I'll be joining him for dinner at a restaurant. If he wants to eat, he can order some take-out. Actually, that's not a bad idea. Keeping him away from the general public is a great idea. Then I won't have to worry about having to fight him again. Tonight, I'm without any sort of power. I should've asked Faith if I could have more.

Within ten minutes, we're all packed into the Jag, Dylan behind the wheel and me next to him in the front seat. Cadence sits in the middle of the backseat before she extends her arm and waves a knife between the seats.

"I'm gonna want this back," she says. "So make sure you get your weapons from Evan."

The knife hilt glitters in the setting sun as I take it and slide it into the empty sheath on my belt. "Thanks. I'm sure Mal wouldn't expect me to stab him if he gets out of control."

She laughs. "I still wish I could've seen his face when you lava-bombed him."

My shoulders shake as I laugh, the memory nowhere near as traumatizing as it would've been had I done it years ago. "You'd think he'd be used to heat being from Hell and all."

Dylan pulls into a parking space outside of the beachfront hotel, and anxiety seizes my chest when I spot Evan sitting on a bench near the door. The last thing I wanted was for him to see my friends, the ones that used to be his, too. They shouldn't see him in this state. Only I should have to bear that sort of burden.

"He looks different," Cadence whispers from the backseat. "Think we should say hi?"

I cringe at the thought. "Definitely not. It's best if you

get back before sundown. The last thing I want is to end up having to introduce you to my dad."

Cadence presses her lips together. "You make a good point."

Leaning over, I kiss Dylan's cheek. He turns before I have a chance to back away and kisses me on the lips. My heart rams so hard against my chest, but I don't pull back even though I can sense the heat of Evan's jealousy through the glass and metal of the car.

I slowly pull away and smile. "I won't be long."

His eyes flicker toward Evan. I can't even force myself to follow his line of sight. "Keep your guard up, love."

I can only nod as I exit the car. Standing firmly in place, I watch as Dylan pulls away and waves once over his shoulder. Maybe I'll stand in this spot until Malicevile arrives. I'm not usually so awkward when it comes to confrontation, but meeting Evan's icy eyes after knowing he watched me and Dylan kiss—well, I can think of a million things I'd rather do. Running from a pack of angry hellhounds is one of them.

I smell his scent before he reaches me. "If you're trying to drive me crazy, it worked."

I spin around to meet Evan's playful eyes. The fire I imagined in them is only the glow of the sun as it sets. He reaches out and pushes my dark hair from my face. I remain utterly still. I'm not sure my heart can handle being pulled in two different directions. It's not as strong as my soul.

Reaching up, I pull his hand down. He doesn't let go of my fingers when I drop my hand to my side. Flames erupt between our fingers, and he smiles as I automatically take his power into my hand. I toss the fireball up and down.

"Remember how fun it was to practice? I bet no one spars like I do," he says.

Instead of snuffing the flames out, I let the power sink into my skin. "You're right about that. Too bad those days are long past us."

"They don't have to be." He waggles his eyebrows, smiling wide.

"You know they do," I say. "I already have to worry about what the alliance thinks of me. I can't have them assuming I'm working with demons."

"You say it like their opinion matters. I thought you'd strayed away from those creature-haters, anyway," he says.

"I did. It's just—"

"Camilla," a smooth voice says, cutting me off. Evan distracted me long enough that I didn't even notice the sun had already disappeared into the horizon. "You came."

I glance over Evan's shoulder as my father stands a few feet away. He's wearing a gray suit with a deep burgundy tie, and I wonder if he has an endless supply of formalwear. At least with Evan wearing jeans and a T-shirt, I don't feel underdressed.

I cross my arms. "Like I had a choice."

"I wouldn't have stolen your soul if you hadn't showed up. I know things got pretty heated between us last night," he says.

"I hit you with a lava bomb," I say.

He moves closer. "Rightfully so. I apologize for my behavior. It's difficult for me to pass up a good opportunity."

My mouth falls open, and I gape at him. Did he really apologize? I almost don't believe it. What kind of devious game is he playing? I wouldn't put it past him to figure out a way to get my guard down so he could punish me for standing up for myself.

"Um, okay. Thanks," I manage to say. "I'd really appreciate it if you kept your demonic business away from me."

He grins, showing off his perfectly white teeth. "I think I can manage that."

"Okay, so now that everything is settled, what do you want to do? I don't have all night to hang out," I say.

He scrunches his brows. "You really are going to make me work for any time with you, aren't you?"

"Yes."

He shakes his head while laughing. "Well, maybe if you enjoy the time with me, it won't be too difficult." He turns to Evan. "Call Gary D. and let him know I need the place tonight. I don't want any interruptions."

Evan tugs his cell phone from his pocket and waltzes away, leaving me alone with my father.

I force myself to keep talking. "So, you already have a plan?"

"I overheard the last bit of your conversation with Evan. I'm going to teach you to fight. I mean, really fight, like a demon." He touches my arm to get me to move toward his car. I notice a leather bag on the backseat and see my cell phone sitting on top. At least I get my stuff back. "It's important you can protect yourself the right way."

I halt in place and put my hands on my hips. "I'm plenty capable of taking care of myself."

His green eyes shine even though the light of the building is dim. "I suppose we'll find out, won't we?"

BROKEN TRUST

"KEEP FOCUS, CAMILLA. Don't blink. Don't breathe. Don't back down. The worst thing you can do while fighting a demon is give them the opportunity to strike when you're not ready." Malicevile rolls his shoulders, standing three feet away.

I repeat his words in my head a few times. My vision blurs as I rock on my feet. Without the element of surprise, I suck at sparring. I haven't even gotten in a single punch—not like I could from this distance.

Sweat beads on my forehead, rolling into my eyes, and I use the back of my hand to wipe it away. A flash of light jolts me, knocking me off my feet again. Stretching my back, I somersault backward and land on my feet in a lop-sided arch, the movement more suited for a toddler. The moment my eyes find Malicevile, it's already too late. Another energy ball soars through the air, knocking me back again.

My neck and cheeks burn with embarrassment, and I'm sure I'm brighter than the fires of Hell. I thought I stood a chance, that I could at least avoid everything my demonic dad had to throw at me, but I was sorely mistaken.

Annoyance pulls my lips downward. My father has really been taking it easy on me all these years. I swore he'd fought with his all to get to me, but he was playing a game of cat and mouse, chasing Alana and me for the fun of it. Because he could.

He's admitted in the past that he allowed Alana to live because I cared for her. I thought he was just trying to manipulate me. But he could've had me long ago. I guess he didn't force me after I learned some of the truth about the Veiled Realm because he was already my enemy. Alana didn't take me to the academy, and we were fine. He never had to really worry. He let her raise me through my adolescence.

"Get up. The longer you stay down, the more at risk you'll be of never getting back up again," he says. His footsteps sound out as he moves closer. "Get up, Camilla, before I zap you back to your feet."

"If you'd just let me use my dagger," I say. I never even

had the chance to surprise him with it before he stole it right from its sheath at my side. It was before we had even gotten out of the car.

He wags his finger. "Uh-uh. Human weapons make you look weak."

I sneer, not only because he claims weapons make me look weak, but because I feel weak no matter what under his stare. "Maybe that's what I want. Demons are quicker to underestimate me."

He rubs his chin for a second. "Still, you need to learn to rely on yourself."

He has a point—one I won't admit to any time soon. Being self-reliant has been hard to do with so many people wanting to protect me. My mind wanders to Alana and how she refused to even teach me to do anything other than evade demons. Fighting was a last resort, and she did most of the grunt work. It wasn't until these last few months that it became obvious that my life wasn't normal. A demon every few months turned into a demon almost every day. I wonder if Alana would change things if she could go back. I know I would.

"Camilla, how many times do I have to tell you to focus?" Malicevile asks, forcing my attention to return to the present.

I throw my hands up. "A dozen more."

He sighs, dropping his hands to his sides instead of attacking me again with another burst of power.

Taking this small moment of reprieve from his power blasts, I pull myself together enough to find my ability. Without waiting for him to make a move, I bend my knees and launch at him through the air. He opens his arms wide, expecting me, but instead of ramming into him, I propel a bit higher and use his shoulders to push myself up and over him.

Flicking my fingers open, I ignite the small burst of power I had taken from Evan earlier in my hand. I chuck it at Malicevile as he spins around. It hits him square in the shoulder, singeing the cotton fabric of his black T-shirt, burning a hole in it. It wasn't enough to knock him off balance or even slow him down, but still, I got him.

I flip midair and land on my feet. "Finally!" An hour is way too long to finally say that I hit my mark. I wave my arms over my head and glide a few feet back, gloating. I can't help it. It feels good not to be on the floor from another blast of his power.

I smile and point at his shirt. "Take that, Dad! That burn on your shoulder is proof that I'm not as weak as you thought."

Malicevile's expression morphs from intense to pleased in a split second, and the words that just fell from my mouth come back to taunt me in my mind. I can't believe I just said that. I can't believe I called him Dad. I've been referring to him as my father for months, but that's different. To actually say it to his face—holy crap. I need to get out of here. This was a bad idea agreeing to come here. I should've risked not showing up. I hate myself a bit for letting my guard down.

He rubs his hands together, a spark of crackling electricity erupting in between his palms. "I'll admit, that was a surprising move."

"You mean an awesome move," I say, trying to play it cool. If I don't draw attention to what I said, maybe he'll forget it. I'm sure he's dancing on the inside, thinking he's getting to me. It was a mistake, though. I was caught up in the moment. *Then stop reassuring yourself.*

The door to the gym swings open, and Evan steps in carrying a box of pizza. He couldn't have had better timing. Not only am I exhausted, but I'm starving and need to put something other than my foot in my mouth. I've had enough alone time with Malicevile to last me the rest of my life.

"Thank God," I say as Evan approaches. He smiles as I close the distance. I'd be self-conscious about the sweat pouring from me, but I'm beyond caring at this point.

Malicevile watches me in his peripheral vision as he stays at my side. "What for? Why not just thank Evan? He brought the pizza."

A laugh bubbles in my throat, and I press my lips together, trying to force my amusement away. He needs to quit sounding so human. Like seriously. This is getting out of control. I shouldn't be laughing and smiling and actually enjoying myself.

I swallow back my oncoming laughter. "It's an expression." I grin at Evan because I can't help it. He looks so irresistible in his tank top and sweats, his muscles bulging from his arms. "Come on. You know that was funny."

He smirks back at me. "I see you hit your target, Cami," he says, nodding his head at Malicevile. "I knew you had it in you."

I gaze at him for a long moment. "Well, I did learn from the greatest."

"He's slightly above average at best," Malicevile says from behind me. "I'm surprised he survived all these years to be honest. His mother deserved to die if she couldn't even manage to survive a fight against someone of his—well, probably more like your—skill level."

I glower. "Hey! I've killed plenty of demons. Once without any power or weapons."

He tilts his head and smiles at me like I've said the most amusing thing in the world. His expression gets under my skin, and I wish I could get close enough to smack it right off his face. In a matter of seconds I've gone from proud of myself to feeling like a speck of demon bait.

"Not a demon of my caliber, though, dear Camilla." He raises a piece of pizza to his lips and bites off the end.

"I'm sure I could if I tried." I take the slice of pizza Evan offers me. "Do you want me to prove it?"

Evan turns his head away, hiding his smile. "Now

you've done it," he says to himself.

Malicevile shakes his head. "No, that won't be necessary. I think I'll take your word for it."

Our conversation turns into heavy silence between us. I prefer sparring with Malicevile much more than conversing. When he's throwing energy orbs my way, he still feels completely and terrifyingly demonic. But watching him eat a slice of pizza makes me question everything I know about him. It makes me question everything I know about myself.

I think about Faith and Raphael and wonder how often they have simple conversations like this one. I think about Melanie. She and Malicevile probably shared a fair amount of secrets and inside jokes. *Stop it, Cami. Remember who your father is. Remember what he's done.*

Evan should be enough of a reminder, but God, he looks almost like the boy I fell in love with. He looks like he belongs here.

My smile falls from my lips as I repeat a list of all the horrible things Malicevile has done to me—to the people I love. It's the only thing that keeps me from falling under his charm for the millionth time tonight.

I force myself to eat a piece a pizza, slowly chewing each bite like it's my sole purpose in life. It keeps my mouth busy and makes things less awkward as Evan and Malicevile make small talk like old buddies. I force myself to smile when Malicevile comments about how I should eat more to keep up my strength. I would if my stomach weren't in knots.

After the box of pizza is empty, and the awkwardness feels like it'll never break, Malicevile says, "Well, my dear, I had fun tonight. I do hope you'll agree to join me again for another evening. There's still so much to teach you."

His words hang in the air when I don't respond. Do I really want more lessons from my father? Opening this door is like opening the gates of Hell and asking to be invited in. It'll also take time away from what I really want to spend my nights doing—helping those tainted and broken by demons. What would my friends think if I agree? The last two nights were obligations. The next would be by my own freewill.

I gnaw on my bottom lip, annoyed that I'm worried I'll hurt my father's feelings. Finally, I say, "I'll think about it, okay?"

He pulls me into a hug, his cinnamon and clove scent driving away the scent of sweat and pizza that clings to the empty gym. "That's all I ask." He turns to Evan. "Will you see to it that she gets home safely? I have a meeting in an hour."

Evan nods, and my father spins on his heels and strides from the gym, leaving me in a tornado of my own conflicting emotions.

"I've never seen Malicevile so happy," Evan comments. He reaches out and touches my shoulder. "You look pretty happy, too, you know."

I grimace. "This isn't right."

"Why?"

"Because he's supposed to be the bad guy."

No one greets me at the door of the safe house after I stroll up the path running through the middle of a sleepy flower bed. Evan dropped me off a mile away on a busy corner, because there was no way I was giving up my current residence. Not with a household full of werewolves Malicevile would love to pick from.

I plop down on the porch bench and lean my elbows on my knees. The mile walk helped clear my head, but I still have so much to think about. If I go inside now, I'll be forced to socialize with the pack. It's rude if I hide out in my room every second of every day.

Malicevile showed a side of himself to me that I've never seen before. He let his guard down and let me in. For the first time in my life, I understand what Melanie saw in him. She saw past his demonic ways to a man who actually had feelings. *Can demons even feel?*

In this moment, I know Malicevile was right about siphoning part of my humanity. But in the end, is it really enough? Humanity isn't all good. It has its bad side—the side that fuels the evil in the world. I'm not exactly sure how humanity affects a demon.

My cell phone buzzes from my pocket, and I read a text message from Dylan. *Ready to be picked up yet?*

I quickly reply, *Already here. Sitting outside. I'm ready to go when you are.*

Seconds later, Dylan comes shuffling out from the house. His black hair flops over his eyes when he smiles at me, and I reach out my hands so he can pull me to my feet. Wrapping his arms around me, he rests his chin on my shoulder. It's like he knows how confused everything makes me. I wish I could tell him how I feel, but I'm not so sure he won't automatically blow it off and try to reassure me that it's all part of Malicevile's plan to get to my soul.

"How long have you been here?" he asks into my hair.

"A couple minutes." I suck in a breath of his comforting scent, squeezing him tighter.

"Everything all right?" He runs his fingers through my unruly hair.

Instead of answering, I bury my face in his chest. He holds me without prying, and a gentle breeze caresses my skin as he unfurls his wings and wraps them around the both of us. I wish I could slink through the house unnoticed and hide in my room until daylight. Maybe the sun will erase the demon confusion from my thoughts. But unfortunately, I can't hide. I have a job to do.

People count on me to be strong. I won't let them down.

A few minutes go by, and I finally find the strength I need to get back in my groove to do what I promised I'd do for the werewolf pack. Even if it's only one hellhound we're attempting to save, it's still one life and that life could mean the world to others.

"Wanna grab Cadence and meet me at the car?" I ask, adjusting my leather jacket that Malicevile had cleaned.

He kisses my cheek. "Sure, love." He pauses. "You know, you can tell me anything, right?"

I half smile. "Yeah, thanks."

Fifteen minutes later we park in an empty parking lot facing the dark ocean about a mile from Raphael's beach fortress. When I reach the sand, I spot Faith strolling up the beach, the flaming hellhound circling her as she kicks sand up near the water.

Cadence grips her dagger in her fingers, and I push Dylan behind me. He might be my guardian angel, but I'm his demon protector. Until I see the hellhound up close, I can't say for sure whether or not we'll be able to save him.

The scent of burning flesh catches on the breeze and swirls around me. Faith raises her hand in a wave, and the hellhound turns its flaming head to her before narrowing its attention on us. It bolts away, charging down the beach, kicking up sand and smoke as the surf rolls over its legs.

A low, guttural growl sends a shiver up my back, and Faith screams from where she runs after the hellhound.

A gust of wind knocks me forward when Dylan grabs Cadence and launches into the air, taking flight. He swears from above me when my palms hit the ground. A flash of fire sparks in the edge of my vision. I roll over to look above me and watch horror cross both Dylan's and Cadence's faces when a heavy body lands squarely on my chest, knocking the wind from me.

Black, frothy slime drips onto my forehead as the hellhound growls and snaps its razor sharp teeth inches from my face. I press my head into the sand, trying to put as much space between the flaming beast and my face. It weighs a ton, and I can't push it off. All I can do is reach up and dig my fingers into the flaming sludge of its hackles.

"Get off her!" Faith yells. "Don't make me hurt you."

The weight shifts off me, and I suck in a breath of ocean air. The hellhound circles me twice before returning to Faith's side. It sits back on its haunches and growls again.

"If you don't stop, we're not going to help you," I say. I know well enough that the beast understands me. It has the mind of a human trapped in the body of a flaming beast. That's what's so sad about hellhounds, especially the ones not completely broken.

"This is the girl I told you about, Flamey." Faith pats the top of the hellhound's head with her gloved fingers. It relaxes under her touch and then plops down in the sand, resting its head on its paws.

A soft thud sounds next to me when Dylan lands on the sand. He moves next to me, and Cadence glances from Faith to our surroundings. Her job is to be a look-out. Demonic activity attracts other demons. That's the last thing we need.

I clomp through the sand, closer to Faith, and then crouch in front of the hellhound. Flames lick its skin, sending up a steady stream of black smoke into the air. I reach out and let the beast sniff the back of my hand.

"Dylan is half-angel," I tell Flamey. "He's not immune to fire, so if you want our help, you need to put it out. Can you do that?"

The hellhound whines in answer. It rolls in the sand a few times, snuffing the flames out. But just as it stops rolling, the flames reignite. With both hellhounds before, they were exhausted and hurt. Getting this hellhound to stop flaming might be tougher than I thought.

I frown at Dylan as he watches the hellhound like he might consider attempting to heal its soul despite its fiery skin. "I don't want you to burn yourself."

We stare at each other in silent thought. I kind of hate that we have to make things up as we go.

"Let's move to the water," he finally says after a moment. "It might keep the flames away long enough."

Cadence and Faith stand near each other while watching us without talking. Neither of them has probably ever seen a nephilim at work. I wish I could stand back and watch Dylan. He never fails to impress me.

I wave to the hellhound to follow us into the surf. I stroll into the freezing water first, shivering as a wave knocks into me, soaking me up to my waist. My skin steams against the cool sea as it fights to keep my temperature up. Another wave hits me, causing me to stumble. Dylan laughs as he grabs onto my jacket, and my face hovers a few inches over the rolling tide. Nearly face-planting in the water isn't exactly how I saw myself ending the evening, but it's better than all the possible alternatives.

The hellhound whimpers as it eases into the water, its flesh sizzling and steaming as the salty ocean extinguishes the flames. I'm sure the water is ten times more uncomfortable for its hot body than the water is to me.

Rubbing my fingers along its back, I pet the beast as it continues to whine. "This is almost over. Just hang on for a few more minutes. I know it's cold."

Dylan flanks one side of the hellhound while I stand on the other, doing my best to hold the broken werewolf still in the rolling waves. Dylan's brows scrunch together when he presses his fingers to the still hot flesh of the beast. He groans through the pain, his normally glowing skin turning pale, but he doesn't flinch away. After a long moment, he squeezes his eyes shut as he expands his wings. Waves crash right through them, unable to stop their ethereal glow.

Bones crack and shift under my fingers as the hellhound's body starts to react to Dylan's healing abilities. The soft whimpers turn into an agonizing sound as the hellhound releases a loud, high-pitched howl. I startle, nearly jumping from my skin at the horrifying noise loud enough to draw probably the whole town's attention. It echoes over the roaring ocean, and fear slides over me. I gently cup one of my hands around the broken wolf's muzzle, trying my best to mute the sound before some brave or crazy soul comes to investigate.

Tufts of fur sprout through the smoldering slime and disappear just as quickly. As the waves roll over us, the black sludge washes away from the hellhound, leaving behind smooth, bare skin the color of dark chocolate. The half-man, half beast, wails in agony as he completes the transformation, and a moment later, Dylan yanks away and falls into a wave. I cry out as he's swept back to shore.

A scream sounds out from the beach, but I can't look up. Watching the transformation is enough to make anyone scream and cry. The naked man slides from my fingers, sinking into the ocean. I dip lower and hook my arms through his and fight the best I can to keep his unconscious head above the water.

"Almost there," I say more to myself. Another wave crashes against us as I drag him to the sand, and he's ripped away. The ground disappears out from under me as I float in the water as the wave takes me back to shore.

Strong hands pull me from the surf and to my feet, and I catch sight of the reborn wolf ten feet away, lying on his back, staring up at the night sky.

"Cami," a small voice says.

I close my eyes, leaning my weight against the solid body holding me. "It's okay, Faith. It's over," I say in the direction the voice came from as I rub the saltwater from my eyes. An unfamiliar scent washes over me, like gasoline and cigarettes, and I stiffen.

"Cami!" Faith screams, sending me into action.

I jerk my head up and stare into the hard, brown eyes of a man with a buzz cut and trimmed beard. His wet, black shirt clings to his toned body, and I elbow him in the jaw. Spinning on my feet, I upper cut him before he has a chance to fight back.

Faith stands in the sand nearby, a glowing, red orb in her hands. She's poised to throw it at our attackers but something holds her back.

Cadence shifts in the sand with her hands up, her dagger dropped at her feet as a woman with black hair points a gun at her. Dylan lies in the sand, unmoving, just out of the reach of the waves.

Anger rushes over me when I realize what's happening, and I'm in complete and utter shock. "How dare you aim a gun at an alliance leader's daughter," I say, looking between the hunter and Cadence.

I point to the man who babies his bloody nose. "And you. Who do you think you are? You both have a lot of nerve."

The woman shifts her gun to me. I'm no match for bullets. While I heal faster than a normal human, I'm not invincible. I'd prefer to fight a demon than a hunter any day.

"We're here on behalf of the alliance. The leaders have

been notified of an undocumented demi-demon. We're here to extract her from her demonic environment. If you do not cooperate, I will shoot you." The woman aims the gun at my head.

I raise my hands as rage rushes over me, the dark feeling gripping my soul, begging me to put up all the fight I have left in me.

The only thing that stops me from trying is that my life isn't the only one in danger.

Sucking in a breath to clear my mind, I try to run through my options. Why is this happening? It shouldn't be happening. Faith isn't a threat to anyone. She wasn't taken against her will by a demon. And I'm almost positive she's never willingly hurt anyone in her life.

How dare the alliance leaders think they can come here and meddle in a situation I had complete control over?

Faith stiffens, readying herself to attack. "I don't want to hurt you, but I'm not letting you take me."

The woman steps closer to me. "If you don't, I'll kill your friend."

I clench my fingers into fists. "Faith, do what you have to do. I understand." Closing my eyes, I wait for the inevitable. The girl barely knows me. Why should she give up her freedom to save my life?

When nothing happens, I peek through my eyelashes. Faith strolls past me, her hands at her sides, and she lets the male hunter take her arm. Three other figures, clad in dark clothing, stand near the parking lot—all armed and ready to fight.

Tears brand streaks down Faith's cheeks as the hunter pulls her away and toward a waiting car. The woman glares at me once more, silently daring me to do something to stop her, but I don't move.

"Faith!" I yell. "Faith, listen to me."

She peers over her shoulder.

"No matter what, don't use your power on them, okay? Don't give them a reason to hurt you. I'll come for you. I promise."

She nods through her tears, and I stand frozen as the hunters load her up in their black, unmarked car. They peel away, screeching their tires as they speed from the parking lot. Once their headlights disappear, I drop to my knees in the sand and cover my face.

"What just happened?" I ask more to myself.

Twisting my torso, I search the beach for answers that won't come. The naked man sits in the sand, shivering, and Dylan climbs to his feet and dusts himself off. Cadence rushes to my side and hugs me.

"It's going to be okay, Cami. I'll call my dad. We'll get this figured out," she says.

I tug away from her. "Your dad is the one responsible!"

Her eyes widen. "What about Alana? She's one of them, too."

My heart sinks into my stomach. Alana. She was the

only one outside of the three of us who I told about Faith. She warned me to be careful. I never imagined in a million years that she'd do something this crazy. She betrayed me. She's broken my trust.

She's turned against me.

I swipe the tears from my face. "You're right. It was her."

Cadence slings her arms around me again. "I'm sorry, Cami. What should we do now? I doubt the alliance will let us get within a mile of Faith."

I tilt my head and look at the stars. "Well, first things first. I need to tell Faith's father."

"Are you insane?" Dylan calls out from his place next to the man, now wearing Dylan's jacket. "He'll kill you."

I rub my lips together, tasting the sour taste of the saltwater. "I hope not, because he's going to need me."

A silence falls over us as we think about what's to come next.

I just hope we survive it.

I hope my soul remains intact.

LOYALTY

MY CELL PHONE rings the moment we pull into the driveway of the safe house, but I don't answer it. I ignore it altogether and leave it in my pocket.

The reborn werewolf shivers in the backseat despite the heater blasting hot air throughout the car. The garage door hums as it opens, and Cadence pulls into it instead of parking in the driveway.

The moment she kills the engine, the garage door closes, and the cavernous space fills with members of the pack as they rush to see if we were successful. Joshua flings the back door open and helps the man out of the car. A woman covers his shoulders with a blanket, and everyone's smiling.

What's supposed to be a happy moment for me is filled with such despair. I can't even force a smile when Joshua squeezes me in a tight hug, kissing both my cheeks. He spins me around before whacking Dylan on the back a few times and then hugging Cadence.

"You don't know the gift you've given us with Sean's return. For once in our history, there's hope for the broken. My pack, every pack, will speak your names for the rest of time." He squeezes my shoulder again. "Thank you, Cami."

I can only nod. Who knew this night would be one that would go down in werewolf history? But the tale won't include the young girl who went against her father to help them. No one will know of Faith. Not if I can't get her back.

Joshua strolls to the door. "Come on now. It's time to celebrate."

"We'll be there soon. Promise."

He leaves the three of us standing in the garage. Howls and laughter erupt from the other side of the door as the celebration starts.

Tears threaten to spill onto my cheeks as the memory of the night lingers in my mind. I've let down a lot of people in my life, but I had never in my wildest dreams thought Faith would end up somewhere against her will.

Dylan wraps his arms around me. "We'll get things figured out. You know this is alliance protocol." His words sting, like it's somehow okay that they took Faith.

"But she wasn't in danger!" My voice bounces off the concrete walls.

"Cami, she'll be okay. Don't freak out. They won't hurt her," he says.

I turn to Cadence, my eyes wide and wild. "Is he defending them?" Because it sure sounds like it. I thought he was on my side. He chose to leave the alliance to be with me. He talked about our future, even. But here he is standing up for the people who ruined my life.

Cadence raises her hands up in surrender and spins to look at the wall instead of taking my side like I expect her to.

"Love, please," Dylan says. "Calm down."

I don't look at him. I can't stand the fury sweeping through me as my friends—the ones who're always supposed to be on my side and by my side—try to rationalize the situation. The alliance's actions are inexcusable in my book. They threatened our lives for Heaven's sake. And with my history, they'd have been good on their word. It's not like they'd care if something happened to me. They'd be relieved to finally get rid of me.

My brows knit together as I stare at Cadence's back long enough for her to get uncomfortable under my stare. I wish my best friend would turn to face me instead of avoiding this conversation. It's making me feel even worse. In this moment, I feel alone with my fears.

I place my hands on my hips. "Do you agree with him,

Cadence?"

She doesn't answer.

Dylan reaches for me, but I jerk away, putting a few feet of distance between us.

"Cadence, look at me," I say.

She sighs as she turns around. "My opinion doesn't matter. I'm here because you're my friend, and I trust your decisions when it comes to demons. You're the expert."

I brush my hair from my face. "You didn't answer my question."

She throws up her hands. "What am I supposed to say? You're upset. Anything I say will piss you off."

"It's the alliance who pisses me off," I mutter.

"But why? Wasn't this the plan? Save Faith from her demonic father? You were so set on saving her that night. What changed? Who cares if she thinks her dad is a nice guy. It doesn't change the fact that he's a demon." Her hands tremble as she wrings them in front of her.

But it does! It changes everything. I don't say the words out loud. No matter how I try to explain it, Cadence will never understand. Dylan won't either. They don't know what it's like to have a demon as a father.

I cover my face for a second and suck in a few deep breaths. Instead of losing control and lashing out at them, I jog to the back door and slam my hand against the garage door opener. The door hums open, allowing in the crisp ocean air. It cools the heat coursing through my veins.

I push past Dylan, smacking his hands away as he tries to grab me again. There's no point getting them involved if they only stand with me because of our friendship. I need their hearts to be in it, and they're clearly not.

"Cami, where are you going?" Dylan asks as I reach the sidewalk.

"Where do you think? I have a demon to tell that I'm responsible for the kidnapping of his daughter." I cross my arms and pick up my pace. I peer over my shoulder. "Don't wait up. I don't know what's going to happen next."

"Cami, please. Don't go," Dylan says. "You're acting irrational and reckless. Nothing's going to change tonight. You're going to end up getting yourself hurt or worse."

His words sink in. Terror slows me down but doesn't stop me. What if Raphael doesn't even give me the chance to explain myself? What if he forces me into a deal for my soul? So many things could go wrong.

"We can work together. You don't have to go," Cadence adds. She steps closer to me, but something stops her in her tracks.

Not something. Me. Maybe my demonic side is showing enough to cause her to hesitate. I turn away, so she won't look in my eyes any longer. "But I do."

My words get lost on the wind as I whisper goodbye to my best friend and my guardian angel. I just hope I'll get to see them again.

Pulling my cell phone from my pocket, I see the missed

call from Evan I ignored earlier. I hit the call button and press the phone to my ear.

He answers on the first ring. "Cami?"

My lip trembles as I say, "Hey, can you pick me up? I need you."

<hr>

Evan pulls to the curb where he dropped me off only a few hours ago. He leans across the front seat and pushes open the door for me, and I slide onto the cool leather seat. When I shut the door, he doesn't put the car into drive and instead idles the engine.

He reaches over and touches my knee. "You're upset."

Tears burst from my eyes the moment he says the words. I sob into my hands, my chest heaving as I try to catch my breath. Leaning forward, I grip my knees as I think about how I left things with Dylan. And here I am, calling the boy who had my heart and tore it to pieces to save my life.

Evan slides his arm over my shoulders and half hugs me. He doesn't need empathy or compassion to see the emotions marring my face. The glimpse of my reflection in the side mirror shows a stranger I don't even recognize in myself. No wonder Cadence hesitated. I'm terrifying with my vibrant green eyes, shining with angry tears and my wild hair. I swear I see a pinprick of fire in my gaze.

Evan doesn't say anything as I bawl my eyes out. He just hugs me and waits for me to pull myself together. It's more than I could have ever hoped for from him. With as cold as he's been in regards to my emotions, I didn't even expect a tissue let alone an attempt at acting like he cares.

I sniffle, wiping my face with my sleeve. "I'm sorry. I shouldn't have called you."

He squeezes my arm. "I'm glad you did."

"Things are a mess."

"It's about Faith, isn't it?" he asks.

I nod. "How'd you know?"

"Raphael accused you of taking her. Threatened your father," he says.

Great. Just great. Of course I'd be the first person he'd want to go after. I was the one to show up at his door with half a plan in the first place. Raphael will never believe that I didn't want this. I'm not even sure my father will either.

I puff a breath of air through my lips, blowing my hair from my face. "It wasn't me. I knew Faith wanted to stay with her dad. I only offered my friendship."

"But you do know what happened to her," he says.

Through a quivering breath, I say, "The Hunter's Alliance."

He swears, smacking his free hand against the steering wheel. "You told them about Faith," he accuses. "You're basically responsible. Why couldn't you just stay out of it, Cami? Your father warned you about interfering in demonic affairs."

I groan. I might've wanted to interfere in Faith's life

but not for the reasons Malicevile assumes. I don't even really know why. I just wanted her to know that she wasn't alone. I wanted to tell her the secrets that no one would tell me when I was her age. I was trying to right the wrongs that happened to me. And, apart from Faith, I was trying to make a difference. "I didn't think Alana would tell. She betrayed me. I never wanted this to happen."

He shifts to stare at me in the eyes. "But it did." His accusatory gaze gets to me. I feel guilty enough as it is. My life is one big pool of guilt that I can't seem to climb out of. I'll drown in it before too long.

I smack his arm. "Stop. Just stop." I don't need this.

"Raphael's looking for you. If he finds you, he'll kill you and take your soul. Malicevile wants us to run. He's entrusted your wellbeing to me. If you die, I'll die. I don't want that to happen."

I'm not sure if he's saying it because of self-preservation or because he really doesn't want me to die. Either way, a shaky laugh erupts from my mouth. After all these years, after wearing me down and convincing me that he has my best interests in mind, Malicevile can't even bother to protect me himself. All of his efforts seem pointless.

I close my eyes so I don't have to stare at the blurry world. "Why won't he protect me himself?"

Evan's quiet for a minute. "This is him protecting you. He just needs time to figure things out. Demonic affairs are serious."

I smack my hands a few times on the dashboard. Malicevile is powerful. I bet he could kill Raphael. I don't mention it though. What's the point? "I can't run forever, Evan. I'm tired of running. I need to fix this."

"It's okay to think about yourself sometimes, you know," he says as he starts the car.

I still hide behind my closed eyes instead of looking at him. "I am thinking about myself. Now will you help me?"

His warm hand covers mine. "Always."

⁂

The moment Evan merges onto the freeway, he cuts across three lanes and races well over the speed limit, heading south on Interstate 5 toward San Diego.

Gripping the grab handle for dear life, I stare out the window as the world zooms by switching between dense cities, browning hills, and pitch darkness where the ocean expands for what looks like forever.

"We need to make a quick stop before we reach the academy," I say after a moment.

He glances at me in the corner of his eye. "For what? We're running out of night. The place will be swarming with hunters come dawn."

"I need to see someone."

He switches lanes and passes a car that doesn't merge out of our way. "I'll call your father. He might be able to send in some reinforcements, but he won't be happy that we came here."

I glower at the expanse of empty road in front of us. "Do I look like I care?"

After a quick phone call and a long, quiet car ride, Evan pulls over and parks the car a few blocks from my—Alana's house. I doubt she'll be home this time of night, especially since the hunters took Faith. The best I can hope for is that she'll come home for a change of clothes and a shower. She's probably expecting us to show up at the academy—she's probably counting on it—and that's why it's best to be here first. I know her well enough to predict what she'll do. I just hope I'm right.

Evan holds my hand on our jog to Alana's. He sends bursts of his power into me, and I relish in how good it feels to have a piece of him touch my soul again. It doesn't feel dark and evil or out of control. It just feels like Evan, exactly how I remember him.

The dark house greets us with utter silence as we sneak around the back to the window that leads to my room. Evan covers his hand with his sleeve and punches the glass, shattering it. He clears off the sill and hops in and then offers his hand out to help me in.

My room is exactly how I left it with Evan's clothes scattered across the floor. I'm almost embarrassed that he gets to see the mess I've left behind. He bends down and picks up a few of his T-shirts and smiles at me.

"You kept my stuff," he comments.

I shrug. "I've always had hope that I'd get you back."

"And you did." He sounds so certain about it that I almost believe him. But what he doesn't realize is that he's not exactly the person I wanted back. I wanted the old Evan back. The one who cared about the same things I cared about. The one who loved me because he felt it in his heart and soul and not just the faint memory of our past.

He closes the distance between us and cups my face in his hands. "You don't believe it?"

I shrug again. "You're here with me, but I don't have you back. Not really. It just isn't the same as before."

He brushes his finger over my bottom lip. "We can change that."

I instinctively levitate up to his level, my lips a mere inch away from his. The heat of his breath caresses my lips, and I close my eyes, just soaking in the feeling of being so close to him. Neither of us moves, and I'm not even sure I'm breathing.

"Cami," Evan whispers. "Can I kiss you?"

His question jolts me back into reality and out of the past. The last time we kissed—on the beach in front of Faith—didn't turn out so well. I'm not sure my heart can handle that again. Not now. Not when my trust is stuck in this fragile state.

After a long moment, I pull away. "No, Evan. I'm sorry. Please, understand."

"Because of Dylan?" he asks.

Yes. No. I don't know. "Because of you," I finally say.

His mouth opens and closes for a second, but he doesn't answer. He doesn't have the chance. The door to the bedroom flies open, hitting the wall, and Alana stands in the doorway with David hovering in the hallway behind her.

Her dagger glints in the faint moonlight coming in through my broken window, and she relaxes, dropping her arm to her side. "Cami, you scared us!" She rushes into the room and freezes. "E-Evan," she stammers.

He stiffens instead of cracking a smile. "Alana. David." He nods to the man who raised him as if they were never partners. He nods like David never meant anything at all.

David steps in and places his hands on Alana's shoulders. "We didn't expect you to be here tonight."

"Why wouldn't we be? You sent hunters to collect Faith. How did you even find us?" I ask.

Alana stands frozen with her mouth hanging open as she tries to think of a response.

"Don't play stupid, Alana. You're the only one I told." My fingers clench at my sides as I wait for her to answer me. I glide a foot closer, expecting her to flinch at my sudden movement, but she straightens her shoulders to stare at me dead on.

"Aston tracked Cadence's phone," Alana answers like it isn't a big deal that Cadence's father keeps tabs on her. If she had known, she'd have thrown it away and gotten a new one.

Heat blossoms from my chest, coming straight from my heart as it burns with the intense desire to lash out at my former guardian. "You betrayed me, Alana. How could you? How could you put me in this position? Those hunters held a gun on me. They would've killed me had Faith not cooperated. Is that what you wanted? For me to die?"

Her face falls as my words sink in. "How could you even think that? They wouldn't have killed you." Is she serious? What happened to her? It's like she's forgotten the last few weeks altogether. Of course the hunters would've killed me.

"You're delusional if you believe that. Has the alliance really warped your mind so much? What happened to the woman who went on the run with me? Where did she go? She wouldn't have wanted Faith to be taken to the academy."

She tugs on the ends of her short hair. "I'm still me. I'd do anything to keep that innocent girl out of the hands of a demon even if it means she's at the academy. If I could go back in time, I would've brought you there, too. I regret my decision to run every day. If I hadn't, you'd have never been in this position. You'd have never seen reason in a demon's actions."

Rage explodes within me, and I fly at Alana, knocking her into David, sending them both into the wall behind them. I grip Alana's shoulders and glare into her startled, steel-gray eyes. David slumps to the floor beneath us, but I don't even flinch.

Heat warms my palms as power licks just below my skin. "You know nothing."

She clenches her teeth. "I know you've changed. I know what it looks like when someone falls under a demon's spell. I know what it looks like when someone's soul is heading straight for Hell."

Surprisingly, her words don't bother me. "I'm not your sister, Alana. I'm not working for demons. I'm here because you took a girl against her will to join an organization she doesn't want to be a part of. You're no better than the monsters you're trying to protect her against." I dig my fingers deeper into her shoulders. "Now, listen to me carefully. You're going to return Faith to me, and you're going to leave us alone. Got it?"

She doesn't respond.

"Don't make me do something I don't want to do," I say.

She licks her lips. "Cami, please."

I glare. "Don't. My soul is on the line because of you. Faith's father is hunting me as we speak, and I'm running out of time. If he catches me, he'll surely kill me. Taking Faith means I'll have to rely on Malicevile. Do you know what price I'll have to pay? Do you want that?"

She swallows. "You should've never gotten involved."

I blink away the hurt, trying to suppress my anger. "So, this is how it's going to be? You're choosing a girl you don't even know over me? I thought you cared about me. We're supposed to be family, remember?"

"Of course I care," she whispers. "But my hands are tied. You made your stance clear, and she's so young."

"Cami," Evan says from behind me. "Let's just finish this." A flame erupts in his fingers.

Alana closes her eyes. "Just do it."

I push her back. Flames spark in my palms, but I keep my arms at my side. "Unlike you, I don't want to see you dead. I do care about you. Since you're not going to help us, you have to stay out of the way. This is the one warning I can give you. If you don't, there's no protecting you. You understand? If you care about me at all, you won't stand in my way."

"Think about what you're doing for one second. The alliance will hunt you like a demon. They won't care you're only half. I'm trying to save your life," she says, pleading.

"And you think they're the good guys? You know, after all these years, Malicevile could've killed you on any occasion? He could kill you faster than you can even blink. But he hasn't. Do you know why?" I ask.

She's silent for a second before she says, "It's not because he's good."

"No, you're right about that. He's not. But he didn't because of me, and he still wouldn't. That's loyalty. You can't say the same about the alliance."

Tears line her eyes. "It's about the bigger picture."

"But it's the small stuff that matters most."

Her shoulders lower in defeat. "I love you, Cami. I wish things wouldn't have turned out like this. I've failed you and now I have to live with it."

"A lot of people have failed me," I say. I can't help it.

She sighs. "You know, I don't agree with you or what you're implying about your demon, but I won't stand in your way. Don't expect my protection, though. It's something I can't give you under these circumstances. I can't watch you run straight down the path of evil."

I turn away and take Evan's hand, ignoring her remarks. All I know is that she won't stand in my way. "Thank you," I say as I pull Evan toward the front door. I peer over my shoulder as Alana kneels next to David. "Alana?"

She glances at me.

"I'll protect you with my last breath, you know. You don't have to worry about your life. I guess loyalty runs in my blood."

I leave her crying in the hallway. Our relationship, like most of the others in my life, is ruined. My relationship with Alana is more than ruined. It's broken beyond repair.

When I exit the house, I'm sobbing. Evan wraps his arm around my shoulders, half carrying me as I fight my emotions from taking control. They're leaving me weak when I need to be strong.

"You can turn them off, Cami. Push them away. Don't

let them control you," Evan whispers.

I suck in a deep breath. "I can't."

"You can."

"No," I whisper. "My humanity is all I have left."

DON'T FALL

STEAM RISES FROM my hot skin as we stand outside the giant wall that surrounds the perimeter of the Hunter's Academy. Evan has given me enough power that I could burn the entire place down if I wanted to, but I don't. All I want to do is slip in and out as quietly as I can without hurting anyone.

"This is a terrible idea, love. Please, just hang tight and wait for me. We can run together. I can keep you just as safe as Evan. You don't have to put your life on the line. We can figure out a different plan to get Faith back," Dylan says, breathing into the line.

I shake my head even though he can't see me. "We

can't wait. You know how hard it is to run from a demon. I'm only alive today because my father never wanted to kill me." I glance at Evan who quietly listens. "And I won't risk you getting hurt or killed because of me."

Dylan sighs. "It's a risk I'm willing to take."

"But it's one I'm not."

"Please, Cami," he says, desperation lining his words. "Don't do this. This isn't what you really want. You're not a murderer. If you go in there, you'll have to fight. Hunters don't fight to injure, remember? The last thing I want is for you to fall from your own good grace. Your soul might be on the side of Hell, but you're still filled with so much good."

I kick the soft ground. "I love you."

"No, you can't say it like that—you can't say it like this is it for you. I can't lose you. Not like this. I'll follow you to Hell if I have to. If you go, then I'll go, too."

"Dylan…" He doesn't know what he's saying. He's crazy to think I'd even let him. "I love you," I repeat.

"Remember what I said. Don't fall. Remember who you are. You're more than a demon's daughter."

"Goodbye, Dylan."

"Cami—"

I hang up before he can argue. My heart splits into pieces thinking about how this is the worst possible way things could end with Dylan, but what else am I supposed to do? Not only is my life on the line, but I have to do this for Faith. I made her a promise.

I tuck my phone back into my pocket and turn to Evan. "I'm sorry you had to hear that."

He tosses a small fireball in his hand. "Whatever. I guess someone had to replace me."

I cringe at his words, doing my best to brush them off. "I could never replace you."

"I'm sorry," he says after a moment. "That was uncalled for. I swear, when I'm around you, it's like I can feel things again. I haven't felt this way in weeks." He snuffs the fire out in his hands and motions for me to move closer. "You make me feel alive again."

Tears prickle the edges of my vision. Wrapping my arms around him, I squeeze him against me and wait for him to hug me back. This is different from all the other times he tried to play with my emotions. He's genuine. I can feel it deep down.

He breathes into my hair, holding me against him, and then looks down into my eyes. "I'll kill anyone I have to for you. Would Dylan do that?"

I don't know the answer to that. I don't even know if his angel blood would allow it. "That's the last thing I want. For anyone. If we can get out of here without blood on our hands..." I let my voice trail off. I'm not so sure that's even an option.

He presses his lips to the top of my head. "If it comes down to it, the blood will be on my hands, okay? Dylan's not the only one who can save your soul."

His warm scent fills my lungs as I suck in a deep breath. I won't admit it to him, but I want to protect him, too. Even if his soul no longer belongs to him, I don't want him to have any regrets for when I figure out how to get it back from my father—which I will.

After a long moment, he releases me even though I don't want to let him go. I'd prefer to stay here in this spot instead of climb the mountainous wall and sneak through the groves and onto the campus.

"You ready?" Evan asks, unzipping a leather duffle bag full of weapons. Some I have no clue how to use—all probably from Malicevile's collection of trophies he keeps from those who lose to him, just like the ones decorating Raphael's house. Evan hands me a dagger and a belt of throwing knives. "Want anything else?"

I peer into the bag. "No. This will do."

Evan arms himself with a few different blades and then nestles the bag in a bush near the wall. He strolls to the wall and presses his hands against it. There's no way he could climb it without a ladder, so I levitate to the top, lock my arms in place over the edge, and let him use me to climb up. His weight nearly pulls me to the ground, but as soon as his hand touches the top of the wall, he swings himself up and over and lands with a thud on the other side.

He opens his arms to catch me as I levitate down even though he doesn't need to break my fall. Setting me back on my feet, he lets his hands linger on my hips for a moment before searching around the lemon grove.

The scent of wet dirt and citrus wafts through the air and catches on a cool breeze that stirs my sweat-dampened hair. Silently, we move through the lemon grove, using the trees for cover. A rustling sound echoes through the grove, and I pull Evan to a stop and search the area.

A lemon zooms through the air and smacks me in the shoulder. Reaching down, I pick it off the ground and toss it up and down in my hand. "You can come out, Annabelle. It's me. We're not going to hurt you." I haven't seen the forest nymph since I left the academy.

"Demon," she hisses, appearing from behind a tree.

"It's me Cami," I say.

She chucks another lemon at me. "Demons don't deserve names."

Evan sighs next to me. "We don't have time for this." Before I have a chance to stop him, fire erupts in his palm, and he launches a fireball in Annabelle's direction.

My scream mirrors hers as the fireball hits her in the stomach, knocking her back into the tree. Tears escape my eyes as I rush forward to her lifeless body, sprawled on the ground. Grabbing a handful of dirt, I put out the flames singeing the otherworldly fabric of her dress. The skin on her stomach puckers with blisters, and I wish I knew what to do to help her.

I glare at Evan from over my shoulder. "How could

you? She was armed with lemons."

He rolls his eyes. "She isn't dead, and she'll heal quickly. It's not a big deal. We don't have time to reason with the unreasonable."

I sigh. What's the point of arguing? He's going to do what he wants regardless. I'm thankful he didn't kill her. I'd have felt guilty about it the rest of my life—maybe even for all eternity.

"Now, come on," Evan adds, grabbing the back of my jacket to tug me to my feet. "Time's running out. If Dylan was right about them keeping her in the dorm with a guard, it'll take at least twenty minutes to get there and get her out."

Without hesitating a moment longer, I dash after him through the lemon grove, leaving Annabelle passed out in the dirt. When we reach the small fence that divides the groves from the sprawling lawns of the backside of campus, I tug Evan to a halt so we have the chance to search the area.

The campus is quiet as students sleep, keeping a normal human schedule. Most hunters are out for the night, claiming to keep the world safe from monsters. It was easy enough to evade those protecting the outside of campus. They're not worried about humans sneaking onto the grounds. Humans they can handle. It's the demons. But even if a demon managed to get close enough, they'd never get in.

Without the cover of trees, anyone could spot us as we cross campus, so I'm thankful it's pretty much dead this time of night. I pray that we don't run into anyone at all.

Instead of cutting across the lawn, which would be the fastest way, we stay along the perimeter and pass the buildings used for classrooms. Staying in the shadows, we move from building to building, stopping once as a faculty member exits one of the buildings and heads toward the apartments.

I raise my finger to my lips, stopping Evan from talking, and I listen as the door to the building closes.

"How many rooms in the dorm?" I whisper.

"Forty," he says. "We'll have to check all of them."

"Do not hurt any of the students," I say. "I mean it."

He presses his lips into a thin line. "What if they attack first?"

"I'll handle it, okay?"

"Okay," he says, shrugging.

Leaning out just enough to peer around the corner of the building, I inspect the front of the dorms to make sure it's clear. Evan links his fingers with mine, and we run together toward the building. He veers me to the left toward the far side of the building instead of the front where I had planned to just walk up the steps and head inside.

He stops outside the last window. "We'll go through here. It's the laundry room."

Without giving me a second to catch my breath, he

pops the screen from the window and uses a knife to pry it open enough for him to get his fingers in to slide it open all the way. Within the academy, the leaders don't believe in locking windows or doors. It's a safe place and crime doesn't usually exist here. Until now. They might reconsider their stance after we take Faith back.

Evan peeks his head in first before climbing through and helping me into the building. None of the washers or dryers are in use this time of night so we don't have to worry about someone coming in to discover us.

I'm pretty sure everyone in the building will be asleep for at least another hour if not more.

"I think we should split up," I say as Evan sticks his head into the hallway. "We'll get through faster."

His forehead crinkles as his eyebrows lower over his dazzling blue eyes. "It'd be safer to stay together."

"Safe isn't my priority," I argue, sliding up next to him to peer into the empty hallway myself. "Let's start upstairs. I doubt they'd put her on the ground floor."

As quietly as possible, we enter the hallway and push the door open for the stairs that sit directly across the hall from the laundry room. The place feels like a hotel with the patterned carpet and the gilded framed paintings lining the walls. The doors are numbered, even on one side of the hall and odd on the other, and I motion for Evan to start at room twenty-one while I take twenty-two.

My hand shakes as I touch the brass doorknob. Taking

a deep breath to relax my nerves, I twist the knob until it clicks and ease it open to peer into a dark room with a figure fast asleep on the twin bed. I don't have to go inside, though. The place reeks like musk and dirty laundry. Nothing like the sweet sugary scent that clings to Faith.

As quickly as I opened the door, I close it and rush to the next one. Evan shakes his head when he stands opposite of me. I check the next few doors on my side of the hall with no luck, and it leaves just one more. The last one at the end. Evan follows my lead to check his last door as well, and I take a breath and say a prayer.

I ease open the door, the scent of vanilla and nutmeg wafting around me, sending relief to my very core. Faith sits at the end of the bed with the small desk light on, and a woman in all black sits on a chair with her nose in a book. Neither of them notices me.

I hold up one of my throwing knives. If I hit the woman just right in the leg, I can stop her from chasing us without killing her.

I take a quiet breath and count to myself. *One. Two. Three.*

A scream rips through the air from behind me, and my knife flies from my hand hitting the wall next to the hunter's head. Faith jumps to her feet, a glowing orb in her fingers, and when she sees me, she smiles.

Evan curses from behind me, tugging the back of my jacket, and I lose my balance just as a rock the size of a baseball propels past my head toward Faith. She ducks just in time, and the rock crashes through the window.

Whoever is throwing rocks at us from the room behind me distracts me long enough that I don't see the hunter coming at me with her dagger drawn until she's a mere foot from me.

I block her arm before she can stab me and push her back.

"Faith, come on!" I yell.

Faith dodges the woman, but the hunter is much faster and grabs her by the back of her hair. She holds her dagger against Faith's throat, and I freeze.

A rock thuds against the wall next to me. "What's going on, Evan?" I'm too afraid to shift my eyes away from the hunter and Faith.

"I startled a halfie," he says, hitting his back against mine. "If she doesn't stop, I'll hurt her."

I suck in a breath. "Do what you have to," I finally say.

Faith's eyes never waver from mine, but the hunter's eyes widen and look past me at Evan in the hallway.

A scream sounds out from behind me and then stops just as quickly. A second later, Evan pushes me forward, forcing me into the room with Faith and the hunter. He closes the door behind us.

"That woke up the floor," he says. "Time to finish this."

I reach out and grab his hand, snuffing out the fireball

before he can throw it at the hunter holding Faith.

"Let Faith go. She doesn't want to be here with you," I say. "We don't want to have to hurt you or anyone. Is one girl really worth that much to you?"

The hunter doesn't respond.

An alarm sounds through the building. The place will be swarming with more hunters soon enough.

I step forward, flames glowing in my palms. "I guess you've made your decision."

I raise my hand, knowing very well that I'll hit Faith in the process, but I'd rather her be injured and with me instead of safe and imprisoned.

Faith squeezes her eyes shut.

A moment later, the hunter wails in agonizing pain and pushes Faith away from her before I even have the chance to throw a fireball. The woman waves her arms around, now smoking and glowing red, and I realize that Faith has used her own power.

Faith dashes to me, wrapping her arms around my waist, and I hug her against me.

From behind us, someone bangs on the door, and Evan waves us toward the window. We're two stories up, but I can levitate, so I'll take my chances jumping. Levitating as I cross the room, I pick up the metal lamp from the nightstand and swing it at the screaming hunter, knocking her back into the wall. I use the same lamp and swing it at the window, shattering the broken glass completely, and use the blanket from the bed to clear the remaining shards away.

I turn to Faith. "We're going out the window."

She clings to me. "I'm scared. I can't jump."

I grip her shoulder, drawing my attention to the door, shaking at its hinges. "You have to trust me."

She nods as I step out of the window first and brace myself on the small ledge. From here, I can see the commotion running through the academy as the stupid alarm continues to blare. Luckily, none of the hunters have looked up yet. They're too worried about the threat sneaking around at ground level.

When a group of hunters pass by under the window and turn the corner to head to the front entrance, I motion for Evan to join me on the ledge. It's barely big enough for the both of us, but I'm going to do my best to soften all of our falls.

I peer at Faith from over my shoulder. "Wrap your arms around my neck and hold on, okay? Don't let go."

Her trembling fingers lock around my neck nearly choking me when the door booms open from behind us.

I jump at the same time as Evan with Faith clinging to my back, and I levitate, concentrating on soaring up instead of descending, knowing the weight of both Faith and Evan will drag us all down if I stop.

Evan lets go of me halfway down, hitting the ground in a crouch. It slows the fall enough that my stomach doesn't rise in my throat at the sudden change in gravity.

"We have to hurry," Evan says. He takes Faith from me, and she jumps on his back instead, leaving me open to protect us as we run.

"You're not going anywhere," a deep voice says, chilling my blood.

I spin to face the threat from behind and meet the eyes of six hunters. We're outnumbered but not outmatched. All of them are human.

"We don't want to fight," I say. "We're just taking Faith and going."

The man, who looks so familiar, but I can't place him, steps forward. "Not happening. Put the girl down and surrender. If you do, I might let you live like I did your guardian."

My mouth falls open as recognition sets in. This hunter—this vile, wretched human—slit Alana's throat to get to me. She's only alive because he didn't cut through a major artery. And he didn't let her live. He just sucked at trying to kill her.

Rage rushes over me as I stare into the eyes of a monster worse than my own demonic father. Fire explodes in my palms as I lose control. I don't care about trying to keep others safe. I don't even care if I get blood on my hands.

This man has to pay for what he did.

He should feel the pain I did as I watched Alana bleed out onto the dirt.

And I'll be the one to make sure he gets what is coming to him.

He has to die.

LETTING GO

THE WORLD SLOWS as I gather all the power within me like I'm siphoning it straight from the depths of Hell. The six hunters stand before me without an ounce of fear in their eyes. They gather their confidence from their numbers instead of their abilities. Through training, hunters learn to suppress their fear so demons can't feed upon it and make them weak. The weaker the prey, the more likely a demon will engage.

What they don't know is that a good dose of fear would keep them alive. I admit I'm afraid of demons, and I'm afraid of losing my soul. My fear of demons makes me fearless of hunters. I'd rather die by the hands of a hunter than a demon if I had a choice about how I was going to die—but I don't. And I don't plan on dying any time soon.

The massive fireball, the size of a basketball, rests between my hands. The hunters are far enough away that they'll scatter the moment I toss it. So I don't toss it. Instead, I glide closer, levitating an inch above the ground just to try to freak them out.

The hunters behind the man inch backwards, and I grin at how quickly they display their self-preservation, leaving their leader in the open.

"You have a death wish, I see," I say, lowering my voice as I close the distance.

Evan remains behind me with Faith. If something was to happen, and the hunters suddenly pull themselves together to fight as a group, I hope that Evan abandons me to take Faith to safety.

"You don't have it in you to kill me," the man says.

Now he's egging me on, begging for me to do something. Encouraging me to snuff his tiny little life out.

I separate a small portion of the fireball and chuck it at him, hitting him in the stomach. His shirt smolders under the heat, and he jumps back, smacking at the burning fabric. He loses his dagger in the process, and his colleagues don't move to intervene.

I throw another fireball, this time at the ground, and his dagger glows a vibrant red. It's too hot for him to try to acquire. I've left him out of options. He'll either have to try to fight me by hand or flee.

"Cami, please," Faith says from behind me. "Don't kill him."

Her small voice tugs me from my own deadly inner thoughts. It's enough to knock some sense into me. Unlike Evan, Faith still clings onto her innocence and naivety. She doesn't understand the truth of the world her demonic father brought her into. She has no clue what these hunters are capable of. The old motto of *Humans Come First* is still quite dominant within hunters no matter what anyone says.

"They'll hunt you forever. They'll kill your father. Is that what you want?" I try to reason my desires to Faith. I shouldn't even have to explain myself.

"My father is capable of taking care of me—and himself," she says.

I sigh but don't snuff out the fireball. "You're right," I say to her without taking my eyes off the hunters. I straighten my shoulders and lift the fireball toward them. "If you follow, I won't kill you, but I will let Evan do it if he wants."

Evan chuckles from behind me, the deep unsettling sound sending a shiver through me. "Oh, I want to. I might even bring home a souvenir for your father."

Please, let that be a joke.

A man on the outside of the line of hunters spins and starts running in the other direction. At least someone has a brain and a need to survive.

"Go on, Evan. I'll catch up in a minute," I say.

Evan pauses for a second. "Let me help."

I shake my head. "Get Faith out of here."

He sighs before he leaves me with five nervous hunters. If I wasn't worried about them attacking me as I turn my back away, I would have fled with him. Now, I'm not sure what to do since they're not fleeing like their colleague.

I look each hunter in the eyes, all of them familiar from my time here, but none of them close enough to me for me to care what happens to them. If I can't turn and run, I have to do something to stop them from following me, because I don't believe they're taking me seriously, though their fear is clear.

"I swear, if any of you follow me, you'll regret it," I say again, taking a step back.

"You'll regret ever showing your face here in the first place." The leader, the weaponless man Faith begged me to spare, cracks his knuckles. He's trying to push me over the edge again.

Rage swallows most of my reason and most of my need to retreat without hurting another person. I swing my arm out, shooting the fireball at the hunters in an arc of flames that hits them all across their shins. The scent of sweat and smoke and burning flesh catches on the breeze around me, and I only stay long enough to watch the hunters fall to the ground, rolling in the dewy grass to put out the flames that'll stop them from following me while allowing them to live.

I spin around and bolt in the direction where Evan was heading. There's no point in sneaking around any longer. I have to catch up to Evan and get us out of here. Then, I have to leave and never look back.

I race through the dark grounds, heading straight for the front entrance of the academy. Evan's heading in the only reasonable direction since there is no way he can climb the perimeter wall with Faith to escape, especially if I can't catch up. He'll have to fight to get out. I just hope I'm not too late.

The world flies by me as I half-run and half-levitate across the still quiet campus. Someone cut off the alarm, so I only have to deal with the ringing in my ears. Sweat beads on my forehead as I exert myself as much as I can even though exhaustion threatens to slow me down. After all of this is over, I'll be happy to pass out anywhere and sleep for a few days.

Commotion breaks out in front of me, and a fire explodes from the guard house near the gate. Bright orange and yellow flames dance across the building, consuming it with the same feral hunger that lingers in the back of my soul.

I try to summon even an ounce of the power Evan gave me but nothing happens. My palms remain cold and empty. I used it all to disable the hunters back at the dorm. All I have now are my knives to rely on.

"Let us through!" Evan shouts, another fireball glowing in his hands. "You've lost. Faith isn't staying here with you."

A single man blocks the exit. "I can't let you take her. Look what happened to you. Look at Cami. The sight of the both of you kills me."

"Why? Because we see the truth? You're an idiot, David, if for one second you believe I'm worse off now than I was before. I lived a mindless life, hunting and killing demons, and nothing more. I had no purpose. This place uses people like me, and the second we're no longer useful, they murder us."

"You know that's not true. Your purpose was to save innocent souls." David doesn't back down. He steps a foot closer.

"Innocent souls? Those who seek out demons are far from innocent. Demons go after those who need to be punished." Evan throws another fireball, hitting the wall next to David. If he wanted to kill his old partner, he would've. A small ounce of hope rises through me. Maybe he isn't as lost as I thought.

I slow my pace and search the area behind him. Alana swore she'd stay out of our way. I didn't want to have to face her again. I can't stand to look into her eyes, knowing she's given up on me.

But Alana is nowhere in sight. It's only David.

"David," I say. "Move out of the way."

He clenches his knife at his side. "I can't. I couldn't live with myself if I let any of you go."

My brows furrow together as I frown. "You don't have a choice. What do you think will happen if you stop us from leaving?"

Tears shine in his eyes. "I can protect you from the demons. I can save your souls."

A sudden laugh escapes from Evan's mouth at how ridiculous David sounds. "The alliance will murder us."

"They will save you," he argues.

I step closer. "Evan's soul belongs to Malicevile. There is no saving him."

"A demon watcher can intervene. Deals can be broken." He straightens his shoulders. "I'd rather he be dead and free than alive and working for a demon." Dead and in Hell is not exactly free in my book. Deals can be broken, sure, but it's too late for Evan. He was with Malicevile for too long. He's not innocent.

Evan tenses. "Death isn't an option."

"You know I had a plan. You know I was going to fix this." I step another few feet closer.

"How? Are you going to trade your soul for his?" David moves back and stands just outside the gate.

"My father won't make the trade," I whisper.

David narrows his eyes. "This is all your fault! Alana should've left you in that burning house for your father to take. She should've listened to me when I told her to give you to the alliance. I warned her that she was playing a dangerous game. I told her it'd come back around to destroy us. Look what you've done to him!" He waves at Evan. "How can you even live with yourself?"

Before I have a chance to defend myself, Evan throws a fireball directly at David. Bending my knees, I propel forward, knocking into David. The fireball hits my back, pushing me forward, and I fall with David to the ground.

"Hurry, Evan. Grab Faith," I say.

David grits his teeth as he shifts under me. He raises his hand, wrapping his fingers around my neck, and squeezes, cutting off my air. I struggle in his grasp, my throat burning as I try to force air into my lungs, but it doesn't come. He's too strong to beat off and levitating only makes him squeeze tighter.

The edges of my vision darken as my heart pounds in my ears. This can't be happening. After everything I've been through, after all the good I've done in the world, my life is about to end by the hand of a man I trusted. A man who had fought to protect me before.

But David isn't that same man. Losing Evan changed him like it changed all of us. His hurt and anger shines in his teary eyes as I stare him down while my vision threatens to darken and leave me blind in my final moments.

Strong fingers slide around my back, yanking me away from David, and I gasp a deep, burning breath as air flows into my lungs. I fall hard to the ground, the back of my head scraping across the gritty dirt.

Evan scoops me into his arms, pulling me against his chest. David moans from a few feet away, and I blink the haze from my eyes. Faith cries out from beside me, and horror and despair course through me when my gaze finally pauses on the figure before me.

Raphael, in all his demonic glory, hoists David from the ground by his neck. Fire flashes from the demon's eyes, and his horns shine like black onyx as they protrude from his head. Fear courses through me as I stare at the demon, not because of what he looks like, but because of what he's doing.

"Dad, no!" Faith screams from next to me. "Dad, you can't!"

Raphael flares his nostrils as he looks in Faith's direction. But he doesn't stop. I wriggle from Evan's arms and glide across the dirt, closer to the demon. He snarls at me as I reach out and grab his arm.

"Let him go, Raphael," I say. "If you kill this man, your daughter will turn against you."

"This is your fault!" His eyes glow a vibrant red as he roars the words at me. He's right. Everything is my fault. Losing Evan's soul, Faith getting kidnapped, my own soul choosing the side of evil. I can't even deny his words. But I'm trying my best to fix things. I have to try.

His sugar and nutmeg scent blows over me, and I crinkle my nose at the sweet smell. "Yeah, it is. I take all the blame. It's my fault your daughter is here. It's my fault Evan's soul is in a demon's possession. But it'll be your fault if Faith turns her back on you. Look what you're doing. This man isn't on a path to Hell. He doesn't need to be punished for anything. If you want to salvage whatever relationship you have left with Faith, you'll release him."

Raphael growls and snaps his sharp teeth in David's face before dropping him to the ground. His horns sink back into his head as his human façade hides the monster lurking under his skin. Faith cries as she rushes to her father, hugging him as he lifts her into his arms.

I sigh a long breath of relief and turn to Evan. "Let's get out of here."

Evan nods as he takes my hand, but something catches my attention, freezing me in place. David jumps to his feet with a dagger clutched in his hand. He charges at Raphael, determined to kill the upper-level demon alone. Before I can even open my mouth to scream, Raphael launches a lava-bomb toward David's chest. David's eyes widen as the power shoots at him.

I bend my knees and propel forward, hoping to catch the glowing orb before it hits David. Our eyes meet as I fly forward, and he raises his hand, throwing his dagger a moment before Raphael's power sinks into his skin and consumes him in blinding red flames.

Tears burst from my eyes as David disappears into blood and fire and smoke right before my eyes. A loud wail escapes my lips as I fall to my knees. The pain in my heart threatens to consume me.

And then I feel it.

Hot pain swells from my stomach, the shock of losing David preventing me from feeling the knife protruding from my skin. My eyes widen as I wrap my fingers around the hilt, my own blood coating my hands and clothing.

"Cami!" Evan yells from behind me.

But I can't move.

I can't do anything except watch as blood pours from the stab wound caused by the man I tried so hard to save. I never thought it would end like this. Even in the final moments as I fought so hard to save him, he wasn't going to let me go. He was never going to forgive me for the circumstances that led to Evan's soul falling into Malicevile's hands.

Flashes of my life pass through my mind. For the first time in a long time, I can imagine my mom and dad. They hold each other as they look at me, smiles on their faces. I hold up my hand to reach for them, but they disappear into a cloud of black smoke and vibrant flames.

"Cami, hold on. You have to hold on," Evan pleads, his voice cutting through the darkness.

But there's nothing to hold onto. My life is over and there's nothing anyone can do about it. My soul burns as the smoke starts to clear from my vision. Heat courses over my skin, and I feel it more intensely than I've ever felt it before.

The world shifts as the black ground trembles under my feet. Visions of flames and fire consume all my thoughts as the world as I knew it explodes into a vast, dark world lit by firelight.

I knew I was Hell-bound. I should've seen this coming. But I had hoped I could get myself out of this mess. There's no redeeming me now. I've never felt so empty and alone in my life. Not even Dylan, the boy I should've never abandoned, can save me now. *Dylan, I'm sorry...*

Pushing all the grief and heartache from my mind, I stand before the gates of Hell, waiting for the devil himself to welcome me among his minions. I brought this upon myself. My own soul knew this is where I belonged. I'm to blame for everything bad that happened around me. *Stop that. You're not at fault. The alliance is. They turned you into this.*

I can't ignore the new, much louder voice in my head. *They're the enemy.*

"They're the enemy," I whisper.

A bright light flashes through the flames of Hell, and the scent of apple and rain wraps around me, tugging onto my consciousness. The feathery softness of Dylan's wings hug my soul, and for a split second, all my pain and despair fades away.

It's only me and him in a place of nothingness.

"Cami," Dylan whispers.

I can't see him, but I can feel him.

"Stay strong, love. Just hold on to me. It'll be over soon."

My very soul trembles. "No, I can't. I'm not ready."

"I wish there were a choice."

There is. Let go now, a voice commands. It's my own thoughts.

A second later, a dark force enters our space of nothingness, coiling around me, trying to pull me from Dylan. A flash of light encompasses me, searing my soul, and I push away as hard as I can. Though I can't see my surroundings, my stomach drops as I freefall through the darkness with nothing to hold on to. A flash of light cuts through the air above me and disappears along with the warm comfort Dylan's presence had given me. He's gone.

My last ounce of hope disappears, and the only thing left is a loud voice that rings in my ears. *Let go of it all!*

I obey the voice.

I let go.

ON THE SAME SIDE

A COLD EMPTINESS settles over me as I open my eyes in an unfamiliar room. My back aches as I shift to my side and stare at my frightened expression reflecting back at me from the black marble floor. A strange heat, unlike anything I've ever felt, radiates through the room, and sweat beads on my temples.

My stomach screams in pain as I sit up, and I nearly faint when I see the gaping wound caused by David's dagger in my stomach. Blood congeals around the wound, but no more pours from me, so I doubt I'll bleed to death...I hope.

I peer around the room in confusion. The last thing I remember is the darkness and the flash of Dylan's wings, and the voice—the one that told me to let it all go. It wasn't until that moment that things disappeared, and I woke up here. *Am I dead? Is this Hell? It sure isn't Heaven.*

I pinch myself, expecting nothing to happen, but I definitely felt the gesture. The pain is still real to me. I thought it went away after death, but maybe I'm being punished. I am a demi-demon with a Hell-bound soul after all.

I gather my courage to get to my feet and wince through the pain. Shuffling across the gleaming floor, I make my way to the curtained window and thrust it open. Fear settles in my soul as I stare out into a world that looks similar to my own, but is slightly different, like looking at the world through orange-tinted glasses.

The sun hangs in the sky, bigger than I've ever seen it before, and casts golden hues across the fluffy clouds. Brown grass and dead flowers surround a black-stone path that leads to a cracked and broken street.

A sinking feeling settles in my stomach as I watch as a demon that looks like a cross between a giant armadillo and a beaver with razor sharp teeth circle around and around in the decrepit street like it can't move more than a few feet. Where ever I am, demons can remain in the sunlight.

"Where am I?" I ask out loud to myself.

"Welcome to our wonderful daylight prison," a masculine voice says from behind me.

I jerk around to find Raphael hovering in the doorway of the room. He combs his fingers through his blond hair, staring at me like I'm some mysterious wonder he discovered in a sideshow at a circus.

My forehead crinkles as shock causes my heart to skip a beat. "What?"

He shrugs. "I'm just as surprised as you are."

A million thoughts race through my mind. I turn back toward the window, staring out. How can I be trapped in the daylight realm among demons when I'm only half? I don't understand. I should be dead. I should be anywhere else but here.

"But I'm not a demon," I say.

"Tell that to the force that pulled you here with me." He strolls into the room and looks down on me like he can somehow find the answer within my green eyes. He studies me for a moment. "I don't know why I didn't see it before. You have your father's eyes. All this time I thought you were a silly human with a protection amulet."

It's not until this moment that I realize the sun stone is gone from my neck. I grip the window frame. "What are you going to do to me?"

He scoffs, spinning me around so I have to face him. In one quick motion, he slides his hand to my throat and straightens my back, stretching my wounded stomach. If he wasn't holding me up, I would double over in pain. "I should cut you to pieces with my nails." He drops me to the floor. "But I'm not, because we're on the same side. Finding you at the academy, saving my daughter, was the last thing I expected."

I clutch my stomach as the pain fades away. Slowly lifting my shirt, I peer at the healing skin. I release a short breath. "Well, what did you expect?"

"For you to run," he says.

"I gave up running a while ago. How did you know Faith was taken to the academy, anyway?" I ask, wondering what he thought he'd accomplish by going there. He can't get through the blessed barrier.

"The same way I always track you, my dear Camilla." I turn my gaze to my father, who stands outside the room. His emerald eyes shine even brighter in this realm, and he's just as mesmerizing as ever as he glides into the room. "You carry my blood, like his daughter carries his."

He holds out his hand for me to take, and after a moment of consideration, I let him help me to my feet. His gaze travels from my face to my boots, and then he tugs at the hem of my brown-stained shirt, tilting his head slightly.

I smooth the crusty fabric. "A hunter stabbed me in the stomach."

"It was a fatal blow, Malicevile," Raphael says, coming up beside him. "I saw it with my own eyes. The hunter's dead, though. You're welcome."

A frown crosses my face as I remember David throwing the dagger at me as Raphael's demonic power consumed him. But that's all I remember. Not a single emotion stirs within me. It's like someone hit the off button on all my grief and heartache, sparing me from myself. The memory feels more like another life altogether—one I want to forget and never think about again.

"I was dying," I say, rubbing my hands up and down my arms. "I think I even saw the gates of Hell. But then my—" I snap my mouth closed for a minute.

Am I here because of Dylan? He said he'd follow me to Hell if he had to...

"Your what?" Raphael asks.

The words stay lodged in my throat. The last thing I want is to bring Dylan into this. "I don't know. I saw a light."

Malicevile twists his lips to the side. "Probably the sun."

"There was also this nagging voice telling me to let go. I woke up here." I close my eyes, trying my best to remember Dylan in the darkness. I can only really recall his apple and rain scent.

Malicevile wraps his arm around my shoulders. "I think you ended up here because you weren't ready to die, Camilla. You forced yourself through an unheard of transformation. Do you know what this means?" It makes sense, but I didn't do it alone. Angel Boy helped me when he was trying to save my soul. For once, I have my own secret to hold. One I could use. *Now you're thinking like a...*

My mouth drops open. "You mean..."

He grins. "You're a fully fledged demon, Camilla.

You're just like me."

⚜

Raking my hands through my dark curls as I pace the room, I let Malicevile's words sink in. I'm a demon. Being stuck in this lame sunlight prison is the only proof I need.

Now what?

I ask the question over and over again. What does this mean for me? Surprisingly, I'm not scared or upset or any-thing—I'm actually happy to be alive. Confused? No doubt about it. But this doesn't exactly feel like a bad thing. I feel more alive than ever, and the things I worried about last night don't even get a second thought from me now.

I stare out the window for the millionth time. The sun moves across the sky much faster than I expect it to. Time doesn't tick by at the same speed as it does in the earth realm. But doing nothing but sitting in this empty room makes me anxious. How am I going to deal with this every day? I don't even know what lies beyond the wall.

Footsteps sound from the hallway. Malicevile waltzes into the room, a smile playing on his lips, and he holds open his arms. I cross my arms over my chest and remain in place. He's crazy to think I'm going to start showing affec-tion for him just because I'm a demon. Actually, all I can think about is what I can get from him. How I can use him to make my life easier.

"Oh, Camilla, why must you always be so stubborn," he says as he drops his arms to his sides. "Would it kill you to lighten up a little? I didn't do this to you. You can't hold it against me."

"I'm your spawn," I mutter. "You're the sole reason I'm in this position."

He covers his forehead with his hand while sighing. "I'm sure you're feeling out of con—"

I hold up my hand. "Don't act like you know what I'm going through. And for your information, I'm not feeling anything at all."

He steps closer and hugs me to him, surprising me. "That'll change come sunset. This realm is devoid of all humanity and emotion. It's basically a holding cell where demons recharge and heal. It's also how we can move from location to location without having to worry about showing up in the same spot if we don't want to—and that, my dear, is only possible for upper-level demons."

"How do you even know that's what I am? Don't I have to work my way up or something?" I ask.

What if I enter the human world as an animalistic demon? What if I'm no longer me at all except for in this place? I know deep down I'm asking myself these questions because I know it would suck, but for some reason, the thought of appearing in the human world as a creepy, mindless demon doesn't bother me. Maybe it'd be better than having to figure out what's going to happen in my life.

He squeezes me against him, his cinnamon and clove scent surrounding us. I wonder what I smell like. I've never been brave enough to ask anyone. "Of course you're an upper-level demon. You carry my blood. Consider yourself royalty, my dear. The human and demon worlds are now at your fingertips."

I frown. "What if I don't want that?"

"You will. Just wait. When the sun sets, the world will be a different place for you. But don't worry, my dear. You'll always have a place at my side. I'm your father after all."

A smile crosses my lips. "Thanks, Dad."

Something within me shifts as the sun arcs across the sky. The lower it gets to the horizon, the more different emotions penetrate through the invisible wall protecting me from my humanity.

After a moment, I pull away from Malicevile. "You said the emotions will be worse, but what about my humanity? What happens to you?"

He shrugs. "It's a mystery. You were mortal. I'm sure it lingers within you somewhere. You still have a soul. I can see it."

"Well, this sucks. I'm a demon in possession of my own soul. You sure I can't stay in this realm forever? I think I should be afraid when we enter the earth realm," I say. Having a soul means that the weird haze cutting me off from everything that had hurt me before might dissipate and leave me vulnerable.

"You can fix that by turning it all off and letting your

demonic blood protect you," he says, patting my shoulder reassuringly. "But you need to be careful. Certain people can get to you."

"Like who? I need to know so I can stay far, far away."

"The nephilim, Camilla," he says. "If you want to survive as a demon and live up to your potential, he has to go. You can't trust him."

Like the prick of a needle, something stings within my soul. My feelings are so muddled that I can't really grasp what I'm feeling, but I don't like it. I love Dylan. I know I do. And I know the last thing I'd want in the world would be to kill him, like Malicevile implies.

But what if he gets to you and opens your soul? Can you survive with those feelings of being a demon? I shake my head, pushing my thoughts away. "Dylan's harmless, Dad. Plus, you know who my heart really belongs to. This proves it." I only call him Dad because I know how it affects him. Even after all the crap I put him through as a human, he's obviously proud to have a demon child.

"Well, we'll see how things play out, okay, Camilla?"

I press my lips together. "Okay."

Raphael comes to the door and hovers in the hallway. He's rigid when Malicevile brings his gaze to him but doesn't back away. He tucks his hands under his arms, rocking back on his heels before saying, "It's time to head out."

I frown. "Where are we going?"

"Home. We're going home."

FALL FROM GRACE

WITHOUT TRANSPORTATION, I stroll behind Malicevile and Raphael as they lead me to wherever we're going that'll take us back to the earth realm and away from the academy entrance. The last thing I need is to reappear at the gate of the organization that'll do anything to kill a demon—like myself. It's strange that I'll be thinking this way from now on.

I've fallen so far from grace—both Heaven's and my own—that there's nothing I can do except accept my life and live it the best I can and the way I want to, which entails standing by my father's side and helping him destroy the Hunter's Alliance and everything it stands for. They stole everything from me. They turned me into the creature they despise most in the world. They can't blame anyone but themselves for what happens next. I'm not beneath them like they think. I do come first. I'll always come first. I yearn to see the alliance leaders' reactions when they come to that realization. They don't even have a precious army of angels to protect them—and the nephilim, who they've kept on pedestals, are useless when it comes to fighting.

After a few miles on foot, Malicevile stops in a clearing within a forest of dead trees with twisted roots that poke from the ground, trying to strangle the other trees around them. The setting sun shines from the west, casting its glow around us. Shadows crawl along the trees, making it look as if screaming faces lie within the cracked, white bark. I pull one of my throwing knives from my belt and carve a slice of wood from the trunk, almost expecting it to bleed, but the pieces only disintegrate in my palm.

Malicevile studies me as I trail my fingers along the otherworldly trees. Their beauty lies in the uniqueness of their gnarled and tangled branches, and I wish my cell phone worked so I could take a picture to show Dylan.

The thought of Dylan comes too easily, and I push it away. Evan was right about how hard old habits are to break. My future with Dylan ended the moment I saw Hell and ended up in this light prison. My heart would break into a thousand pieces if it weren't so tainted. My new fate saves me from ever having to choose between the two boys I love. This is just how it has to be.

The sun burns in the sky as it sinks into the horizon. A golden mist trickles through the air, covering everything in a yellow light. The world around me shimmers, and for the first time all day, fear sneaks into my heart. I feel it with every ounce of my being.

But fear isn't the only thing.

Like a thousand tiny needles pricking my skin, leaving me susceptible, grief, shock, anger, confusion, and pain—a whole lot of pain—seeps through my skin and burrows into my soul. My knees hit the ground before I even realize that my legs had given out on me. The dark night blinks in and out of the golden haze, and a strong hand wraps under my arms and then under my knees and lifts me up.

The scent of cinnamon and clove, which used to send fear flooding through me, now engulfs me in comfort. I rest my cheek against my father's chest as my emotions threaten to consume me and pull me into darkness.

A moan escapes my lips as cold air smacks my face. My skin steams in the chilly night. It's much cooler than last night, and I wonder if it's because I'm hotter. The thought helps pull me away from my out-of-control emotions long enough to realize we're standing in front of Malicevile's plantation-style home only a few miles from the academy.

He doesn't set me on my feet, and I'm glad for it, because I'm unsure if I could even stand. My heavy heart sits in my chest waiting to drag me down to where I belong. As the memory of David dying flashes through my mind, my breath catches and a sob grabs hold of me. I bawl my eyes out on the front of Malicevile's suit jacket, but he doesn't say anything as he struts forward and up the stairs of his house—our home.

A low growl erupts from the left side of the porch and a hellhound slinks to its feet, eyeing Raphael as he comes up beside my father. Malicevile says something to the hound in a language I don't know or understand, and the beast retreats back to its spot.

The sight of the broken werewolf sends me over the edge, and I scream out, clawing and smacking my hands against Malicevile until he has no choice but to set me down on the porch. The front door flies open and a figure stands tall, haloed in the light of the chandelier in the foyer, and then a familiar voice wraps around me at the same time a pair of strong arms do.

"You're alive, Cami. I don't believe it," Evan says, kissing my hair.

I sink against him, savoring the comfort he brings me. He helps push away all the bad emotions refusing to let me go. I sniffle, clinging to his neck, and the world shifts as he takes me inside.

"Evan, I'm a—I'm a—" The words just won't come. I'd accepted them not long ago, but now that I'm back in the human world with access to all my human emotions, I can't stand the thought of what I've become. I wish I would've just died by David's hands. It'd be better than having to live with myself. I'm the epitome of evil.

"You're a demon," he finishes for me. "That's where you went when dawn came. You went to the sunlight prison realm."

My loud sobs confirm his statement without me having to say anything. "It saved me."

He adjusts me in his arms until my legs wrap around his waist, and I can look into his eyes. Through my blurry tears, I see Evan exactly as I remember him—strong, brooding, and utterly human. Even without his humanity, I can see the good hiding under all of my father's demonic taint.

"So why are you crying?" he asks, smiling at me like my meltdown is the most ridiculous thing. "You're alive and safe and now with me."

Malicevile clears his throat from behind, and Evan's gaze flicks past me. "Camilla is a demon with a soul and her humanity. The daylight realm shuts off all emotions, but now that she's back here, they seem to have run amuck. All she has to do is shut off her humanity, and she'll come to her senses."

I sob harder. "I can't! I'm afraid. My humanity is what makes me *me*."

Evan bends his neck to rest his forehead against mine, blocking out the world around us until it's just me and him. I lose myself in his fathomless blue eyes. They're brighter than before, and I can no longer see the dark shadows that used to swirl within them from being demon-bound.

"You're going to be you no matter what, Cami," Evan whispers. "You just won't feel the pain and hurt. You won't even care once you do it. Look how messy your humanity is. Why would you want to keep something that hinders you and leaves you powerless? Please, for the sake of yourself, shut it off. I can't stand to see you like this."

I suck in a deep breath, shuddering as I calm myself down. "You're just saying that. You're not capable of caring, Evan. Malicevile made sure of it."

"Don't say that. I do care about you. You awakened something within me and seeing you like this makes me want to take on the world for you. I love you, Cami," he says. He draws closer, his lips inches from mine, and my body responds as lust tries to push away the pain and heartache.

I kiss him, cupping his face in my hands, and hold onto him like I'll float away otherwise. His arms wrap tighter around me, and I can feel his heartbeat through the thin cotton of his shirt. His kisses numb my emotions, clearing my head. I'm afraid to stop. All I want is to feel his hot body against mine, taste the sweetness of his lips, lose myself in everything that is Evan Whiteshaw.

"Wow," he whispers as he takes a breath.

I smile into his lips. "Wow is right."

Malicevile taps his foot on the tile, drawing our attention to our surroundings. "You can't just replace one emotion with another, my dear. Stop being difficult and get yourself under control in a proper manner."

Heat blossoms up my neck as anger replaces my desire, and I glower at my father. I don't even know how to respond. Instead of making a fool out of myself by claiming there is nothing proper about being a demon, I say, "I can't. What if I forget who I am? What if I stop loving Evan?" I face the boy who holds part of my heart. "Do you want to risk that?"

He blinks once and nods when Malicevile gives him a pointed look. "I want what's best for you, Cami. I want you to accept who you are so you can get rid of all the unnecessary stuff. This is what you're meant to be. Don't torture yourself with the remnants of your human life."

I push from his arms and swipe away my unwanted tears. "But I'm not ready to say goodbye." I cross my arms over my chest, hugging myself. "I think I need a moment alone. Please, excuse me."

I don't wait for either of them to answer, but Evan calls my name as I retreat deeper into the house toward the room Malicevile had given me.

The last thing I hear before I shut the door is Malicevile say, "Let her go. She'll come around."

But I'm not so sure I can.

Or that I want to.

An hour goes by as I sit on the edge of a brand new bed and

count down the time until sunrise. I look forward to it as much as I did as a human, and I can't wait for the sun to sweep me away and back into the mysterious realm that'll take all my suffering away.

A small tapping noise sounds on the door and a soft voice calls my name. "Can I come in?" Faith asks as she cracks the door only wide enough for her to talk to me without intruding on my space.

I wipe my hands across my cheeks and take a deep breath. "Yeah, come on in, Faith."

When Faith enters, she gazes around my neat room with an empty bookcase, a small sitting area, a flat-screen TV, and the four-poster bed with the sheer canopy I've tied up to get it out of the way. Everything in it is brand new and different than before—probably because I tore the place apart.

She pushes her blond hair behind her dainty ears with glittering diamond earrings as she pads across the soft white rug that covers most of the dark wooden floor. She's wearing the same clothes as yesterday, as am I, and I pat the spot next to me on the bed. I scoot over and cross my legs in front of me. Faith is the one person who doesn't stir a million rapid emotions within me. All I feel is happiness when she smiles, crinkling her blue eyes in the corners.

The bed bounces as she sits next to me. "My father went out with yours for a bit. He said it was okay to visit you."

I slide my arm around her back. "I'm glad you're here." I peek over at her. "As long as he didn't send you in to convince me to turn off my humanity."

She frowns. "Why would you want to do that?"

I release a long breath. "Glad you understand."

A silence falls between us, but it's not awkward or uncomfortable. It's just the two of us enjoying each other's presence.

Faith fiddles with the sleeve of her shirt and doesn't meet my eyes when she says, "I'm sorry about the man my dad killed. I'm not defending his actions, but I wanted you to know he didn't really want to kill him."

I sigh. She has no idea what Raphael was thinking. For all I know, he'd have killed David regardless of whether or not he tried to attack him. He could've controlled his power so the blow wasn't fatal. He didn't have to kill the man who raised Evan. The man who tried protecting me until he realized the truth. Maybe he saw my transformation before I could even fathom the possibility. Maybe David was really trying to save me.

I scratch the back of my head, messing with my dark hair. "I know," I say, instead of forcing my thoughts upon her. "I can't be mad that he killed David when David was trying to kill him...and me."

"My dad said you're a demon now," Faith says. "Are you okay?"

I shrug. "I don't know. I should be thankful I'm alive,

right?"

She nods. "I knew you would be. I could feel it. I have a sense for these things."

"I just—" I let my thought remain in my mind. Faith doesn't need me to drown her with my worries. She deserves to have a few more years to grow up like Alana had given me. *Alana...*

Curling her legs to her chest, Faith rests her chin on her knees. "I'm not a fragile little girl. You can talk to me, you know."

I grin at her words. She sounds like I did when I was her age. "I'm sorry. I was just thinking about my guardian."

"Alana," she says. "I met her. She talked about you and said how you attended the Hunter's Academy."

My mouth falls open for a moment. "Did she tell you how they sentenced me to death for something that was out of my control?" I pause when I see her eyes widen. "Never mind. That's in the past."

"It's okay to think about her," Faith says. "She was a nice lady."

Tears prickle my eyes. "She hates me now."

"It didn't sound like it," Faith says. "She was worried."

I press my lips together for a second and say, "David was her husband. Without me and Evan, she's all alone now."

"It doesn't have to be that way. I bet you can explain yourself to her. Families fight all the time. She'll forgive you."

Her idea is crazy, but maybe seeing Alana is what I need. Maybe reminding myself of my past will lessen the hurt I feel now.

I push from the bed. "Maybe you're right."

I cross my room and head to the door.

"Where are you going?" she asks.

I open the door and step into the hallway. "Tell my dad I'll be back. I need to face some of my own personal demons."

23

DEMONIC REALITY

I SNEAK OUT of the house without telling Evan where I'm going. The last thing I need is for him to try to stop me. He'd say I was making a mistake, and that I'm setting myself up for disaster—maybe I am—but I can't just keep going until I see Alana and apologize for last night. I need to be sure she'll be okay without me.

I race through the forest of trees peppering the property and head to the front gate that'll take me to a gravel road that leads to the street. It's a straight shot and much faster than having to travel around the perimeter of the property, jump a wall, and then trek through more forest to the main road.

Branches crack from behind me, and the scent of burning flesh catches on the wind, heading straight toward me. I freeze in place as the glow of the fiery skin of a hellhound slinks from behind a tree. The broken wolf doesn't growl or bark—it doesn't even move.

I take a step in the direction of my escape route. The hellhound follows my lead, trailing behind me but keeping enough distance to not intimidate me. After twenty feet of walking backward, facing the beast, I turn my back toward it to pick up my pace.

Glancing every so often over my shoulder, I watch the hellhound follow me up until I reach the wrought iron gate. The hellhound closes the distance between us when I hook my fingers on an iron bar toward the top to help propel myself over without a running start.

The broken wolf whimpers, and I pause, dangling from the gate, before descending back to my feet and next to the hellhound. It sits on its haunches and rubs its head on the side of my jeans, singeing the fabric enough to turn the blue color brown. I run my hand over the top of its head, staring into its burning, coal-like eyes. There's no saving this beast from its eternity at Malicevile's side, but maybe I can make its life a little better.

"You wanna go for a walk with me, boy?" I ask.

The beast growls.

"Girl?"

She whimpers and licks her black, slimy tongue across

my hand.

I wipe off the slime on my jeans before I crouch. "Come on. You can use my back to hop the gate."

Without a single ounce of hesitation, the broken wolf launches from my back and over the gate. I stumble under her weight, using my hands to stop from falling, and then I jerk my head up and watch the hellhound disappear into the trees.

"Whoops," I say out loud, my voice echoing through the quiet night.

I guess she didn't want to go for a walk with me. She must've only wanted to escape. I don't blame her. I levitate over the gate and land softly on the compacted gravel road. Without touching my boots to the ground, I glide just off the side of the road in case Malicevile comes down the road from wherever he and Raphael disappeared to.

After strolling for a mile, I reach the street and peer in both directions before crossing to the other side. It'll take at least an hour to get to Alana's, if she's even there. I hope she is.

Picking up the pace, I break out into a sprint and follow the road line. Running in the street is much faster than navigating the surrounding forest. I no longer have to worry about demons, so I couldn't care less if some poor human sees me. They'd probably head in the other direction anyway.

After keeping a steady pace for twenty minutes, I slow

down as I come to the intersection of a dead street. The light signal hums as the light changes from green to red, but I don't move from my spot.

Headlights illuminate the street as a truck barrels down the road in my direction. I duck behind a light pole, waiting for it to pass by, but then the light changes red. My stomach flips when I see a pair of hunters searching around the area from the truck.

I press my body to the pole, not because I'm afraid of the hunters, but because I don't feel like confronting them. Not while I'm on my way to Alana's. It's not like I have all day. I don't want to find out what happens if I'm away from Malicevile when the sun rises. I'll be alone in a mysterious world to fend for myself.

The light changes to green, and I relax as the truck lurches forward. When the hunters reach the end of the block, I slide from my spot and dash into the street. A flash of light zooms out from the shadows of the trees near the truck. The sound of screeching brakes rings through the air, and the scent of burning rubber hits me at the same time the smell of burning flesh does.

The hellhound that abandoned me at the front gate of Malicevile's property now races toward the truck. Its massive body stretches as it launches from the ground and lands on the roof. Vicious growls send chills down my back. Hellhounds are trained to protect their demonic masters. I'm not this broken wolf's owner, but she's sure treating me like one. I didn't realize she'd go after anyone in my vicinity. I regret ever letting her out.

I pray the hunters stay inside their vehicle, the thought really wrong in my mind. If they'd just drive, she'd leave them alone, and we could all be on our merry ways. Not all hunters like to deal with hellhounds—most don't—but there's always one.

The passenger's side door flings open.

I sigh. It just had to be this one.

My heart nearly explodes from my chest when I recognize the demi-demon who steps from the truck. It's been weeks since I've seen Jacie, and this was the last place I expected her to be. Jacie gave me a few lessons on how to handle my power. She's the one who told me what I was capable of. She was also a good friend of David's.

After the mess of a plan to break Faith out of the academy, I'm sure the alliance is down in numbers and has brought in hunters from the local areas. I left half a dozen people injured and David dead.

Electricity erupts in Jacie's hands as she confronts the hellhound. She has power similar to Malicevile's and is a great hunter. I wouldn't put it past her to hurt the poor broken wolf. *She's going to free its soul from the demonic bond by sending it to Hell.*

Pushing the nagging thought away, I pull up my hood from under my leather jacket to cover half my face. I used to think that killing hellhounds was a good thing, but a part of me doesn't want my new protector to die.

I straighten my shoulders and strut a few feet closer to the truck before stopping on the lane divider. Placing my hands on my hips, I release a loud whistle, drawing the attention of both Jacie and the hellhound. The beast is faster to return its attention to Jacie, and before she can launch her power, it jumps, knocking her back.

"No! Bad hellhound!" I scream. "Get back here."

I let out another whistle, pounding my boots against the pavement as I rush closer. Smoke rises from Jacie, who remains unmoving on the ground as the hellhound growls, baring its dagger-like teeth.

"Helena, girl, get over here and leave the poor hunter alone," I call. The name just came to me, and when the broken wolf snaps at Jacie once before retreating, I figure she must like the name, too. I pat my knees. "Come on, girl. You're going to get us in trouble."

My gaze darts to Jacie as she jumps to her feet and dusts herself off. Helena ambles her way back to me and circles around my legs before taking a seat at my side. I absently run my hand along her head as Jacie stands frozen next to the truck.

Run. Get out of here before she recognizes you.

I pull my hood lower and race away, cutting through the forest in case Jacie and her partner decide to circle back. If I'm not brave enough to face Jacie, how on earth am I going to show my face to Alana?

I consider turning around and heading home, but Helena whines from behind me when I stop and nudges me with her flaming muzzle.

The only way I can go now is forward.

My hands tremble as I reach the street that leads to Alana's. David's car is parked in the driveway and grief floods over me stronger than before. I reach over, using Helena to brace myself against, and she stiffens to hold my weight. A few minutes pass, and I don't move from my spot in the shadows between a tall hedge and a car parked for the night.

A light shines from the living room and a figure moves across the room. It's Alana. I could identify her unruly blond hair at a glance. Kneeling down to look the hellhound straight in the eyes, I say, "I want you to stay here. Do not, and I mean do not, go after anyone. You understand?"

She whimpers in response, and I take it as a yes when she doesn't move to follow me across the street.

The low hum of a TV sounds through the half opened window in the living room. Alana sits on the couch with her knees to her chest. Tears streak her pink cheeks, and a pile of used tissues scatter the spot next to her, the coffee table in front of her, and all over the floor. She silently cries, not even bothering to wipe her face anymore.

Tears burn in my eyes as I quietly watch her mourn the death of the husband she'd barely gotten back. She'd dropped everything and left him to run with me. She doesn't have to tell me again how much she regretted her decision to do so. I can feel her anguish radiating from her, burrowing deep into my now demonic soul.

I wipe my face on the sleeve of my jacket and clear my throat. "Alana," I say, my voice hoarse as I try to say something more but nothing comes out.

She jumps to her feet and stares through the sheer curtain covering the window. "Cami? Is that you?"

"Yes," I whisper.

She rushes to the door, flings it open, and before I have a chance to prepare myself, she charges me, flinging her arms around my shoulders. We fall to the grass as she clings to me, crying into my jacket and hair. Sobs rip from her mouth, and my own chest heaves as I start bawling my eyes out.

"Alana, I'm so sorry. I'm so, so sorry. I tried to save him. I tried with all my might, but the demon was just too fast." I sputter as the words tumble from my mouth. "He wasn't supposed to be there. Why did he go?"

Alana groans as she rolls off me. "I told him not to but seeing Evan threw him over the edge."

I sniffle. "He blamed me for everything."

She wipes the hair sticking to her cheeks from her face and squeezes my hand. "He was hurt that you left us, too."

I grimace through my tears. "I know. I'm sorry. But I'm here now."

She blinks the tears from her eyes as she pulls herself together. "How? Aston came by just after sunrise. Someone witnessed David stabbing you. They were sure it was fatal by how much blood was left behind."

I sit up on my elbows. How on earth am I going to explain my transformation to Alana?

A horn blares through the air, startling me, and I jump to my feet instead of trying to explain myself. Alana's already to hers as well.

When Jacie's truck screeches to a halt at the curb, she flies from the driver's side, her partner no longer with her. She waves her arms above her head, running toward us.

"Get inside!" she screams. "Hellhound!"

Before I have a chance to do anything, Alana hooks her arm with mine as Jacie rushes past us to open the door. She enters first with Alana behind her, yanking me so quickly that I can't even protest. Dread washes over me the closer I get to the threshold. Something deep within me screams out, begging me to turn around. Maybe I can't stand to be in that house any longer.

Alana gives me one more tug as she enters the house, and pain erupts through my whole body as a dazzling golden light shoots out and shocks me, leaving small burn marks across my hands. Hitting the blessed barrier was like hitting an electric fence, and there's no way I'll ever get past it.

Because I'm a demon.

I'm. A. Demon.

The thought hits me harder than before as I fall back and land on my butt on the cement path. Getting trapped in the sunlight prison felt surreal. It was almost unbelievable that I was a demon. But now, as I stare in shock at Alana and Jacie staring at me in horror from the protection of the blessed house, being a demon is utterly and tragically real.

"Cami," Alana whispers. "What's going on?"

I open and close my mouth a few times as I dig my fingers deep into the grass, looking for something to hold on to.

"I—I can't go inside." My chest heaves as I try to catch my breath. A low growl erupts from behind me. I turn and shake my head at Helena as she slinks back and forth on the sidewalk, just waiting for me to command her to attack.

Alana pales, and Jacie grabs hold of her before she drops to her knees. The demi-demon shoots me a curious look, but her eyes line with a disgust I've only ever seen a hunter have for a demon.

"The hellhound's yours?" Jacie asks. "That was you in the middle of the street on Breeze Hill?"

I force my head to nod even though I want to deny everything. "That was me, but the hellhound is Malicevile's. I didn't break the werewolf."

Alana listens quietly, her eyes shining with more tears. She swallows back a sob and says, "Are you what I think you are?"

I hold myself so I don't fall apart. "It's not what you

think. I'm still me. I still have a soul and my humanity."

"But you're a—you're a—" She presses her lips together for a moment and inhales a long breath through her nose. "Demon," she finally says.

I shrug, unable to deny it. "Looks like it."

DANCING WITH THE DEVIL

JACIE TUGS ALANA deeper into the house like I'll somehow manage to cross the barrier to destroy them both. My lips twist downward as I frown. Jacie knows me—Alana knows me—yet they stand there with terror-lined eyes like I'll drag them to Hell at any second.

I blink away oncoming tears. "I'm not going to hurt you. It's not like I chose this."

"How did this happen? It's not possible." Alana glances at Jacie like she has the answers.

Jacie wrings her hands together. "Come on, Alana. Shut the door. Don't let her fool you. She'll take your soul the moment she has the opportunity."

I glower at Jacie. "Stop it. You don't know anything. I don't even know how to take a soul. Even if I did, I'd never do that."

"She's lying," Jacie says.

Rage warms my skin as I stare at the demi-demon trying to ruin my relationship with Alana. How will I ever get Alana to listen to me and understand with Jacie around?

I ball my hands into fists at my sides while taking a slow, deep breath to calm my intense, unbidden emotions that feel a hundred times more powerful now that I'm dancing with the devil. Jacie stiffens as she studies me, stepping back again. An energy ball erupts in her fingers, and I eye the power glowing in her hands, wishing she'd throw it at me. I almost dare her to.

"Alana," I say, reverting my gaze back to my guardian. "I came here because I care about you. I wanted to be here for you because I know how much pain you're in. You're my family. Please, believe me."

Tears stream down Alana's face. "My family is dead." Her voice cracks as she says it. "My sister's dead because of demons. Evan's gone because of demons. David died by a demon's hands. And now, you're a demon. For the sake of my own soul, I need you to go, Cami. My family is all lost because of demons."

My lip quivers as I breathe a shallow breath. "Alana, no. Don't say that. Please."

"Listen to her," Jacie says.

My hair slaps my face as I shake my head. "No, you need to listen to me. None of this is my fault, and you know that demons are not fully responsible. Evan's gone because he felt he had to trade his soul for my life because the alliance leaders were going to kill me. David died because the alliance kidnapped Faith. And I'm a demon because the alliance made me who I am. They're the reason I'm Hell-bound. They're the reason I never had a chance. It's the alliance you should despise."

Alana's eyes narrow. "Spoken like a true demon." She steps to the edge of the threshold separating us. "Now leave, Cami. Leave before I call the alliance for back up. I can't see you like this anymore."

My heart shreds to pieces in my chest. The edges of my vision darken as her angry words set in. After all these years she spent protecting me. After all the times she vowed to protect me forever. After all the tragedy—after all the good times, too—Alana is turning her back on me. She's forsaken me because of the monster I've turned into all because I refused to die. My shock and hurt is too much to handle. I wish the sun would rise and take me away this second, but the night still grips the world for another few hours.

A million thoughts crowd my head as I think of something to say. If only I can reason with her, she'll listen to me and understand that I might be a demon, but I'm still Cami.

"Alana," I say again. No matter how many times I say

her name, I know she just won't listen. I have to try though. "Don't do this to me. I love you. I'd protect you with my last breath. Don't abandon me."

She strides from the house, crossing the protective barrier, and gets in my face. "I abandoned *you*? You're the one who ran off and left *me*. You chose to immerse yourself in the Veiled Realm among the demons. You knew exactly what you were doing and where you wanted to be."

I hold my face expressionless even though I want to break down and cry. So, I've made some mistakes. People make mistakes all the time. Maybe I should've left everything well enough alone, but how could I turn my back on a pack of werewolves that needed me? All of my dates with demons have been to help others.

I close my eyes after a moment so the world disappears and I don't have to gaze into Alana's accusatory eyes. "I'm sorry. I'm sorry I hurt you. I'm sorry Evan's gone and David's dead. I'm sorry you had to see me like this. If you really want me to go, I'll go. But I want you to remember something." I snap my eyes open. "You turned your back on me. When the world starts to burn around you, and you need someone to lean on, when you turn around, I won't be there. You'll be as alone as you feel. Because that's what you deserve."

Alana swings her hand out and slaps me across the face. My head jerks to the side, my hair whipping with the movement, and I raise my hand to cup my stinging cheek.

A low growl echoes from behind me as Helena lurches closer to go after Alana.

I raise my hand to the hellhound. "Stay back, Helena. I'm okay."

Alana screams as the hellhound retreats again and rushes me, slamming her hands into my chest to knock me off my feet. I levitate before I can fall and raise my arms to protect my face as she lashes out at me again.

"You monster!" she screams. "You won't be here because I'm going to send you where you belong!"

Alana slides a dagger from her sheath as she charges me, a darkness in her steel-gray eyes that I've never seen before. She swipes the knife out, aiming for my heart, but I jump out of the way and fly forward to grab her wrist. I squeeze as hard as I can, and she cries out, dropping the knife.

It doesn't stop her though. She rushes at me with her bare hands, and I swivel out of the way, keeping space between us. A blinding light soars in my direction as Jacie steps onto the porch to help Alana, and anger rolls over me as the demi-demon's power shocks me before I have a chance to absorb it.

She throws another energy ball, but this time I'm ready, and I allow the power to flow to my soul where I store it. The small distraction leaves me open, and Alana charges me again, knocking me off my feet with no time to levitate. My back hits the cement walkway hard enough to force the air from my lungs.

She laces her fingers around my neck and squeezes. While demons are immortal, they can still be sent back to Hell where they remain imprisoned for failing to do what they were supposed to do on earth. At least, that's what I've been taught by the people who really know nothing about demons. Who really knows what happens once a demon is destroyed. *Your father...*

But I'm not going to find out tonight.

I reach out and lock my fingers through Alana's hair and yank her head forehead, head-butting her. She wails as blood spurts from her forehead, a deep gash cutting across her once smooth skin. Fire and rage burn through me when I get to my feet. Steam wafts from my skin, and every single negative emotion that runs through me escalates, making it hard to think of anything good in my life.

Jacie throws another energy ball at me as I hover over Alana, standing tall because of my levitation. I glower down at her as she straightens her shoulders with the dagger I knocked from her moments ago now gripped in her hand.

I point my finger at her. "This needs to stop!"

Alana spreads her legs in a fighting stance. When she looks at me with her intense gaze, I can't help but despise her. I didn't want to have to hurt her. I didn't want to fight. I came here to console her, hoping to try to mend the tears in our relationship. What I found was a changed woman. One filled with so much anger and darkness, even a tainted soul looks good in comparison.

And then I see it.

Her beautiful, shining soul peeks out from her skin, glowing around her like a golden halo. Seeing a soul with my own eyes leaves me frozen in wonder. It's reminiscent of Dylan's ethereal wings, and all I want to do is reach out to touch it.

Jacie hits me with another blast of electricity, but I don't waver. I can't turn my eyes away from Alana's beautiful soul. Small shadows streak through its golden color like black fissures threatening to break it apart. I imagine breaking it apart piece by piece to carry a bit with me.

My hand reaches out idly, almost as if it has a mind of its own, and I crave to touch Alana's soul. I can't stop myself.

Alana stands frozen as my fingers brush her chin.

"It's so beautiful," I say.

"Alana," Jacie says, fear shaking her voice. "Get back."

Alana doesn't move. She just stares at me in shock and awe.

As I reach out my other hand to cup Alana's face, Jacie rushes forward, smashing into my side, breaking my concentration. Alana's soul disappears from sight, and a rage like nothing I've ever felt before courses through my veins. I clench my fingers while summoning the power Jacie had thrown at me. I roar as I throw it in the demi-demon's direction. It's enough to rock her backward in surprise, and she stumbles.

"How dare you!" I scream.

The sound of my voice pulls Alana out of her trance, and she races toward me, dagger raised to stab, and all I can think about is her soul and how much I want it. I meet Alana head on, rip the dagger from her hand, and throw it at Jacie before she can manage to launch another bout of power at me. The blade sinks deep into her shoulder, and she cries out, hitting her back on the side of the house.

I turn my blood-tinted vision to Alana, my teeth clenched so hard together that I'm sure they'll break at any second. I open my palm and blast a small amount of electricity at her, and her eyes widen as she's shocked.

She drops to her knees, but I don't let go of her. I clamp my fingers to her shoulders, stopping her from wobbling, and burn my heated gaze into her. Her bottom lip quivers in fear as she shuts her eyes so she doesn't have to meet my gaze.

"This ends here, Alana. If you can't accept what I am, then so be it. But I'm not letting you go back to the alliance so you can gather others to hunt me down." I shake her until she opens her eyes. "Do you understand?"

"Yes," she whispers. "Do it quickly."

An eerie calm falls over me. "I'm not going to kill you. I have a better idea. I want to make a deal. I'll spare your life if you keep my secret. The alliance cannot know about me," I say.

"You're going to let me live?" she asks in a whisper.

I nod. "Yes. But remember my words. If you tell anyone about my transformation, I won't only kill you. I'll take your soul. Do we have a deal?"

Her face contorts as she grimaces. "No."

"Make the deal, Alana," I say, moving my hands from her shoulders to her neck. It'd be so easy to snuff her life from her.

"I can't."

With her words, I squeeze, watching as the light dims in her steely eyes. Tears pour down my cheeks as I steal the life from the woman who had done everything to protect me from this fate. But it has to be done. I can't risk the alliance coming after me. I need to protect myself.

"Cami, no," a smooth voice says from near the street. "This isn't you. Fight it, love."

I lessen my grip as the familiar voice wraps around me. Jerking my head up, I catch my reflection in the window. My green eyes reflect like cat eyes, and a faint orange sheen coats my skin, like fire burns within my veins. A crown of tiny horns juts from my forehead, hiding beneath my wild curls, and I reach up and run my sharp nailed fingers over them. It's enough to send me reeling back and away from Alana.

"Run!" I scream. "Get inside and stay there!"

Without hesitating, Alana jumps to her feet and races toward Jacie, grabbing her from the ground and tugging her inside.

My breathing quickens as I suck in rapid breaths to control the demon that has finally shown itself. It no longer slithers within me, coiling around my heart, squeezing my soul. It peeks through my very flesh, waiting to consume everything human that was left of me.

"Cami, it's going to be okay," Dylan says.

I swivel on my feet to face him. He flies twenty feet in the air right above Helena as she growls below him. Something about him has changed. His usual translucent wings shine so brightly that they sting my eyes. I shade my vision so I can stare up into his dark eyes. *He hasn't changed. You have.*

I levitate a few feet in the air, but I can't get close enough to meet him on his level. I can only get so high. "How? Look at me! I'm a demon!"

His eyebrows lower over his eyes as pain crosses his face. He feels what I'm feeling, being one of the few people who truly understands me. He descends a little, but I wave my hands, needing him to stay back.

"Please, let me look at you, love. You don't scare me. I know you're still you, Cami. No one, not even Hell, can take that away," he says. He offers out his hand. "Now come with me. We can figure this out."

I close my eyes and hold up my hand. When our fingers touch, a pain so intense it takes my breath away consumes me to my soul. It's like I can feel all the sharp edges of every broken piece of myself, and the pain begs to take control. It wants to steal everything else away from me. But I can't let it.

I jerk my hand away. "Stop."

"It has to hurt, love. Pain and relief, grief and happiness, anger and bliss, hate and love—you need to hold onto them. You need to feel them with your entire being. It's the only way to fight the darkness," he says. "You're strong, Cami. You can do this. You need to awaken your soul so it remembers what you are." He waves his hand at me. "This—this isn't you."

He jets his hand out to grab me again, but I drop to the ground. I whistle for Helena to come to my side. Dylan wouldn't dare try to touch me again with a hellhound protecting me.

"You're wrong. This is me. I'm a demon, and it's how things were always supposed to be." Without another word, I turn away from my guardian angel and stroll into the dark night.

I don't look back.

SURVIVING ETERNITY

AS I CUT across Breeze Hill, I don't bother to hide in the shadows. I meander down the center of the street, my boots straddling the center stripes, and count each road reflector I pass. The long walk in the cool air helps clear my mind. It took everything in me to walk away from the people I love, knowing how much I broke their hearts. Alana is completely lost to me. Whatever relationship we had has burned to dust like everything else in my life. Unlike a phoenix rising from the ashes, the remnants of my life and who I was float away on a breeze, slipping from my fingers.

Helena whimpers next to me, her fiery coat lighting our way when the streetlamps thin out as we turn onto the

314

road that'll take us home. I haven't seen a single vehicle since I left Alana's and wonder if she decided against telling the Hunter's Alliance about what happened to me. I've been expecting a team to show up at any second, but I remain alone with my thoughts. Maybe Dylan advised her otherwise. Maybe now that I'm a demon, she'll actually listen to Angel Boy.

A familiar gray Maserati flashes its headlights at me as it speeds down the road. I don't move from the center of the street, and the car stops short, blinding me. Malicevile swings his door open and stands, keeping one of his legs inside.

"Get in the car, Camilla," he says. "We have to go. Sunrise is upon us and we must leave the area."

My face scrunches in confusion. "What? Why?"

He waves me forward. "We'll discuss things in the car. Now hurry."

Just as I take a step forward, a gunshot rings out. Malicevile ducks as it flies over his head, and I stumble before seeing a hunter aiming a gun from a dark car without headlights on. I bend forward and jog to the car. Another shot rings out, and I scream as a bullet clips my shoulder. Evan flings the door open and yanks me into his lap.

Malicevile stomps the throttle before I have a chance to close the door, and the acceleration shuts it for me. I cringe as my skin sizzles where the bullet grazed me. Malicevile yanks the sleeve of my jacket, pulling me close so he can inspect my wound while racing down the empty stretch of road, only steering with one hand.

"That's not going to heal until sunrise. The bullet was blessed," he says.

My eyes widen, and I lean my head back on Evan who rests his hands on my stomach without saying a word. It takes me a minute to realize that Faith and Raphael are sitting together in the back. Faith's eyes shine red from tears, and Raphael sits sullenly, peering out the window like someone took away his favorite toy.

Evan presses his lips into a thin line, his jaw tight enough to even give me a toothache, and a flash of fire draws my attention out the back window.

My stomach clenches when I spot Helena racing after us by foot, falling farther and farther behind. "Dad, you have to stop. Helena is back there. We can't leave her behind."

He shifts his gaze to the rearview mirror. "You named the hound?"

"You didn't?" I ask.

He shakes his head. "Of course not. And we're not stopping. If she's fit to be by our sides, she'll survive on her own and return to us."

"Please, I don't want her to die," I beg.

He doesn't stop. Instead he raises an eyebrow and says, "If we stop, the hunters will catch up. That'll put Faith at risk if it happens at sunrise. You don't want her to be taken again, do you? And besides, I thought you were against hellhounds."

I gulp a breath to calm my nerves. "I can't believe we're running from hunters," I say, ignoring his remark about the hellhounds. I am against them, but it doesn't mean I want Helena to die. "What happened to my all-powerful demon father?"

"I've managed to survive all these years because I know when to back down. You can't honestly think you can fight off an entire army? That's not how we work. Yes, it's occasionally fun to spar a hunter but seeking them out to fight? We have people for that. There are so many better things for us to do." He doesn't signal when he drifts right, fishtailing onto the street that will lead to the freeway.

"So you just abandon your house and let them win?" I don't know why I ask. It's not the first time he gave up that house.

He sighs. "You ask a lot of questions, but none of them are the right ones."

"Like?"

"Like why would the alliance send an army of hunters to our door?"

Oh. That. It's not my questions he wants to answer. He wants to know what the heck happened. I clear my throat, rubbing my hands on my dirty knees. I guess Alana did tell the alliance after all. Instead of hunting me down directly, they went after my father. The only way they knew about his house was because I told Alana about it when Evan traded his soul. I should've known she'd use that information against me.

I lean my head against the cold window. "I saw Alana," I say. "I went over there to make amends."

"And?"

"It didn't go so well."

"I see."

I expect him to tell me that I was an idiot, that I put us all in danger, and that I need to accept who I am and forget about my past and everyone who was a part of it. I expect him to yell and make me feel tiny. I expect a lot of harsh things—I deserve it—but he doesn't say anything else.

I slouch against Evan, pulling my knees to my chest. "I saw her soul. I never wanted anything so badly."

He tilts his head slightly. "Really?"

I frown. "Why do you sound so surprised."

"Because that means your former guardian is no longer pure. Demons can only see the souls of the corrupt. Unless a pure soul seeks us out for a negotiation, they're off limits. Alana's soul is now free for the taking."

Dread trickles down my back. "No, she's not," I say. "I won't allow it."

"She sent an army after us. Why do you still feel the need to protect her?" he asks.

Tears line my eyes. He's right. I shouldn't feel like I owe Alana anything, but just the thought of her soul ending up in the hands of a demon—my father—pains me to my core. That's the last thing I want to see.

"She started a war, Cami," Evan says, speaking up. "She brought this on herself."

I clench my fingers into fists. "This isn't a discussion. My word is final. Alana is mine."

Neither my father nor Evan argues. There's nothing either of them can say to change my mind. It's the least I can do for Alana no matter how hurt and angry I am at her.

I shift uncomfortably in Evan's lap and stare out the windshield as we speed down the freeway. All I can think of is surviving the night, but a more prominent question settles in my mind.

How am I going to survive all eternity?

<hr>

Raphael's beach fortress is a lot less ominous and terrifying when I enter through the front door. His dress shoes snap against the tile as he waves his arm around the elegant foyer with gleaming marble floors and a sparkling light fixture above us.

The weapons of dead hunters don't sink my heart into my stomach either. It's one less person I have to worry about and one less weapon to hurt me like the blessed bullet that grazed my shoulder, leaving me with an annoying burning sensation I'm not used to, considering I don't feel the heat of fire at all.

"Evan, I need you to patrol the area for signs of the alliance," Malicevile says, handing Evan his car keys.

Evan nods his head and turns to go.

I saunter next to him. "I want to go, too."

"Absolutely not. Haven't you caused enough trouble?" Malicevile asks from behind me.

I spin around. "Hey! All this trouble was to save Faith. I'm sorry if I don't want to hide in some fortress like a fragile princess. I want to help."

"You can help by staying with Faith, Camilla...princess," he says. His words lace with a mixture of sarcasm, annoyance, and command.

I grind my teeth. With the sunrise upon us, I have a few more things I need to do before I'm trapped for another half-day. Malicevile should know by now that I'm not one to take orders, especially from him, unless I'm obligated by a demonic deal. I'm practically an adult and have been treated like one for a while. I don't need Malicevile's parental guidance. *Maybe just a little demonic guidance...*

"I'm not her babysitter," I half-whisper, half-hiss. "Isn't that what minions are for?"

He scoffs. "You killed the help."

I roll my eyes. "Not my problem." Without another word, I hook my arm through Evan's and pull him toward the door.

"Camilla, get back here!" he yells, his voice bouncing off the vaulted ceiling.

I ignore him.

"Camilla!"

A blast of power knocks me off my feet, sending me sprawling to the marble floor. Evan continues striding to the door, leaving me to face the wrath of my demonic father alone. I glare through my tears as he exits, leaving the door open behind him.

I can't believe he left me. He should've stood up for me, or at least stopped to make sure I was okay. I flip over to face my father in time to see him gathering another ball of energy in his hands.

I scramble back, not because I'm afraid of being blasted, but because if he closes the distance between us, he could easily physically restrain me.

As I reach the threshold, Malicevile chucks his power at me. I catch it, but the force knocks me back again. I somersault out the door and back on my feet on the porch. Evan revs the engine from the driveway, and I glance once at Malicevile's raging eyes as I race to the car and hop in the backseat because I'm afraid running around front would take too long.

"Drive!" I scream even though Evan's already reversing.

Glancing out the rear window, I watch as my father punches the air in our direction all the while kicking the ground like some angry toddler. He doesn't follow though, and when we reach the main street, I release a long breath.

I sling on my seatbelt and sit up straighter. "Thanks a lot for not standing up for me."

Evan's jaw twitches. "What'd you want me to do? He's your father. Only you can pull shit like that and get away with it. I'll be lucky if he doesn't kill me when we get back for waiting in the driveway."

Fear fills my heart. "He wouldn't."

Evan brushes his hand through his blond hair. "He would. He'd do it to get to you. Did you know he and Raphael were discussing ways to get you to turn off your humanity? Malicevile has plans for you."

I scrunch my brows together. "What? He's crazy."

Evan turns right to make his way toward Beach Way, which runs along the ocean. "Is he? Don't you get it, Cami? You were a demi-demon who transformed into a demon. Other demons are going to want to know how. They're going to want help and will pay big. You know demons don't usually band together, but look how Raphael and Malicevile are now working together without paying each other off. They're doing it for the good of both you and Faith. Things are going to shift. Taking control of the human world will come sooner than anyone thought."

My mouth goes dry as I try to process his words. Demons already have the upper hand in the world. I can't imagine what it'll be like if my father got his way. *Why do you even care?*

The question swirls around my mind as I try to think of a million reasons why I care so much about the people who've turned against me. Why should I fight for humans?

Even the one closest to my heart wants me dead. Alana will never see past me being a demon.

"Can I use your phone?" I ask. I'm desperate for some advice and guidance, and there's only one person left that I haven't seen.

Evan hands me his phone.

I dial one of the few numbers I have memorized, but it goes to voicemail. I squeeze my teary eyes shut and when the line beeps for me to leave a message, I say, "I hope you're still in town. I'm sorry for how we left things. Can we talk? I'll be on the beach outside the safe house until sunrise."

I set the phone in the cup holder. "Can you drop me off at the next corner?" I ask.

Evan grips the steering wheel. "I can come with you."

I shake my head. "I need to do this alone."

Without arguing, he pulls the car to the curb, and I hop out.

I don't look back as I stroll down to the sand. If Cadence doesn't show, I don't know what I'll do. I don't even know what I'll do if she does show.

AS THE WORLD CHANGES

A SLENDER FIGURE stands down the beach, away from the safe house, staring into the roaring dark ocean. Cadence's purple hair looks black in the night, and her hips sparkle with the hilts of several daggers.

She doesn't move as a wave washes around her feet, drawing her closer to the ominous ocean. The moon casts a sparkling glow on the water, and I wish I could follow the silver path away from here.

"Cadence," I say, my voice cracking.

My best friend turns to me, her black mascara streaking her face, and then she pulls a dagger from her belt.

My heart sinks, and I freeze. Raising my hands up in

surrender, I do my best to plead with my eyes. Cadence doesn't look like the fierce hunter I know her to be. Her puffy eyes and slumped shoulders make her look defeated. My heart aches for her the longer we share a quiet gaze.

"I guess you heard the news," I say. "But please, I need you. You're my best friend. I'm not some heartless monster. I still have my humanity. Don't turn your back on me like everyone else."

She sheaths her dagger after hearing my words and rushes to me. We embrace each other, crying into each other's shoulders, and I never knew I could feel such relief.

She pulls away, her eyes turning angry. Her fingers clamp my shoulders and she shakes me. "I'm so angry with you, Cami. Do you know what you've put me through? First I find out you've died, then my dad calls me and tells me you're alive, and then he breaks the news that you're a full-blown demon."

I sigh. "It's unbelievable, isn't it?"

She shakes her head. "What's unbelievable is that you didn't call me once in the last twenty-four hours, and Angel Boy abandoned me here with the pack."

I kick my boot through the sand. "I'm so sorry. The daylight prison realm doesn't exactly have cell reception, and I've been on the run since Alana tried to murder me. I shouldn't even be here, you know. Malicevile might come looking. He's turned into an overprotective father."

"So you're staying with him?" she asks.

"What else am I supposed to do? He's one of the few not trying to send me back to Hell," I say.

Her perfect brows arch. "Back?" She licks her lips. "Never mind, I don't want to think about that. But you should know I'm not trying to kill you. We can run."

She's offering me the same out that Dylan had when he tried to get to my soul through my demonic exterior. The pain of him touching me was unbearable, and I can't imagine ever going through that again. But with Cadence it's different. She's human. She can't hurt me the way Dylan did.

Then the memory of Alana's soul flashes in my mind, reminding me exactly what I am. Stepping away from my best friend, I swipe my hair from my face and peer at the shining stars overhead. "As much as I want to run with you, Cadence, I can't. I'd be putting you in danger."

She rolls her eyes. "I'm not afraid of the alliance. They can kiss my ass. They've been nothing but trouble, and I told my dad that."

I wring my hands together. "It's not the alliance I'm afraid of for you. It's the entire demonic world. I'm a demon. I could accidentally claim your soul."

She places her hands on her hips. "I'm not afraid of any demon—especially not you."

I rub my lips together without saying a word. There's no point in arguing. She'll have a reason to dispute my excuses or fears regardless. Cadence, like me, likes to do things her way without other people trying to influence her.

"Plus, we can't leave Dylan behind. He'd watch out for me if you went a little devilish. You were wrong about him not wanting to be with you because of it, you know?"

She smirks, and I can't help the smile that creeps on my face. It's always like her to say something ridiculous at a time when the world seems so bleak. She's the one to not only laugh in the face of danger, but also make fun of it.

I almost consider her makeshift plan. It's not like our lives will revolve around worrying about finding a safe house that'll take us in, not when I can't cross a blessed threshold. But something inside me stops me from agreeing.

I pout my lip. "Cadence."

She glares at me. "Don't say it. Just agree with me, and I'll go back inside, grab my bag, and we can go."

"What about the daytime?" I ask.

She purses her lips. "We'll figure it out."

"I can't do this."

"Cami, please."

I close my eyes for a second, wishing for her to understand. When I open my eyes, dread sinks into my stomach, and I take an automatic step back.

Joshua, followed by his entire pack, steps onto the back patio and leaves the safety of the blessed house. They trudge through the sand in our direction, weapons and teeth shining in the night, their expressions fearless. It's rare to see werewolves so confident after sundown, but maybe they don't realize what's happened to me. They should be shaking.

"You're no longer welcome here, Cami," Joshua says. "I have to ask you to leave. If you do not, I can guarantee that we'll make you."

Cadence raises her hand, palm out, toward the pack. "She's okay. She's not a threat. Give us ten minutes, and we'll both go."

"You're not going with that demon," Joshua says. "I promised your father. He promised my pack protection in return."

Cadence gasps and pulls a blade from her belt. "Stay back."

Joshua doesn't stop. He picks up his pace, his pack at his back, and he rushes forward. I step in front of Cadence, electricity igniting in my hands, and it's enough to halt the charging werewolves in their tracks.

"I don't want to hurt you," I say. "I'm not your enemy."

"Then tell your friend to come back to us and go on your way," Joshua says.

I've never felt so alone in my life. How could the whole world I fought so hard to stay in, the world I cherished and loved, turn against me? Cadence clearly doesn't want to go with the pack, and I can't make her, but I don't want to fight these men and women either.

"Cadence," I say quietly. "I don't want to fight them."

"Cami, we can—"

Before she has a chance to finish her sentence, a werewolf with brooding good looks, muscular arms, and a vicious smile charges forward and wraps his arms around Cadence. His sheer size is enough to prevent her from fighting as he drags her back. She thrashes like a fish on dry land, but it does nothing to loosen the werewolf's grip.

Someone smashes into me from the side, tearing my attention away from Cadence as she screams, and I collide with the sand. A hard fist hits me in the cheek, sending pain exploding through my face and head. I dig my fingers into the man and jolt him with a burst of energy.

He howls as he rolls off me, scuttling to his feet, and another firm hand grabs me by the shoulders, digging long nails into the wound where the bullet grazed me. As much as I want to electrocute this werewolf, something holds me back. I can't show them my demon self. I can't hurt them. Because if I do, I'm not so sure I could live with my humanity for much longer. The last thing I need is to be tempted to turn it off.

"Get off me!" I scream.

As my hands push against the werewolf, a ball of fire blasts above me, catching the man's shirt on fire. He hollers as he hits the sand, rolling around to put out the flames. It doesn't take long for the rest of the pack to join in the fight. I watch in horror as Joshua rushes Evan alongside another werewolf I didn't care to learn the name of, with a gun raised.

If he shoots him, Evan will die. If he dies, there will be no saving his soul.

I gather an energy orb in my fingers and toss it at the two werewolves, knocking them off their feet. Evan offers me a dazzling smile, but I can't share in his excitement. I can't smile and watch as these werewolves fall by our hands.

A woman collides with me, tangling her fingers in my hair, catching me before I hit the sand. She snarls in my ear while jerking my head back, and a sparkle of light glints off the blade she holds to my neck.

I close my eyes and wait for the sting of the blade, but it doesn't come. A low growl echoes through the night, and I can't stop from opening my eyes. A black-coated wolf kicks up dirt as it charges my way. The woman squeezes me tighter, laughing in my ear, as I stare in horror as the wolf opens its mouth, flashing its sharp teeth, and prepares to launch at my chest.

Instead of hitting me, the wolf jumps past the woman and bites her on the back of the knee. Her legs buckle under her, sending her sprawling into the sand, and it gives me enough time to rush back, pulling Evan with me.

The wolf stands between us and the rest of his pack, and I see Cadence cry as a man holds her over his shoulder while taking her to the house. They pass the threshold, and I clench my fingers at my sides. I can't save her. I can't even get in the door.

The transformed wolf growls and snaps his teeth, and the pack steps back. His bones crack as he snarls while making the transformation back to his human form. Standing naked before me is the boy—Greg—that I saved from Malicevile the night of our dinner date. He turned on his own pack to protect me, and I don't think I can ever repay him.

"You stand against your own pack for a demon?" Joshua asks as he recovers from the burst of energy I sent his way. His deep voice echoes through the night, stirring something strange within me.

Greg crosses his arms over his chest, not caring that he's naked and facing a whole lot of trouble. "She saved my life. I won't let you end hers. So, yes, I stand by her."

The sound of the ocean disappears, leaving me in utter silence. Something dark crashes through me, and a bright light erupts from my fingers, setting the dark night aglow. Greg spins on his heels to face me, surprise and wonder in his eyes, and he reaches out his hand like he's caught in a trance.

When our fingers touch, his expression morphs from awe to horror, and fire explodes from his core, sweeping over his skin, leaving black slime in its place. He falls to the ground, his back arching while his screams turn to into whimpers as he loses his humanity and breaks under my demonic influence.

My mouth falls open in surprise as I stare at the flaming hellhound before me. Greg growls and snaps at his pack, charging at them until they flee back to the safety of their blessed house.

My heart slams against my ribcage as the hellhound—Greg—returns to my side and sits back on his haunches. My breathing quickens as his coal-like eyes stare at me. I can't believe this happened. I broke a werewolf and transformed him into my own pet—a guard against those who threatened me.

I rub my hands into my eyes. "No. Please, God. What have I done? No. No. No."

I tilt my head to the sky, praying for an answer, but nothing happens. And this time, it's different. The response isn't someone who's quietly listening—it's a void. An absence that burrows deep into my heart and soul.

I tug at my hair and scream at the dark ocean as regret and grief engulf me, along with an emptiness so bleak it threatens to destroy me.

Evan wraps his arms around me, pulling me to him. The world feels so wrong. I know I don't belong here anymore.

"Cami, turn it off. You have to let it go," Evan whispers. "Don't let your humanity control you. Please, I can't stand to see you in pain. I'd give anything to change things—to turn back time to the way things were—but I can't. You have to turn it off. I can't lose you."

"Look what I've done!" I scream, waving my arm at the

hellhound. "I can't live with myself."

"Then turn it off," he says into my ear. "Let it all go."

His eyes shine when I meet his gaze. I could lose myself in their endless blue depths. In this moment, I know Evan isn't asking me to shut off my humanity because he wants me to be the demon I'm supposed to be. He wants me to shut it off to save myself from all the pain and horror that being what I am brings.

And he's right. I can't do this anymore.

Closing my eyes, I suppress every emotion within me. I gather all the pain and grief—the love, the hate, the happiness, the anger—I take it all and shove it into an imaginary box and lock it up tight in my soul.

A sweet, comforting calmness washes over me when I open my eyes. The world changes right before me, and I now see it for what it is—a place I have to take and make my own. The people who want to destroy me only do so because they crave what everyone craves deep down—control and power. And now, I have it all.

No one can stand in my way.

I shift my gaze to Evan as he rights me on my feet. Running my fingers up his arms and over his shoulder, I lean up on my tiptoes and brush my lips against his. He devours my kiss, pulling me closer, taking me into his arms, showering me with a need so intense, I want nothing more than to give him what he wants. Because I want it, too.

I tilt my head back to gaze up as the sky lightens above

us. "Let's get out of here."

He takes my hand in his and guides me down the beach. My new hellhound saunters behind us, and I smile at his loyalty. I don't know why I was so upset. Greg chose to be by my side. He chose to protect me and now he will forever.

I glance over my shoulder one last time, catching sight of Cadence hovering on the patio of the beach house. She raises her hands, waving me down, but I just turn my back on her. She doesn't want me to reach my full potential now. She wants to run.

And I don't.

I'm ready to be who I am. Without my past holding me back, I'm finally free. Being a demon isn't as bad as I thought. It's better than I could've ever imagined.

The world is there for my taking, and I'll enjoy claiming every single piece of it.

LOST FOREVER

BRIGHT SUNSHINE STINGS my eyes as I peer around a decaying garden overrun with weeds and dead plants. The air permeates with the scent of fresh apple, and if I couldn't see the sky, I'd think it had just rained.

Running my fingers over a dead rose bush, I pluck a dried rose, now blackened with time, and cup it in my hand.

One moment I was sparring with my father, and in the next, I woke up here. The sunrise isn't for another few hours, so I must be dreaming. I forgot what it felt like—to dream. The only time I ever really close my eyes is when I'm dying of sheer boredom as Malicevile tries to teach me something about demonic hierarchy and how I must act when I'm allowed to follow him to "business meetings."

It's only been a dozen nights since I turned my back on my humanity, but it feels like it's been forever. I don't even remember what it feels like to care anymore. The only feelings I allow into my Hell-bound heart are the ones that make me feel utterly alive. And Evan does that to me every time I appear back in the human world. I can always count on him no matter what.

I thought I'd change the moment I turned everything off, and I did in a way. I'm a hundred times better. I'm stronger, more in control, and my bond to both Evan and Malicevile has grown so strong, I'd kill for either of them. I'd die for them, too, but that isn't happening. I'd say I'd feel bad for the poor soul who tried, but I'd like to see how it works out for them.

"Cami," a smooth voice whispers from behind me.

I crumble the dried rose petals in my fingers and scatter them across the dead grass beneath my feet. "I should've known you'd show up." I swivel on my feet to face Dylan. I haven't seen him since he tried to mend my soul at Alana's—which didn't work because I wasn't broken.

"I've been looking everywhere for you, love. I can't visit your dreams if you never sleep. I thought I'd lost you forever." He strolls forward, eyeing me as he draws near like I'll suddenly lash out at him.

I stiffen when he reaches out and touches my chin, tilting my face so I have to look into his eyes. I bat his hand away and cross my arms over my chest. "You can't do that anymore," I say. "I don't want you here."

He cringes at my words, tears shining in his eyes. I never thought I'd see the day when an angel—nephilim—cried on my behalf. The gesture pokes something deep within me, threatening to awaken the humanity I keep locked away. My father warned me this could happen. Dylan puts my whole world at risk.

"That's not you talking," he says, stepping closer while I step back.

I smirk. "Sure sounds like me." I reach out and grab another dead rose and smash it between my hands. "And I meant what I said. You need to leave. You were right to think you lost me forever. Let's keep it that way."

His face falls as I turn my back on him. If he won't leave my dream, I won't acknowledge his existence, and he might give up.

Soft footsteps sound from behind me, and I ignore them until Dylan's hands grab onto my shoulders and spin me around. Before I have a chance to protest, he leans down, presses his lips to mine and embraces me in a hug.

I stand frozen, feeling the softness of Dylan's lips against mine, the coolness of his hands as they cup my face. My heart races as I sink into him, the faint memory of my love for my Angel Boy stirring in the back of my mind, begging for my full attention.

I stiffen in his embrace when his wings expand on his back, their ethereal light outshining the sun in my dream world, blinding me as I pull away from Dylan's loving kiss. Sheer pain explodes through me as he wraps me in their heavenly light, and I scream as they sear the bare skin of my arms.

With all my strength, I push Dylan back. He stumbles, catching himself before he hits the ground.

"What in the Hell are you doing?" I glare as he straightens his shoulders.

"I'm saving you, Cami. You have to let me in," he says. "You felt something, didn't you? I know you still love me somewhere deep in your soul. That armor you've built around you isn't saving you. It's imprisoning you."

I hold my hand up. "I don't need to be saved!" My voice echoes through the air. "Now get out of here. Save your love for someone who cares."

The world shakes around us, and when the ground splits, I jump feet first into the void. Whatever Dylan did to me was enough to fissure the wall protecting me, and I imagine building my armor twice as thick until the faint memory of how I felt about him disappears altogether.

I snap my eyes open and vault to my feet. Electricity erupts in my palms, and I spin around.

"Welcome back, Sleeping Beauty," Malicevile says, resting his elbows on the empty reception counter of the gym. "I thought you'd be out until dawn."

I growl as I throw an energy ball at him, but he catches it easily enough. "I told you to stop." I couldn't hold anymore demonic power within me even if I tried. Static clings to my clothes, my curly hair flying around my face.

"You need to be prepared, Camilla. I can't take any chances." He waltzes forward, closing the distance.

Rolling up my sleeves, I notice puckering black skin in the shape of feathers running from my wrists to my elbows. I'm sure they continue up my arms to my back. Not only did Dylan nearly burn me alive in my dream world with his heavenly grace, he managed to get to me in the physical world.

I crinkle my nose and pull my sleeves down before my father can see. I'm in no mood for an angel hunt even though Dylan deserves to face my wrath in the physical world. Being near him leaves me vulnerable and weak. I'm a demon now. Those feelings are unacceptable, as Malicevile would say.

"Think you're feeling strong enough to run an errand for me?" he asks, sliding his arm over my shoulder, drawing my attention away from my thoughts. He pauses for a second, sniffing the air, but doesn't say anything.

I bob my head, keeping my face straight despite the eagerness to get out of the gym to have a little bit of fun. "Definitely."

"I want you to take Evan."

I don't argue. I had planned on taking him regardless.

Reaching into his pocket, he pulls out a slip of paper and hands it to me. I stare at his beautiful calligraphy handwriting, one of the only things I'm jealous that he didn't pass on to me. The note contains the name and a nearby address of a man I've never met.

"You're letting me meet another demon alone?" I ask, my eyes widening. It'd be the first of many promised introductions.

He laughs. "No, definitely not tonight or alone. This, my dear, is the name of a man who owes me his soul. I want you to make the collection and bring him in."

My lips form an O-shape. "I see. Sure, I can handle it."

"I know." He kisses the top of my head before nudging me to the door. "And if you hurry, I'll let you have the rest of the night to yourself."

I beam my best smile. "You're the best. I won't disappoint you."

I rush toward the door, pulling my bag from the floor as I push the door open. Evan steps from his place against the wall, closing the distance between us. I kiss him while dragging him with me toward the parking lot. The cool night air clings to my hot skin, sending steam misting through the air.

"Camilla?" my father says from the doorway as we race to my convertible Mustang.

"Yeah?"

"Watch your back tonight. The alliance is out in full

force."

I click my key fob, and the lights to my Mustang blink as the alarm turns off. Evan opens the door for me, and I turn to Malicevile. "Good," I say, grinning. "Maybe I won't bring back only one soul tonight. Maybe I'll make it two."

With the alliance doubling their hunters, we've been doubling our own army with all the tainted souls we can manage. It was a lot easier than I thought. All it takes is a little nudge to the side of evil to darken a person's thoughts enough to bargain for their souls.

Hunters are no different. They're not above anyone. They're just human.

If the alliance wants a war, they'll have one. I won't stop until every single last one of them begs for me to spare their lives. And then, I'll take their souls.

To be continued...

ACKNOWLEDGMENTS

MANY THANKS TO my editorial team, whose knowledge and guidance have turned Haunted into the book I imagined. Jan, Katie, and Jamie, you all have helped me so much, and I'm forever grateful.

I also want to thank Nikki Godwin and Courtney Whittamore for befriending me and offering me moral support when I need it. With you two, this writing journey is a lot less lonely. You're awesome!

Thanks to Jaz, whose sassiness and devotion I used to mold Cadence into the best BFF ever to Cami. Your enthusiasm and love for me help me get through the tough times. Thanks for always being here for me and for letting me send you thousands of snaps of my manuscripts as I write.

As always, thanks to my family, who have been so supportive of all my endeavors. You guys mean the world to me.

And lastly, thanks to those who have showed such enthusiasm for the *Demon Within* series and the rest of my books. Thank you for sharing your thoughts with me and for also reviewing. Thanks for sharing with me whose team you're on and how much you relate to Cami. And mostly, thanks for reading! You're why I've decided to share these characters with the world.

GINNA MORAN IS a writer from sunny Southern California. She started writing poetry as a teenager in a spiral notebook that she still has tucked away on her desk today. Her love of writing grew after she graduated high school, and she completed her first unpublished manuscript at age eighteen.

When she realized her love of writing was her life's passion, she studied literature at Mira Costa College in Northern San Diego. Besides writing novels, she was senior editor, content manager, and image coordinator for Crescent House Publishing Inc. for four years.

Aside from Ginna's professional life, she enjoys binge watching television shows, playing pretend with her daughter, and cuddling with her dogs. Some of her favorite things include chocolate, anything that glitters, cheesy jokes, and organizing her bookshelf.

Ginna Moran loves to hear from her readers so visit her online at www.GinnaMoran.com. You can also find her on Facebook, Twitter, Instagram, and Snapchat (@Ginna Moran). To stay up-to-date on new releases, sign up to her newsletter. You'll not only get a FREE book, but you'll be able to participate in monthly giveaways!

Ginna Moran is currently hard at work on her next novel.

MORE BY GINNA MORAN

PARANORMAL

Destined for Dreams Series
Demon Within Series
Finding Nate Series
Going Ghostly Series
Spark of Life Series
When Souls Collide Series
Demon Watcher Series
Call of the Ocean Series

CONTEMPORARY

Falling into Fame Series

STANDALONES

Life After Lila